SATOSHI
WAGAHARA
ILLUSTRATION BY ■ 029
(ONIKU)

THE DEVIL IS A PART-TIMER!

RÉSUMÉ

NAME
HANZOU URUSHIHARA

DATE OF BIRTH
I — dont — know

AGE
doesnt matter

"And you still call yourself Devil King, Maou?"

ADDRESS
Devils Castle
Villa Rosa #201
Sasazuka x-x-x, Shibuya-ku, Tokyo

← THAT'S "ZUKA." —MAOU

TELEPHONE NUMBER
050-xxxx-xxxx

← Wh-when did you...! —

PAST EXPERIENCE

angel

Great Demon General Lucifer [Hanzo Urushihara]

Once an assassin sent from Ente Isla to eliminate Maou and the Hero, he has rejoined Maou's force after a pitched battle. Now he's an unemployed shut-in who spends all day surfing the Net.

-IN.
He sure is. —As

awful

shihara

QUALIFICAT
none

← I ca...   ave a PC.
—MAou   Wh   ushihara

SKILL
Int

PERSON
ork can a

COMMU
I am n

Maou!

F GUA
Maou!

LY PROTEST. —MAou

RÉSUMÉ

NAME
Suzuno Kamazuki

DATE OF BIRTH
Fall XXXX, Ignora 1211

AGE
2~~0~~

GENDER
F

ADDRESS
Villa Rosa #~~
Sasazuka~~
Shi~~

DUDE, JUST WRITE ~~MA~~

PAST EXPERIENCE

"Emi, are you in a close relationship, perhaps, with Maou?"

born as ~~ st ~~oreido, We~~ ~~d

graduated ~~College (major:~~

assigned to diplom~~ ~~f Church

↑ JOBLESS. —MAO~~

QUALIFICATIONS/CERTIFICATIONS
Japan Kanji Aptitude Test, Level Pr~~orate~~
certification; bishop certification

SKILLS/HOBBIES
gardening, kimono maintenance, cooki~~

**REASON~~
worl~~

Crestia Bell [Suzuno Kamazuki]

The young woman who moves into the apartment next to Devil's Castle. Thoroughly prim, proper, and polite, she provides vital food to the continually cash-starved castle, a development that makes both Chiho and the Hero shiver in fear.

~~
It was~~ ~~me.
Gate.~~

COM~~ ~~/DEPENDENTS
~~t need any

**NAME ~~
Orgot R~~

"Kimonos alone aren't good enough...?"

"No, it'd be a lot better if you wore something besides those sometimes!"

CHIHO SASAKI

A second-year high school student in love with Maou. She works part-time at the MgRonald fast-food outlet in front of the Hatagaya station, the same one Maou works in.

"Why do I have to go on this shopping trip, too...!"

EMILIA THE HERO
EMI YUSA
A heroic fighter who traveled to Japan from the world of Ente Isla in pursuit of the Devil King. Works as a call-center operator in order to support herself.

The girls in Shinjuku

"THIS NATION IS AS GOOD AS CONQUERED BY ME ALREADY!"

Hwa-hah-hah-ha!

"Your Demonic Highness...!"

The boys in Sasazuka

MgRonald

CONTENTS

SATOSHI
WAGAHARA
ILLUSTRATED BY ■ 029
(ONIKU)

2

YEN
ON
NEW YORK

THE DEVIL IS A PART-TIMER!, Volume 2
SATOSHI WAGAHARA, ILLUSTRATION BY 029 (ONIKU)

Translation by Kevin Gifford

HATARAKU MAOSAMA!, Volume 2
©SATOSHI WAGAHARA 2011
All rights reserved.
Edited by ASCII MEDIA WORKS
First published in 2011 by KADOKAWA
CORPORATION, Tokyo.

English translation rights arranged with
KADOKAWA CORPORATION, Tokyo,
through Tuttle-Mori Agency, Inc., Tokyo.
English translation © 2015 Hachette Book
Group, Inc.

Yen On
Hachette Book Group
1290 Avenue of the Americas
New York, NY 10104

www.hachettebookgroup.com
www.yenpress.com

Yen On is an imprint of
Hachette Book Group, Inc.
The Yen On name and logo are
trademarks of Hachette Book
Group, Inc.

First Yen On edition:
August 2015

ISBN: 978-0-316-38501-5

10 9 8 7 6 5 4 3 2 1

RRD-C

Printed in the United
States of America

THE DEVIL'S FINANCES ARE SHORED UP BY A HELPFUL NEIGHBOR

The coals glowed white-hot as they seared the sizzling strips of meat.

The oily drippings from the finely sliced pieces of flesh caused the fire to roar even stronger, further punishing the meat with its burning vengeance.

The room was filled with the smell of flesh and bone charring from the edges inward, along with enough smoke to hide even the death-scream-like sizzle.

He looked on at the sight, licking his lips as he did. The smile surfacing across his face was like that of a demonic beast possessed by sheer, overpowering greed.

"Heh-heh-heh… How does it feel, then? Being seared by the flames of hell without even a moment's chance of escape?"

The dark voice, even restrained, could not conceal the innate, profound cruelty its owner was aiming at the meat as it wailed its last amid the flames.

"Now I will consume you whole. Your meat, your entrails, your very bones! And you will provide the energy I need to fulfill my great mission! So just rest easy and let the life escape you…heh-heh-heh…"

"Your Demonic Highness…"

A quizzical voice sounded above the smoke and flame. He paid it no mind.

"Ah, give me a moment. No need to hurry this. I'm not gonna be happy with this unless it's charred to a crisp."

"No, Your Demonic Highness, I mean…"

"Now! Let the great feast begin! Let's start with the organ meat, shall we? …But look at you! What is the meaning of this? Cowering in the corner like a scared child?!"

"……"

"There is no longer any escape for you! You shall have the honor of being the first sacrifice offered to my lordly presence!"

With a final shout of glee, he nimbly brought the chopsticks in his right hand to the ready.

The edges of these two traditional weapons swiftly found their target, a well-cooked piece of beef laid bare on the grill. Ferrying it to a bowl of hot-and-spicy sauce as red as a blood-filled cesspit of hell, he drowned the tidbit inside before ruthlessly bringing it to his mouth.

"Heh-heh-heh… A delectable treat indeed!"

An evil look of self-satisfaction crossed his face as he finished off the mouthful.

"…My liege?"

"What, Ashiya?"

In a flash, his facial expression returned to normal as he turned forward, toward the unwelcome attention-seeker.

"If I may, could I convince my Devil King to enjoy his meal a little more quietly? You're going to disturb the other diners around us."

Across the undersized table, the tall man known as Ashiya peered through the rising smoke, eyebrows furrowed in apparent distress.

"Mm? Oh. Right. Guess I was getting too into this for my own good, huh? Sorry if I was too loud."

The so-called Devil King, a perfectly normal young man in appearance, glanced about his surroundings.

"Also, there's no need to become so passionate about some organ meat at a *yakiniku* restaurant. You're acting like this is the first decent meal you've had all year."

"Well, I'm not *trying* to act like that, but if you're like me and you live off junk food and scratch-'n'-dent groceries, it's kinda natural to get excited about eating someplace fancy, you know?"

The Devil King deftly transferred a selection of meat, organs, and vegetable bits from the grill to his plate as he spoke.

"I gotta be honest with you, I never really understood why all the other demons loved feasting on the organs of their victims up to now. This stuff's really good! Like, what's this bit? Veal heart or whatever? It's so rich and melt-in-your-mouth *yum*. And I love how the pork belly and chicken cartilage crunch against my teeth! And what's this stuff? Beef tripe? It looks pretty weird, but it's not bad!"

"...I am glad, my liege."

Ashiya nodded, his face still muddled with concern as he gave up the idea of calming down the Devil King anytime soon.

It was a weekend evening. Only a few chairs were empty in the restaurant, with the smoke of barbecued meat wafting up to the air vents. None of the nearby customers were demonstrating visible annoyance at the Devil King's revved-up commentary, but internally, Ashiya regretted being so strictly frugal (okay, cheap) with the food he bought and prepared for his companion.

The pair lived in the "Devil's Castle"—aka Room 201 of the Villa Rosa Sasazuka apartments, a rickety wooden structure built sixty years ago in a spot five minutes' walking distance from Sasazuka rail station, which offered quick access to the rest of Tokyo's Shibuya ward via the Keio line. A ten-minute hike from the Devil's Castle brought them to the 100th Street shopping district, home to a *horumon*-style *yakitori* restaurant well-known to the local crowd.

As part of a campaign to celebrate ten years in business, the restaurant was offering one free drink and 390-yen deals on most plates during weeknights in the early dinner hours. To Satan, the Devil King—more likely to answer to the name Sadao Maou these days—it was a deal worth dragging his companion to.

He had just received his paycheck, which took the heat off his finances for the time being. And since certain earlier events made a "celebration" seem in order anyway, the Great Demon General Alciel—much better known around the neighborhood as Shiro

Ashiya—had agreed to relax his iron grip on the Devil's Castle's finances for one night.

Sipping on his free mug of oolong tea, Ashiya set his side salad in front of him.

"Your Demonic Highness, you need to eat some vegetables in addition to all that meat. These days, if we wanted to eat this many vegetables at home, it would take far more than three hundred ninety yen."

Briskly, he attempted to transfer some of his salad into Maou's bowl.

"Oh, yeah, I heard that produce was startin' to get expensive."

"It is madness, my liege. A head of cabbage has risen to three hundred fifty yen."

"Well, it doesn't really matter, does it? I'm pretty much a born carnivore anyway."

"It 'doesn't matter' only if you think a sound nutritional balance doesn't matter. It would be nice if we could at least cook some fish, but we don't have a fish grill for the Devil's Castle stove, and our puny ventilation fan would be no match for all the smoke and stink we'd generate."

The pair of arch-demons commiserated over their oolong teas about the more poverty-stricken aspects of their lifestyle.

"Oh, speaking of which, we better buy some dinner for Urushihara, right? I think they have takeout bento boxes here."

A small box on the side of the menu Maou took into hand listed the *yakiniku* bento options available. The *galbi* marinated beef option was priced at an extremely reasonable six hundred yen.

But Ashiya scrunched up his face and shook his head at the proposal. He sorted through the remains of his salad and had a waiter take the bowl away.

"No need. We can just buy a regular-sized pork rice bowl at the Sugiya on the way home."

"Huh?"

Surprised at the unexpectedly cold response, Maou watched as Ashiya indignantly finished up his salad.

"Urushihara's started to get into online shopping, if you haven't noticed. He's never worked a day of his life here, and yet he commandeers your credit card to fritter away our monthly budget. He never spends a great deal of money on each individual purchase, but if we let it pass unmentioned, we'll all pay for it someday."

"Wha? He's been buying stuff?"

"I noticed on the past month's credit card bill that there were quite a few more purchases made besides the computer and Internet installation we bought. Unless it was one of us wasting our money, which I doubt, it had to be him."

"...Oh. Yeah, you know, I kinda had the impression that laptop's gotten a lot more decked out since I bought it..."

The computer, a device that was undeniably the most state-of-the-art cultural artifact in the lives of all the Devil's Castle denizens, was a gift funded by Maou in hopes of encouraging Urushihara's computer skills.

"I kinda wanted to go easy on him. He can't really go outside, and I don't want him getting so stressed that he starts thinking about double-crossing me again. But if he's going too far, I better read him the riot act, huh?"

"I earnestly hope you do, Your Demonic Highness. The iron hammer of justice needs to be struck, and quickly."

Ashiya's face was still locked in a frown, but it seemed to loosen a bit at Maou's encouraging words. It did not last.

"Okay, well, if we got some free money, then how 'bout we splurge a little?"

"Ha?"

Ashiya's chopsticks froze in the air as Maou suddenly shifted gears, menu already open.

"I kept this on the cheap side 'cause I thought we'd need to save some money for Urushihara's portion, but if not, how 'bout we get one order of prime *galbi*, huh? What do you think? One prime *galbi*!"

Even with the early-bird special, the prime-grade *galbi*, tripe, and *harami* meat each cost 490 yen a plate.

Ashiya hung his head in resignation.

"...Well, if you insist. But just today, and just this once! There will be no more ordering tonight."

"Yesss!!"

Maou pumped a fist in the air as he caught a nearby waiter, made his order, and requested the check. Watching his leader drool with excitement over a single serving of spiced beef, Ashiya couldn't decide if the sight was heartwarming or soul-crushingly pathetic. He raised a glass to his lips to drown the pangs of barren emptiness. All that remained was ice.

✻

The world of Ente Isla, the Land of the Holy Cross, was fabled to be watched over personally by the gods themselves. It was composed of five vast continents, spread out in a cross formation over the Ocean of Ignora. And the king of demons, the supreme ruler of evil in this world, now lived here in the Sasazuka neighborhood of Shibuya ward, Tokyo, Japan.

Satan, the Devil King, was the iron-fist tyrant of the world of demons, a stained land infested with the writhing minions of darkness. His very name was synonymous with depraved cruelty and terror.

Together with his close-knit band of trustworthy Great Demon Generals, Satan had demolished Ente Isla's human forces, to the point where he was just one step away from wholly conquering the land.

But then there appeared a Hero, one powerful enough to crush the Devil King's ambitions and protect her motherland. Her name was Emilia Justina. After a climactic battle, the Devil King was defeated and forced to jump through a Gate connecting to another world, in a frantic attempt to make good his escape.

In his wounded, exhausted state, he could do little more than let the Gate's flow take him to an unknown world, one that called itself "Earth." It was much larger than Ente Isla, its civilization far more advanced—and, most distasteful of all, it was under the supreme rule of the human race.

Finding themselves in "Japan," one of Earth's nations, Satan and Alciel quickly realized they could no longer retain their high-level demon forms. The magical force that so naturally bubbled out of every pore of Ente Isla's fabric did not exist at all in this world. To regain their powers and return home, the pair of arch-demons decided to live with the humans in this strange nation, bereft of both holy and demonic force to live off of, and search for a way to safely regain their magical energy.

And by the time one Earth year had passed, the two arch-demons had found themselves a worthy position in Japanese society—the few, the proud, the menial part-time workers!

The Devil King Satan, who had taken on the name Sadao Maou, was now an A-level crew member at the MgRonald fast-food chain location in front of the Hatagaya rail station.

Alciel, his Great Demon General who now went by Shiro Ashiya in Japan, served as his de facto househusband, giving his all to support Maou's new lifestyle.

The two established their temporary Devil's Castle in Room 201 of Villa Rosa Sasazuka, a wooden apartment building in the Sasazuka neighborhood of Shibuya, Tokyo, that was a surefire nominee for the Rat-Infested Dump Hall of Fame. There they lived their days, just a pair of kind, energetic, law-abiding citizens trying to make their way in the world.

It was not the sort of life one would expect from a demon with dreams of world domination, but Maou was content enough with it. That changed one rainy day, when he lent an umbrella to a young woman caught in the rain on his way to work.

The woman was none other than Emilia Justina, the Hero herself, who had followed the Devil King to Earth in order to strike the final, decisive blow.

The sudden appearance of his greatest foe flustered Maou at first. But Emilia, too, was just as powerless and isolated in Japan as he was, living under the name Emi Yusa and painstakingly building up a part-time work résumé of her own.

Despite these natural enemies rediscovering each other, neither had the freedom to use their otherworldly powers with reckless abandon on Earth. Thus they glared helplessly at each other, forced to continue living as members of Japan's underemployed young working class.

One day, the two of them were attacked by someone calling himself an "assassin from Ente Isla," a nemesis who swore that he would dispose of both the Hero and Devil King in Japan.

The assassin was actually a pair. One was the fallen angel Lucifer, a Great Demon General who Maou had thought was defeated at the hands of Emilia the Hero. His partner: Olba Meiyer, Emilia's close confidant and a powerful archbishop in the Church that ruled over the human race in Ente Isla.

Sent on the run by Lucifer and Olba's barrage of destruction, Maou and Emi were forced into battle, nearly losing their lives on multiple occasions.

But following a last-ditch stab in the dark, the Devil King Satan was unleashed once more. Teaming up with the Hero, who released the remaining holy power she had saved within her body, he turned the tables and successfully defeated the assassins.

With Satan reborn and the Hero's own companions arriving from Ente Isla, the final confrontation between holy and demonic seemed about to unfold.

But instead of waging battle, Satan used his newly recovered force to repair the destroyed city and erase the memories of the many eyewitnesses to the conflict. His powers quickly atrophied once more, and soon he was back to regular old Sadao Maou.

Resolving to keep the Devil King on close watch after he blew his best chance of returning home, Emilia decided to remain in Japan herself. And so the stalemate between holy and demonic continued in the sleepy side alleys of Sasazuka, not exactly the most exalted of divine battlegrounds.

✳

Putting the *yakiniku* restaurant behind them, Maou and Ashiya's lungs were instantly filled by intensely humid air. It was almost enough to make them choke—there was no fog, but it seemed like a cup of water had just been poured down their windpipes.

The season was just about to shift from early summer to *summer* summer. The days had grown long, and the temperature difference between night and day was quickly growing negligible. It was the rainy season, too, and the needles on their respective Annoyed-o-Meters were both about to pop right off their gauges.

"What the hell? It was cooler inside the restaurant! There were literally fires lit across the entire damn room!"

"We owe much to air-conditioning, my liege."

Given how they had taken advantage of the early-bird special, the shopping street was still in the prime of activity. Herds of salarymen returning from work were walking en masse away from Koshu-Kaido Road, which served as Sasazuka station's main exit point.

After purchasing the cheapest pork rice bowl at Sugiya, the beef-and-rice fast-food joint in the middle of the shopping arcade, Maou and Ashiya fought the waves of incoming traffic as they made their way toward the station entrance.

"These guys have to be crazy. It's this friggin' hot, and they still put on those full business suits like it's nothing."

"Well, a lot of those suits are made of much more breathable material these days. Even the discount chains like Akayama and Akaki are starting to sell them."

"I know that, but how stupid do you have to be to want to wear long-sleeved shirts in the summer?"

"Your Demonic Highness, have you forgotten about our attack on the Desert Kingdom on the Southern Island?"

Ashiya's face suddenly turned grim.

It was not quite seven o'clock, but with the long summer days settled in, the sky still retained its twilight colors, the streetlights lining the shopping street casting the unique shades one only sees on languid summer evenings like these.

At the end of the street, upon the intersection with Koshu-Kaido Road, the demons hit a red light.

"The sun can cause terrible damage to one's skin. Do you recall what the people of the desert wore? Their bodies were covered in thick fabric. Japan may not be the searing wasteland you saw in the Southern Island, but then, Earth is quite a different place from Ente Isla."

"Wh-what're you talking about?"

Ashiya grew more impassioned as he continued.

"Overexposure to the sun can lead to sunburn, my liege, and excessive sunburn can cause skin cancer. Aren't you aware that the thinning ozone layer is exposing the cities of Japan to more and more ultraviolet rays every year?!"

"Uh, no? So what?"

Ashiya pointed a finger toward the sky.

"Even on cloudy days, or evenings like these where the sun isn't out, those UV rays are still raining down upon us. They are the direct cause of skin cancer and cataracts, and in places like Australia that are closer to the Antarctic ozone hole, some states even require children to wear protective glasses as they travel to school."

Ashiya was careful to not let the rice bowl in his hand bump into anyone passing by as he continued his soapbox rant.

"My point, Your Demonic Highness, is that even in the summertime, it is no longer strictly the wisest move to go around in short sleeves. If I could at least convince you to add a baseball tee and some sunglasses to your wardrobe, that would put me a great deal more at ease with regard to your long-term health."

"Dude, baseball tees are one thing, but I'm *not* going around wearing sunglasses."

It was hard to tell how serious Ashiya felt about the topic. Maou decided to nip it in the bud before it graduated to anything above idle chitchat.

"Hey, it's green. Let's go before that pork bowl gets cold on us."

"Ah. Yes."

The wave of people in the middle of the crossing began to lurch into action. Ashiya quickly turned his attention elsewhere.

The two arch-demons continued talking as they walked among

the countless hundreds of Japanese citizens surrounding them in the large crossing in front of Sasazuka station.

"By the way, Your Demonic Highness, did you know about that *yakiniku* restaurant in days past?"

"Hmm?"

Ashiya spoke up again just as they reached the other side.

"I know it's not along your normal route to work, so I simply wondered how you came to be aware of it."

"Oh… Well, I've kind of gone there before, actually."

Just as he said it, Maou scrambled to explain himself further.

"And before you say anything, it was on someone else's dime, okay? I didn't use any of our money!"

He dared a glimpse at Ashiya's face, only to find it perfectly serene.

"I would hardly be angry about that sort of thing."

This was a total lie. If he told him he paid his own way, Ashiya would yell at him all night, then force him into a drastic rationed diet to make up the financial deficit. He had to be hiding something behind that shady smile of his!

"A-anyway, the first time I went—today's the second time—Ms. Kisaki brought me over."

Mayumi Kisaki. The manager of the MgRonald in front of Hatagaya station. Maou's boss and the keystone of the Devil's Castle economy.

"I see. A private employee party or some such, then? Come to think of it, I do recall you venturing by yourself eight months and seventeen days ago, stating that you didn't need me to prepare dinner."

"You know, the way you instantly recall dates like that is pretty damn scary."

Maou knitted his brows.

The crowds quickly grew sparse once they passed by the station's main entrance. They were approaching the latticework of extended back alleys that comprised Sasazuka's old residential area.

"Ms. Kisaki called it, like, a welcome party for me. She said she knew some people who worked at the place. It was me, her, and a few other folks, but she wound up paying the whole tab."

"A grandly generous manager as always, I see. So this wasn't your first time trying *horumon*-style *yakiniku*?"

"Welllll, I kinda didn't wanna pig out the first time, since it was her treat and everything. To be honest, I don't really remember exactly what I ate."

It was, perhaps, the most pathetically sniveling thing a Devil King has ever uttered.

"Still…it's not like I didn't want it, but I'm not totally cool with how Ms. Kisaki sprung it on me."

The thought gave Maou's expression an odd air of depression. Ashiya, meanwhile, seemed honestly happy for his companion.

"It merely shows how much trust she's placed in you, Your Demonic Highness. It hasn't even been a year since she hired you. Quite the exceptional promotion, is it not?"

Maou listlessly shook his head in response.

"Yeah, maybe, but I'm still just as hourly as always."

"Perhaps it is for restricted periods of time, my liege, and perhaps involving only a small number of people, but you are *ruling over* human beings! Surely it is something to be commemorated!"

"You say that, but…do you really mean it?"

"I would hardly have taken you out to eat if I didn't. What kind of servant would I be, my liege, if I did not celebrate your grand promotion?"

"Shift supervisor?"

The words had fallen out of Kisaki's lips right after Maou changed out of his uniform postclosing.

Just as he was nearly out the door, his manager had stopped him with some sudden news—she wanted him to be shift supervisor for the afternoon hours.

"So, you mean…"

"Right. You'll be assistant manager during your assigned hours, Marko. You'll get a raise to cover the extra duties, too."

Assistant manager. It had such a fetching ring to it. Maou was unable to hide the shock.

"To be honest with you, the franchise bosses are calling me out for managerial training. Which, frankly, is a huge pain in the ass for me, because it means I'm gonna have to be away from here during the late shift for about a week, starting next weekend."

Maou internally marveled at this. What kind of training could this whirlwind of region-beating sales figures possibly need?

"I know you haven't even been here a year yet, Marko, but I think you've got some serious talent. I thought about calling for another full-timer to fill in for me, but if I'm going to leave this location in someone else's hands for half the day, I'd rather leave it to someone I know's up to the task instead of rolling the dice with some guy I've never even met. So what do you think? Can I count on you?"

This was faint praise indeed for someone who once had the entire demon netherworld wrapped around his finger, but to Maou, Kisaki's sincere words were enough to send his heart soaring.

As he himself stated in the past, Maou's ambitions for world domination would begin to formally bear fruit once he became a salaried employee. If he could fulfill his duties well enough in the shift-supervisor role, it would be another solid step forward toward that lofty goal.

"Yes! Absolutely! I'm not gonna let you down!"

So he snapped up the offer. After all, if he failed to live up to Kisaki's expectations, he'd be a failure both as a man and as a Devil King!

Kisaki nodded in response, a warm smile across her face, before suddenly changing the topic.

"By the way, Marko, you know that those pricks at Sentucky Fried Chicken are opening up a new location next to the bookstore across the street, right?"

"Uh? Um, yeah."

Maou blinked at this unexpected gear shift.

Sentucky Fried Chicken, a fierce competitor of MgRonald, was opening soon in the space next to the nearby bookstore, a whopping fifteen seconds' walk away. They were already putting the hard sell on the neighborhood, placing a huge advertisement in front of the under-renovation storefront and even going so far as to put fliers and coupons inside MgRonald's own mailbox.

The serene smile on Kisaki's face was now curled up a bit more, suggesting a wholly different emotion. Her eyes reminded Maou of a hunter marveling at the animal caught in his trap.

"Well, the grand opening's the day my training begins. Hence, why it's a huge pain in the ass for me."

Kisaki ruefully spat the words out. The sharpness around the jagged edges forming every syllable suggested a deep-seated resentment of some sort. Come to think of it, Kisaki brought the SFC ads and coupons in the mail straight over to her portable shredder, didn't she?

Maou thought over this as he nodded his commiseration. The next volley from Kisaki took him a moment to fully comprehend.

"So here it is, Marko. If SFC attracts more total customers during the evening hours than we do, I'm docking your pay ten yen for every guest we're beaten by."

"Uh?"

"If you lose by ten people, one hundred yen! Lose by a hundred… one thousand yen. Right off your hourly wage!"

"Wha— Uh, I, uh, hang on a second!"

As Maou struggled to articulate a response, Kisaki regrouped herself, flashing a razor-sharp smile that'd make even the Hero proud.

"Silence! That's the kind of resolve a shift supervisor needs to survive in retail sales!"

"Yeah, but…I only make one thousand yen an hour! If you take one thousand yen off that, that's basically working for nothing! There has to be something in the labor laws about that…"

"The only constitution that applies here is *me*!"

Not just the law, but the very constitution of the land. Maou began to feel dizzy.

"And you'd be *glad* to work for free, trust me. One of the guys I joined up with lost big to a competitor once. He wound up getting reassigned to Trinidad and Tobago. Last I heard, he's still there. 'At least they speak English,' I remember him saying."

"I don't think that's the problem..."

"Regardless! I officially name you our newest shift supervisor! For one week, I want you to stake your life protecting this place and destroying that godforsaken new SFC location! Defeat means death!"

"N-no way...!"

Maou tried to defend himself, but Kisaki responded by crossing her arms and walking right up to him. Thanks to her already tall stature and the heels she wore, her vantage over Maou was even higher than usual. Her eyes were aglow with an eerie, foreboding light, just as disquieting as the dull flames that roared behind the Devil King's visage.

"What are you trying to say, Marko? Are you saying you want to take all the trust and hope I placed in you and toss it in the septic tank?"

By now, Maou realized there was no escape. It was far too late to do anything, with Kisaki already unloading this great, burdensome commitment onto his shoulders.

Still unable to respond coherently, Maou watched as Kisaki suddenly let the dramatic energy drain from her face, returning to her original serene smile.

"As your boss, I have an obligation to give you the stick sometimes. But every stick needs to have a carrot, too. If you respond to my trust in you and emerge victorious, I'll make sure you're generously rewarded for it."

"...!"

"Depending on how things go with the daily customer and sales figures, I may consider a further raise. And if you can build more experience as a regular shift supervisor and assistant manager, I could even recommend you for a full-time position, too."

It would be fair to say that Maou was completely under Kisaki's spell by this point.

"Yes, ma'am! I'll do it! I promise I won't let you down, Ms. Kisaki!!"
A look of supreme satisfaction spread across her face.

"But how would she even know how many customers visit your rival?"

Ashiya's question interrupted Maou as he retold the story.

"She said the main office is sending observers over to keep tabs on foot traffic. We had a temp job like that once, too, remember? Like, not long after we first came here. They gave us that handheld counter thingy we had to click every time someone passed by us."

"Ah, yes. That was in the dead of summer as well, if I recall. Spending hours under the hot sun counting passersby was nothing short of deadening, both physically and mentally. We had to bring our own drinks and shade as well."

It was hard to imagine a demon that once waged an epic, near-apocalyptic war against the human race on Ente Isla ever reminiscing about crappy summer jobs.

"So in the course of a week, she's teaching me how to do the daily books, how to enter sales figures into the office computer, and how to run the attendance-management system. Then, next weekend, I'm betting my salary on this all-out war. It's making me, like, *crazy* nervous."

"Your Demonic Highness, now is no time to grow weak at the knees. Being granted such a substantial post is nothing short of a high honor. I, too, recall the intense pride I felt upon being named supreme commander of the Eastern Island invasion force…!"

Ashiya, hand on chest, was already striding across Ente Isla in his mind as he reminisced. Maou cut in, his voice unnaturally loud.

"Yes! Right! Anyway! There's no weaseling my way out of this now regardless. My work schedule's gonna stay the same, though, so hopefully you'll still be able to cook for me."

Whenever the topic of discussion turned to Ente Isla, Ashiya would inevitably spring into *I want to invade our homeland, stop screwing around, Your Demonic Highness* mode. It was his way of expressing homesickness.

"Y-yes… Certainly, my liege."

Soon, the front light from the Devil's Castle—or, as anyone else would put it, the Villa Rosa Sasazuka apartments—grew visible in the distance. Maou breathed a sigh of relief now that the topic was buried before reaching full fruition.

"Hmm?"

"Hohh…"

Maou and Ashiya both exclaimed out loud.

There were two lights.

One came from the corner apartment upstairs. This was Room 201, the Devil's Castle that Maou and his generals called home.

The other was from Room 202, the apartment next to theirs. Maou's crew were supposed to be the only tenants in Villa Rosa. There couldn't have been any construction or maintenance people onsite at this time of the evening. Oh, no. Had Miki, the landlord, returned?

Miki Shiba, the owner of Villa Rosa Sasazuka, let out every intimation before the battle against Lucifer two months ago that she was fully aware of who Maou and his band of demons really were. Then she up and disappeared.

If the note she left was to be believed, she was somewhere overseas. But what kind of landlord would simply abandon her property for two months?

Not that she was taking great pains to keep a low profile. In fact, despite zero requests from Maou along those lines, Room 201 was receiving letters from her at the rate of two or so per week.

When the first one arrived, in the sort of frilly envelope usually reserved for wedding invitations, he opened it with almost reckless abandon.

What rewarded him was a neatly worded chronicle, written in an elegant, practiced hand, of the joyous vacation she was experiencing on a private beach in Hawaii. Less-than-humble bragging, in other words.

And included in the envelope was a photograph of his landlord, lying on a deck chair underneath a beach umbrella, tropical cocktail in one hand, her rainbow-colored bikini and devil-may-care wrap leaving far more of her wine-barrel-shaped body bare than wholly necessary, tanning herself to a golden brown as she made the most of the Hawaiian climate, in a pose that reminded Maou of a slab of beef covered with bits of multihued barbecue sauce.

The moment they set eyes on the photo, Maou's vision turned sheer white, Ashiya stumbled for the bathroom with one hand covering his mouth, and Urushihara—who had never even met the landlord in person—fainted on the spot, ultimately requiring three days to fully recover.

Ever since that incident, when Maou learned that nuclear terrorism was the last thing Japan had to worry about as long as Miki Shiba was cavorting around beachside unattended, the Devil's Castle was gripped in fear whenever an unexpected piece of mail arrived.

Just as the memory of the now-infamous landlord cheesecake pinup massacre raced across Maou's mind, a truck carrying a container with a giraffe logo passed them by.

Maou and Ashiya exchanged glances. Even though they didn't own a TV to bombard them with the ads, they still knew the logo belonged to a well-known moving company.

"It would appear we have a new neighbor."

"Yeah. Wish he coulda moved in some other time. I'm kinda gonna miss being the only tenants in that whole place."

"Quite true. Hopefully it won't be someone of low morals. The sort of person to play loud music at night or bring their garbage out on the wrong day."

Maou shook his head. Something about a demonic overlord worrying about someone else's morals struck even him as ironic.

"Ah, I'm not really worried about that sort of thing."

"No? Well, considering this apartment is dirt cheap and requires no deposit or advance fees, what kind of people would you expect to move in…? Besides, when we came here, we were homeless, jobless, and dare I say *quite* suspicious."

Maou shook his head once more at Ashiya's concerns.

"Maybe we weren't exactly model tenants, but think about it. Remember what kind of...*lady* is renting this place to us, Ashiya?"

The word "lady" was enough to make the memory of that ghastly photograph grate across Ashiya's brain.

"I, er... I imagine anyone moving in under our landlord's auspices would never seek to get on her bad side, no."

"That's not what I mean, but... Ah, well. What happens, happens. Let's get moving. I don't want Urushihara whining at us."

They were already on apartment property as Maou spoke. The outdoor stairway, the same one that had struck such a lethal blow (in assorted ways) upon the Hero once, seemed even more tilted and decrepit than before.

"...Huh?"

As he placed a foot on the first step, Maou looked up, catching sight of a shadow lurking upstairs.

The figure, standing in front of the fluorescent light over the second-floor corridor, was peering down below.

The backlighting and awkward angle made it impossible to know for sure, but the small size and delicately curved body suggested it was a woman.

"Uh..."

Maou, not expecting this sudden encounter, froze in place, his gaze still pointed upward. The figure upstairs jerked awkwardly, apparently caught in the same reaction. Then:

"Ah..."

"Ah!"

"Ahh!"

All three raised a voice at once—the person upstairs first, Maou second, and Ashiya at the end.

The shadowy figure, resolving to head downstairs, had slipped off the first step.

Her body flew through space for a moment.

"No way...!!"

Instinctively, Maou extended a hand.

Whatever odd angle the figure had flown off the stairs from caused her to fall wildly, limbs flailing, in a virtual bullrush straight toward Maou.

"My liege!"

Ashiya shouted out just before the moment of collision.

"Whoa, that was close…"

Maou muttered to himself after a moment's confusion.

The small, unfamiliar woman was safe within his arms. She was tensed up, eyes open, perhaps still in a state of shock after falling down the stairs without so much as a scream.

That and, for whatever reason, the outfit she chose for the occasion was a Japanese kimono, a long cooking apron, and a triangular head scarf. Her footwear must have slipped off, but instead of socks, she wore traditional Japanese *tabi* with two separate toes. The only people who wore clothing like that these days were the matriarchs of cartoons set in the '60s.

"Uh…umm…" Gingerly, Maou said this to the woman—really a girl—in his arms, who was staring listlessly into space.

Then:

"Danger comes when one least expects it…!"

With that, the girl suddenly closed her eyes, her body growing limp.

"Well, uh, yeah, but that's not the problem here…"

Maou couldn't help but give his take on the now-unconscious girl's non sequitur response.

"Are you…all right?"

Ashiya ran up to them, carrying one of the women's *geta* sandals, which must have flown off her foot.

"You talking about me, or this girl?"

It was difficult to judge which of the two demons was the more baffled.

"So this girl fell from the stairs, and I caught her, and…*now* what?"

"You're late! I'm hungry!"

The complaint was lodged from within the moment Maou, master of the Devil's Castle, opened the front door.

"We came as fast as we could. You could at least say 'Welcome home, master' or something."

Maou and Ashiya bumped against each other as they took off their shoes in the cramped front foyer.

"Here, Lucifer. Got a souvenir for you."

Ashiya offered the bag with the bento dinner inside. It was snapped up by a young man, small in stature, a good head shorter than Maou. Purple eyes peered out from between tendrils of hair, which had gone beyond fashionably long and were threatening to enter the realm of lazy bum.

"Hey, I thought you guys went to a *yakiniku* place. Why'd you get me a Sugiya pork bowl?"

"Oh, uh, sorry, Urushihara. Ask him to give the financial rundown."

The young man, called Lucifer by Ashiya and Urushihara by Maou, followed Maou's finger as it pointed toward Ashiya.

"You could point the finger at yourself, I would say. Your extravagant spending habits as of late are too much for me to tolerate."

Ashiya's glare was just as abrasive as his opening salvo.

"Yeah, but…dude, this is kinda a huge difference, isn't it? I mean, come *on*…" The young man mumbled under his breath, aware enough of what he was being lectured about that he quickly backed off. He removed the plastic bag and pork-bowl cover, tossing them off to the side.

"Lucifer! Don't spread your garbage around the room. Clean it up!"

Ashiya, looking on, angrily picked up the paper wipe that fell out of the plastic bag.

"Also, would you mind cleaning the area around your computer already? All these chip bags and empty juice cans… It's going to be a bug magnet in the summertime!"

Outside, the night had finally progressed from twilight to darkness. Underneath the fluorescent bulb lighting the room, a table holding an outdated notebook computer sat in the corner, an equally outdated fan whirring loudly behind it.

Surrounding this workstation was a pile of empty snack-food boxes and bags, discarded juice cans, and an assortment of devices and cords whose uses were not immediately obvious to the casual observer. Whenever the fan hit the pile of garbage, little bits of food and plastic wafted their way across the tatami-mat floor, raking Ashiya's face as they did.

The young man, nonplussed at Ashiya's tongue-wagging, looked expectantly at the microwave as he spoke, not bothering to turn around.

"I'm hungry, okay? If you're gonna yell at me, do it when I'm done."

He was not quite demonstrating enormous regret for his actions.

The man's name was Hanzou Urushihara. His true identity was Lucifer, one of the four Great Demon Generals and the assassin who was sent to Ente Isla two months ago to rub out Maou and the Hero.

Robbed of his magic force after a violent confrontation, Lucifer had once again returned to Maou's camp—now as Urushihara, a nondescript, listless, sullen Japanese youth.

Olba was detained by the police at the end of the previous battle. He was arrested for violating Japan's weapons laws, thanks to the pistol he was packing beneath his robes, but it likely wouldn't be too long before they realized he was the man behind the string of burglaries that gripped the city in fear a few months back.

Exhausted by the fight and fully aware that the Hero was alive and well in Japan, Olba wasn't likely to try anything else for a while, but there was every chance he would name Lucifer as his accomplice.

In terms of external appearance, the difference between "Lucifer" and "Hanzou Urushihara" wasn't much. Far less than that between the rest of the group's human and demon forms. Until Olba met his fate, whatever it was, Urushihara essentially couldn't take the risk of going outside.

But he had a key asset to his name, one that made his new indoor-oriented lifestyle possible. Two months ago, he went to an Internet café and hacked into the Hero's workplace network. Witnessing this great potential, Maou purchased a notebook PC and Internet connection for Urushihara, hoping he would provide support for them from within Devil's Castle.

The Devil King had ordered him to use his computer skills to gather information about any world culture that may have dabbled in magic powers, in hopes he would uncover a way to refill their demonic energy here on Earth. Yet, his work ethic was proving to be a problem.

"So, did you find anything useful today?"

Maou broke into Urushihara and Ashiya's tête-à-tête, a concerned look on his face.

"I'm not gonna hit pay dirt that easily. You *know* that."

Returning to his computer desk with the pork bowl in hand, Urushihara dug into his dinner, not giving Maou a second (or even first) glance. Even Maou was growing annoyed by the act.

"That's all you've said to me for the past two months, man!"

The remonstration fell on deaf ears.

"Well, what do you want from me? I'm not gonna go on some webpage and find the secrets to all the magic in this world, just like that."

Back before the Devil's Castle joined the infobahn, Ashiya was obliged to do all the legwork himself in his quest to recover his master's magic force. He went through an endless cycle of research, poring through promising-sounding books in libraries, going from museum to museum to evaluate any special showings, hitting the books again, discovering another museum. To Maou, having Internet access at home meant the search would surely be on easy street from now on.

"I mean, look, Maou…"

Urushihara was just as openly hostile to Maou back during the Lucifer era, but even then he used the proper Demonic Highness terminology. Now, in human form, his mentality had shifted to the point where it was just "Maou" by itself. This led to at least one pitched argument with Ashiya per week.

"Do you think that computer and the Net are, like, some kind of magical potion that'll solve all your problems?"

"Nggh."

Maou groaned in frustration. He *did* think that. Correctly gauging this response, Urushihara exhaled a very deliberate sigh, mouth full of freshly microwaved pork bits.

"Heh. Well, look, dude, the Net isn't a miracle machine, okay? Also, maybe you didn't notice, but the government's starting to give out jail time these days if you start screwing around online too much. You want the cops putting their eyes on us any more than they probably are now?"

Maou could no longer resist taking the bait.

"And you call yourself a demon?"

"And *you* call yourself Devil King, Maou?"

Ashiya remained silent, no longer able to drum up the energy to intervene. Silently, Urushihara picked up the garbage strewn around his desk, his face that classic midteenage sort of petulant.

"Like, let's say everything works out and you really did find some museum exhibit that could link us to demonic force. Do you really think we'd just rappel down the wall and steal it like we're in some Hollywood film?"

"I don't know what you're getting at with that example...but, like, maybe you could reprogram the surveillance cameras, or hack out the code to the museum storehouse, or something. Can't you?"

"Pfft. You sound like some kid who's watched too much TV. And we don't even *have* TV in here."

Urushihara showed no mercy.

"I mean, sure, hacking lets you read and mess around with data on whatever computer you gain access to. But you can't just hack right into a museum's entire administration system. And you *definitely* can't do it with this ancient relic."

The PC Urushihara was slamming was the very first purchase Maou had made with his shiny new credit card. To him, it was like taking the plunge into a completely unknown realm, but the way Urushihara put it, he had been sucked into buying old, useless inventory.

"Take a look at this."

"Huh?"

Urushihara called Maou over to the computer. A black-and-white video of something or other was playing on one end of the LCD screen. Maou looked on, unsure what he was watching, when he noticed a car passing by the camera, stuttering forward at a painfully low frame rate. At the same time, he heard a car engine passing by outside the window.

"...Whoa. What's that?"

"I got an old webcam and made it into a surveillance camera. See? Over there."

Urushihara pointed out the window, toward a ball-shaped object perched on top of old, paint-chipped iron grating. A cord snaked out from the plastic device to his computer.

"I bought it 'cause I figured it'd tell us if anyone suspicious was nearby, but...I mean, it's black-and-white and this thing *still* can't keep up with the frame rate. You see what I mean? It's useless."

"I don't appreciate how you expect me to know that intuitively... but that's actually something pretty useful for a change, isn't it? If you have it set up outside, does that mean it can hold up against the weather?"

"Nah. It's old and not waterproof, so I'd have to bring it back in when it rains."

"...Wow. Never mind, then."

Crestfallen, Maou stepped away from the desk. Urushihara launched a parting shot behind him.

"Like, look at it this way. Any target I'd be 'hacking' into would be running on multiple supercomputer-class servers, each loaded with the latest in firewalls and security patches. Meanwhile, I've got a PC with a hard drive under one hundred gigs, a Pentium III processor, and only one USB port. It can barely even run all the crapware that's bundled with it. How am I supposed to compete?"

Maou had only one curt phrase to answer Urushihara's torrent of complaints.

"Dude, speak Japanese."

Any attempt on Urushihara's part to downplay his computer's abilities was totally lost on Maou and his complete lack of any computer knowledge whatsoever. Any attempt to berate his PC-purchasing skills whooshed right over his head.

For a moment, Urushihara was thrown by Maou's completely

ill-informed response, both as Devil King and as a member of modern Internet society. Soon, he pointed a finger back at his PC.

"And more to the point, if I leave this old computer running all day in this heat, it's gonna catch fire sooner or later. I ain't gonna be doing much of anything for a while."

Maou remained quiet. Even he understood that electronics had trouble handling high temperatures.

The environment within the Devil's Castle knew little of such modern marvels as air-conditioning. A bare wisp of wind coursed through the room when all the windows were thrown open. Their only recourse was to hope the fan could amplify the fresh breeze just a little.

Said fan was another purchase from the 100th Street shopping district, this one having run Maou one thousand yen at the thrift shop. That, alongside the bamboo blinds they bought from a home-improvement store to block direct sunlight, allowed them to just barely survive in the heat.

"Hey, by the way, what was all that clattering outside?"

Lucifer asked the question out of the blue, fanning his face with a paper fan festooned with advertisements for a neighborhood pachinko parlor. Maou and Ashiya exchanged glances.

"You've been here the whole time and you didn't notice?"

Maou pointed at the wall they shared with the adjacent apartment.

"Someone moved in next door."

Urushihara looked toward the wall as he nibbled on the pickled ginger included with his meal.

"Huhh?! Are you kidding me? Who would actually *move into* this pile of crap?"

There was no clearer demonstration of how useless the surveillance camera was, not to mention the person controlling it.

"You had to have heard *something* from the other room. There was a moving truck here and everything. Plus, the corridor window is wide-open. Didn't you notice the moving guys or anyone?"

Urushihara shook his head.

"Nope. Sure didn't."

"You were browsing videos and listening to music or whatever, weren't you?"

Maou tried to frown as disapprovingly as possible. Urushihara shook his head as he continued tucking into the pork and rice.

"No, really, I totally didn't notice."

"Quit talking with your mouth full! You're spraying bits of rice all over the place! And throw away that pointless surveillance camera at once!"

Ashiya's running commentary on Urushihara's self-indulgent lifestyle was quickly becoming another hallmark of the summer season around Devil's Castle.

"No way, dude! It cost me five thousand yen with the software!"

The shock waves that price quote sent across the room caused Ashiya's hand to slip as he attempted to tie a garbage bag closed, ripping it open at the mouth instead. Maou brought a hand to his forehead, staring listlessly at the floor.

"So did you run into whoever moved in yet?"

Maou shrugged at the useless Urushihara's question.

"Well...we met, I guess."

Nothing, not even shaking her or slapping her cheek, could get the girl who fell off the stairs earlier to wake up.

With no other option at hand, Maou brought her back upstairs, to the room she (hopefully) was moving into. The entryway to Room 202 was propped open with a door stopper.

The lighted one-hundred-square-foot space, a dead ringer for Devil's Castle next door, was packed to the gills with unmarked, new-looking cardboard boxes, as well as a polished, wooden, valuable-looking clothes chest and (oddly enough for the season) something resembling an open-air brazier.

Her appreciation for the traditional Japanese lifestyle apparently went beyond her wardrobe.

Maou and Ashiya looked at each other for a moment before venturing inside the residence of this strange woman. They brought her to the center of the room, laying her down gently.

She showed no signs of awakening anytime soon, but she was

breathing. After some debate, Maou and Ashiya decided to leave her alone, resolving to check up on her later and call an ambulance if she was still knocked out.

They removed the doorstop for safety's sake, though they naturally had no way to lock the door from the outside.

"The girl must have a hell of a lot of stuff, too. The room was floor-to-ceiling boxes."

"I'm not gonna ask you to stay out of sight since she's right next to us anyway, but try not to get involved with her as much as possible, all right?"

Urushihara's eyes teared up a little after Ashiya finally lost his patience and landed a sledgehammer blow on his head, but it wasn't enough to put him off finishing dinner.

"Huh. So she's young? Must be pretty effed in the head to move someplace like this."

He sat up as he attempted to toss the paper container into the garbage bag.

"How many times have I told you?! You need to wash out containers like that before throwing them away! I've said it a thousand times, if you don't clean them out, they'll stink up the place until the next garbage day!"

Ashiya, like clockwork, went off once again.

Urushihara was clearly peeved, but silently followed his orders and washed the empty bento box. Ashiya shouted at him again shortly for not separating his garbage the way the local authorities demanded, but Urushihara was less receptive to that advice.

"Ah, screw that. C'mon, let's go to the bathhouse! It's dark now!"

As always, he had his own priorities.

The Villa Rosa apartments lacked bathing facilities. That was part of the reason the rent was so cheap, but failing to bathe in Japan's hot, sticky summers was less a matter of being clean or not and more an issue of public health.

Urushihara, usually forbidden from journeying outside, was allowed to accompany Maou and Ashiya to the local public bath as long as it was after dark and he used a cap and his hair to conceal himself.

"Ughh… Give me a sec. I'll be ready once I brush my teeth. Can you get the ticket book out for me?"

The exasperated Ashiya barked the orders to Urushihara as he reached for his toothbrush.

"Sirs!"

The three demons stared at each other.

It was a woman's voice. The trio's eyes turned toward the front door. Then the doorbell rang out a single time.

They all knew a little about "speaking of the devil," being, by and large, devils themselves. The relief that she was alive and well intermixed with a sense of nervousness at having to deal with neighbors for the first time in their lives.

"Wh-what do we do?!"

Maou was stricken with panic. His two minions were far more collected.

"You're the man of the house, Your Demonic Highness."

"It says *Maou* on the card, right? Get your ass out there."

It was just the sort of warm encouragement he needed.

Glaring at his two humble servants, Maou gathered his breath and replied to the visitor outside.

"I-I'll be right there!"

Still gripped by an inexplicable nervousness, Maou opened the door.

"I apologize for intruding so late at night. My name is Suzuno Kamazuki, and I moved into the room next door earlier today."

A large cardboard box stood in front of the door, politely introducing itself to Maou.

"……"

UDON NOODLES —RESTAURANT USE ONLY, the box read.

"Um."

"If I may, about earlier…"

The box of noodles opened its mouth again.

"I must humbly apologize for my abject rudeness upon our first encounter, and for placing such an onerous burden upon you."

The box of noodles that had introduced itself as Suzuno Kamazuki bowed toward Maou, maintaining perfect balance as it pitched forward gracefully.

"Oner...wha? No, uh, it really wasn't anything big... Anyway, my name's Sadao Maou. It's good to meet you."

Failing to find any other option, he bowed lightly toward the industrial-sized package.

"I thank you for your kindness. I hope you will accept this gift, a token of my appreciation for my esteemed neighbor."

The box lurched forward...or, to be exact, was offered to him.

"Um...this is...?"

"I understand that an offering of noodles is the most appropriate and customary method of greeting one's new neighbors."

It was hard to see what was at all appropriate or customary about the gift, or its size, or its qualities, but if the box was really full of udon noodles, the Devil's Castle could very well eat for free the rest of the year.

"Oh...uh, well, thanks for the kind gesture."

His voice wavering as he thanked her, Maou picked up the box.

"Erff!"

It was so startlingly heavy, he almost dropped it on the spot.

Which would make sense. This box, easily big enough to occupy the entire front foyer of his apartment, might just be packed to the brim with udon noodles. One could only guess how many dozens of pounds it weighed.

Grimacing to support the unexpected weight, Maou gingerly placed the box at his feet as he sized up his visitor.

"I do hope it proves to suit your palate. Please; there is no need for modesty."

The young girl who had launched herself in dynamic fashion right into Maou's arms a few hours ago was standing there, now dressed in a somber-colored but nonetheless high-quality kimono and a pair of *zori* sandals.

"I come from an old farming family established long ago in the mountainous countryside. I'm afraid there is much I have yet to learn about city life, but I hope you will be kind enough to put the unfortunate events of before behind you, and provide whatever neighborly support you deign to offer."

Suzuno Kamazuki, no longer a box but now a small, young woman, lowered her head in a deliberate, well-practiced bow.

"Uhmm. Ah, yeah, certainly. You, too."

Maou bowed his own head down in a halfhearted attempt to return the favor.

Incongruous would be the only way to describe the impression she gave.

Judging by her swan dive down the stairs and bizarre parting words subsequently, he imagined she was just a bit touched in the head. Now that he had another good look at her, though, he realized that "just a bit" could be easily removed from that appraisal.

Her eyes were large, the bridge of her nose sharply defined. Her white skin and long, shiny hair were a perfect match for her navy-blue kimono and bright yellow sash. She cut an impressive figure, standing out there in the corridor, exhibiting her effortlessly perfect posture.

The expression on her face, dignified and betraying the strong will that lurked inside of her, added an even more powerful presence to her appearance.

In terms of pure looks, she could easily pass for her early teens, but the sheer practiced perfection of her Japanese wardrobe and mannerisms, coupled with her rather eccentric approach to language, made Maou wonder if she was transported from her home to Sasazuka via time machine.

As she bowed, even Maou's untrained eyes could tell that a great deal of attention had been paid to her hair. A bright red Japanese hairpin, decorated with a four-petaled flower, shone elegantly in the light.

With summer now in full swing, he had seen more and more women dressed in gaudy, fashion-oriented summer kimonos outside. But this

went beyond that. Plainly this was a woman who wore Japanese garments as her de facto first choice.

Looking up, Maou realized that Suzuno's blade-like eyes, brimming with energy, were fixated on his face. For just a few seconds, he flinched at her.

"So you are…Sadao Maou?"

"Huh? Uh, yeah, but…"

Suzuno averted her eyes in thought for a moment, apparently satisfied that it was indeed Maou in front of her. She nodded once, then looked back up at him.

"Is it true that you share your quarters with one Shiro Ashiya?"

"Buh?"

Without thinking, Maou turned his head back behind him. Ashiya looked just as surprised as he approached the front door.

"Um, yes, I am Ashiya. Maou is, ah, an old friend of mine. We are sharing a room together."

"Enchanted to meet you. I am Kamazuki. I have heard much about the both of you."

She's heard *what*, from *whom*? Noticing Ashiya and Maou exchanging glances with each other, Suzuno exhibited a subtle change in expression for the first time so far. Ever so slightly, the area between her eyebrows wrinkled up, as if she were baffled.

"I have yet to meet the landlord here in person. However, a person I believe to be the landlord posted me a letter through her real-estate agent. It read that her only tenant was Sadao Maou, living here with his friend."

So saying, Suzuno produced an envelope from her bosom, the envelope's frilliness more than familiar to the demons at this point. Maou had no idea until now that women stuffed things under their kimonos like that.

"She wrote that the people residing here were kind and sensibly minded, and that I could trust in their aid if I ever came across any difficulty."

It was not the sort of praise that delighted a malicious minion from the underworld.

That, and Maou had little to no interest in taking over any of his landlord's Villa Rosa management duties. Besides, why wasn't Shiba taking responsibility for this new girl, instead of pawning her off on them?

"Ah! There was a photograph included as well. I wanted to ask you, is this really our—"

Suzuno, suddenly reminded, made an attempt to take something else out of the envelope.

"No! No, don't! You don't have to take it out! I don't need to see it! That's her, all right! If you were going to ask whether the lady in that photo is actually human or not, then yep, that's definitely our landlord!"

Maou intuitively stopped her with all the force he could muster. Suzuno's eyes opened a notch wider at the sheer panic Maou exuded.

"Why are you so flustered, if I may ask? It is merely a woman in a colorful pair of glasses, relaxing in a half-submerged inner tube while—"

"Don't describe it! Please!"

Ashiya, for his part, was spooked enough to scurry back into the apartment.

Watching Suzuno reluctantly place the envelope back into her pocket, Maou breathed a sigh of relief. Perhaps the shock was absorbed a bit when someone of the same gender looked upon her. Of course, the question of whether you could even call the landlord a woman was still substantially in doubt, but finding a conclusive answer would achieve nothing for anyone. Thus, Maou resolved to file the whole landlord cheesecake pinup massacre into a padlocked X-file deep in a dark, cobwebbed corner of his mind.

"Uh. Right. But anyway, I'm glad you aren't hurt or anything. Oh, and thanks for the udon noodles. I'm not at home in the daytime usually 'cause I'm working at the MgRonald nearby, but if anything comes up, you can usually find him in here, so…"

Still recovering from his temporary bout of panic, Maou's voice broke slightly as he spoke to Suzuno.

"I know it is not exactly inviting, all of us men in the same room, but please let me know if anything's bothering you."

Ashiya's gentlemanly invitation boomed out from inside.

"Ah...yes. Thank you in advance, then."

Then, while it was hard to glean from her usual stony expression, it seemed to Maou that a flash of surprise crossed Suzuno's face before she turned her head downward.

"Oh, but keep in mind, that guy gets kind of carried away sometimes, so don't be afraid to shoo him away if he gets too annoying."

Maou attempted to put up a defensive wall, out of concern they were tromping too far into their female neighbor's life upon their first encounter.

In times like these, if a man gets too friendly too quickly, bad things happen. They always did to Maou, anyway.

"Oh, certainly not. I was not expecting such a warm reception, perhaps, but it gladdens me to have neighbors I can freely call upon. I look forward to learning all the many ins and outs of communal life from you."

He couldn't tell what was so unexpected about it, but the term *communal life* caught Maou's attention. He'd have to start by teaching her how to speak like someone from this century, for starters.

Despite this response, Suzuno bowed once more, turned her eyes toward the floor Maou was standing on, and let out a slight, startled exhale.

"Is there another among you?"

"Huh?"

"Oh...I simply noticed, there was another, different-sized set of footwear. I apologize if you were entertaining another visitor."

"No, um..."

Maou and Ashiya sized each other up. Trying to hide a roommate from their next-door neighbor would only serve to arouse more suspicion. Urushihara had yet to demonstrate an interest to listening to anyone's advice, besides. It'd be better, Maou thought, to make the first move instead of inviting further unwanted attention.

"We actually took on another roommate recently. But he's, like, a total shut-in, so he shouldn't bother you too much."

"I'm not a shut-in 'cause I *wanna* be, dude! Hey, I'm Urushihara! Nice to see you, finally!"

Said shut-in shouted his greeting from across the apartment. Maou wondered whether he really cared if the police found him or not.

"I see… And you as well."

This was enough to make Suzuno's eyes dart around, as if agitated. Not even the flying leap she took off the stairs changed her rigid expression. What did an unkempt freeloader do to her that *that* couldn't? Was it that strange to her, three grown men living in the same room?

But even that facial tic lasted for a mere instant, as she gave a shallow bow to Urushihara.

"Well, I had best haunt your doorstep no longer. I bid a good evening to you. Farewell for now!"

Then she turned her heels, her sandals squishing against the wooden floor as she returned to her room.

Once he was sure the door was closed, Ashiya crossed his arms, head tilted.

"A rather strange one, wasn't she?"

"I don't think we're in any position to toss *that* word around. But, hey, it's nice to have some generous neighbors, huh? Just like that, we've got some extra food."

He hoisted the box of udon up to his waist as he cheerfully commented on their unexpected visitor.

"*Man*, this is heavy."

The follow-up came out in a low whisper as he struggled with the weight.

✳

The cardboard boxes, large enough to occupy an entire corner of the room by themselves, loomed large over her living space.

She had decided to place the three enormous boxes here in the hall for the time being. Between the apartment's layout and her furniture, there was no place else convenient for them, but even this left only one closet door fully openable.

It was the start of a new week, a hot, humid, and overall oppressive Monday. Emi Yusa, still in her office-casual work outfit, groaned as she pondered over the problem facing her, fingers rested on her forehead. She had wanted to take a shower immediately upon returning home, but Sasuke Express paid her a visit at that exact moment, as if deliberately aiming to bother her.

Flipping on the AC to defend herself against the sickening heat, Emi brushed away the hair sticking to her sweat-soaked forehead as she read the packing slip.

In the *From* box, the word *EMERALDA* was written in characters that looked like a pile of small worms in a petri dish. *Food products* was written in the *contents* section.

At a loss to explain this package delivery, Emi paused for a moment before making her move. Taking out her phone, she called a number stored on it.

"...Hellooooo! This is Emeralda Etuuuuva."

She picked up on the seventh ring, her speech still a little uneasy from nervousness.

"I know. This is Emi... I mean, Emilia speaking."

"Indeed! Even after all this time, it seems I still get nervous with the tellllephone."

"You've had enough time to get used to it by now, haven't you?"

Emi chuckled to herself. She wasn't being serious, of course. There was no way she could expect the woman on the other end of the line to "get used to" such black magic. After all, the girl who introduced herself as Emeralda Etuva wasn't even in Japan. Or, to be exact, on Earth.

"I haven't spent that much time in Japan, soooo..."

Emi eyed the tower of boxes in front of her.

"I just got some packages with your name on them... What *are* they?"

Each of the three boxes was unnaturally heavy, enough so that the

Sasuke Express deliveryman brought each one into the apartment to save Emi and her spindly arms from having to struggle with them.

"It said on the packing slip that it's food, but…"

"Oh, did they make it oooover? Wowwww, that was faaast! I only sent them off yesterday!"

It probably *would* be a surprise to someone becoming familiar with the astonishing speed of Japan's delivery infrastructure for the first time.

"They contain holy energy for youuu! I modified its appearance so it wouldn't look conspicuous storing it within Japan."

"Holy… *What*?"

Emi pushed the table away from her as she rose.

"B-but why's it say *food*, then? They're all, like, super heavy. Is it bags of rice or something?"

"Rice…? Oh, right, the main food staple in Japan? No, not thaaaat. I set it up so it's divided into small portions that're easy to work with! They're famous on Earth, right? Liiiike, one swig fills you up with power, yeah?"

"One swig?"

She raised an eyebrow as she took the packing tape off the topmost package. Tossing it to the side, she opened the box and peered inside.

"Whoa…"

It was packed with a vast array of smaller boxes, wadded-up paper wedged between them. Each one had the logo of a well-known Japanese pharmaceutical company stamped on it. Opening one of them up, Emi's suspicions were confirmed—eleven small brown bottles greeted her, each filled with a clear liquid and with a gold cap affixed to the top.

"'5-Holy Energy B'…?"

"Oh, not a B. That's a β. Beta, y'knoooow? Like, kind of a beta test."

"That's not the point. Emeralda. So if I drink one of these, it'll refill my holy power?"

"You've got it! By the way, Emiliaaaaa…"

The voice on the other end suddenly grew inquisitive.

"What's the Devil King been up to laaaately?"

"Well…"

Emi thought for a moment before answering.

"The same as always, pretty much. We usually wind up arguing whenever we run into each other, but we're both busy with work, so I haven't really had a chance to gauge his private life."

"……"

The indecisiveness was palpable.

"Emiliaaa…do you understand what you're telling meeee?"

"Huh?"

Emi was at a loss. Emeralda chose her words carefully as she continued.

"You sound like someone whining that you're so busy, you're having trouble making time for your lovvvver."

All right. Maybe *carefully* was a stretch. Straight down the middle, in fact. And it still managed to strike Emi right on the noggin.

Emi compared Emeralda's observation with what she just said a moment ago.

"Dah…wha…nragh…"

The phone mike picked up every phase of her raging emotions.

"What're you *talking* about, Emer?! You should *know* it's nothing like that between us! I—I mean, as long as we're both living in Japan, we have to follow Japanese laws, go to Japanese work, make Japanese money, the whole bit! When I say that I can't watch over every waking moment he spends, it doesn't *mean* anything more than… Unnghghh!!"

"I know, I knowww…"

Emeralda cracked up as she picked on her companion. Emi's fury continued unabated, her breath quickening in pace.

"Stop making fun of me! I am the Hero of Ente Isla! And he's the Devil King! He's my sworn enemy, and that *never* changes! The mere thought that we're lo…lo…*lovers* makes me nauseous!"

Indeed, the woman calling herself Emi Yusa was none other than Emilia Justina, the Hero who dispatched the demonic forces serving the Devil King Satan and brought lasting peace back to her world. Just as Satan was now mild-mannered MgRonald burger flipper

Sadao Maou, so, too, was Emilia posing as Emi Yusa, working for Shinjuku-based telephone company Dokodemo as a contracted call-center operator.

Emeralda Etuva, on the other end of the line, was Emilia's traveling companion. The court alchemist for the empire of Saint Aile, the nation that boasted the largest swath of territory on Ente Isla's Western Island, she followed Emilia to Japan as she pursued the Devil King two months ago, just in time to take in the Hero's battle against Lucifer.

After that came to a close, Emi gained a key advantage Maou lacked—the ability to accept support from Emeralda and her companions.

Further, to prevent their regular "idea link"–based conversations from being intercepted by a third party, she had sent her friends Emeralda and Albert a handy device for long-distance verbal communication—a cell phone, in other words—making it easier to exchange information on a more intimate level.

"Ugh… Look, I'll admit I've been a bit lazy with monitoring him. I'll go check him out tomorrow, all right? It'll be a good chance to test out these bottles, besides. Too bad I can't invoice you for the transport costs to *his* place!"

The old wound to Emi's heart, caused by a hapless police officer who mistook her and Maou for a couple having a spat when they were taken to the station one night, continued to fester within her.

"I don't know what you meeean by that, but anyway, greaaat!"

Emeralda's voice suddenly changed tone as she spoke.

"Emer?"

"So…pleeeease, Emiliaaaa?"

Emeralda's normally easygoing verbal pace seemed to slow down even further as she took pains to emphasize each word.

"Pleeeease, don't do anything that would turn me and you into ennnnemies, all riiight?"

"…!"

Emi swallowed nervously. This came as a complete surprise.

"I know about 'Emiiii', and Japaaaan, and Maoooou, too. So pleeeease…"

Her voice was soft and approachable. It made the meaning lurking behind her words all the more powerful.

"I'll take that to heart. Don't worry. I am the Hero. On the name of my mother and father, I swear I will not follow the path of the mistaken."

"Ah, how reassuring to hear thaaaat!"

Nordo, her father, disappeared into the raging flames of the battle between human and demon. And:

"Your moooother, you know… She was suuuuch a nice woman, Emilia!"

"It'd be a bit strange if an angel *wasn't* nice, wouldn't it?"

Her mother was the archangel Laila. Such was the power granted to Emilia Justina, the Hero who bore the power created by her half-angel blood.

"But how have things been over there? I know it's weird how peaceful things are even though the Devil King's running free, but has anything changed with the Church and all the other nations at all?"

"Wellll…"

Emi could hear Emeralda shuffling a large sheaf of papers in her hands.

"The plan to kill you off alongside the Devilllll King was led by only a tiny cabal of high Church officers. And in public, anyway, you and all of us are the heroes that saved the world! So no nation's shown any outward signs, anyway, of sending assassins your waaay."

Emi immediately noticed what Emeralda was trying to tiptoe around.

"Outwardly, you say."

"Indeed, veeery much so!"

She could practically hear Emeralda grin bitterly across the line.

"But even if the main powers don't make a mooove, there's been quite a lot of suspicious actiiiivity from powerful nobles with deep

Church connections, not to mention smaller nations and entities hoping to ingraaatiate themselves with the Chuuurch."

"I wonder what I could've done to make those big shots hate me so much."

"Oh, not like logic works against them. All they care about is protecting themselllves, and their iiinfluence."

The bitterness was now clear in Emeralda's voice.

"I've heard talk about someone enlisting the Assassin's Guillld, and underground bounty hunterrrs, and even the Reconciliation Panel taking aaaction…but that's still firmly in the realm of ruuuumors."

"Panel of…what?"

Emi was offput by the unfamiliar term. Emeralda, apparently realizing this, corrected herself.

"Oh, I'm sorry, I mean the Council of Inquiiisitors. They changed their naaame recently."

"What? The Inquisitors…? Then why would they be targeting me? It's not like they'd bother going after the Devil King at this point, either. Why's that rumor going around?"

"Probably because Olba hasn't returned, I'd saaaay."

Olba Meiyer was one of the six archbishops, the ordained group of ministers that wielded the brunt of power within the Church.

The archbishops were tasked with making all final decisions related to the direction of the Church. Each of its members retained direct and exclusive control of their own section of the Church hierarchy.

Olba was able to gain a position of such confidence with Emilia, accompanying her for most of her conquest against the Devil King, in part because he was in control of the Church's diplomatic and missionary operations.

As archbishop, Olba had extensive experience spreading the tenets of the Church far and wide across foreign lands.

Emilia's travels began in the Western Island, where the Church's grip on power was strongest. Since the Hero still had little exposure to the outside world at that time, Olba—with his talents as a Church administrator and vast knowledge of lands where the gods he served were less known and accepted—was the ideal choice to accompany her as she challenged the Devil King.

The Council of Inquisitors was a somewhat unique subgroup within the Church's missionary department. Their work was the sort that never came into the limelight, but was nonetheless essential to the entire organization, from surveying foreign lands as a sort of vanguard force for the missionaries, to purging the younger clergymen of their corrupt morals should they lose themselves to debauchery during training, to aiding the Church theologists as they nurtured and developed holy doctrine.

On the other hand, they also served as a sort of public police force within the Church bureaucracy, declaring a nontrivial number of people to be heretics in their regular inquisitions. This more public face of the Council saddled them with the sort of dark reputation no political organization enjoyed.

"It sounds like the missionary department is trying to find out what haaaappened to Olba, so it might be that some among them are aware of you, too, Emiliaaaa. Try not to let your guard down, all riiight? Some of them might try pushing things too quickly and start meddling with Japaaaan before long."

"I'll keep that in mind. So are you and Al all right?"

"Oh, they've got their eyyyes on us, what with all the stuff we pulled on 'em. But nothing beyond that's happened to us, noooo."

"Guess there's no rest for the Hero and her companions, huh?"

"Guess notttt."

Neither Emeralda nor Albert was the sort of guileless goody-goody that could be rubbed out of existence by some half-cocked assassin. If she said they were okay, Emi was perfectly fine with believing her.

"Aaanyway, I know talking for too long's gonna rack up your phone bill, so I better hang up, huhhh?"

"I'm not sure if it costs anything past the base fee or not, actually. It's the idea link that's actually connecting our two voices, after all. The phones are just an easier way to access it."

"Welll, just in case, I wouldn't want you going broke on myyy account, sooo..."

"I appreciate the thought. Thanks for the holy magic, anyway. Say hi to Albert for me."

Just as she was about to shut off the call, Emeralda quickly interjected.

"Ooh, wait, I forgot somethiiing! Watch you don't drink too many 5-Holy Energy βs at once, okaaay?"

"Too much? Is there a limit or something?"

Turning the small bottle of liquid in her hand, she noticed that, where the label would usually list up the ingredients, it simply read *Holy power* instead.

"There is! I mean, we can refill our own holy powers here as eaaasily as we breathe. But deliberately ingesting it like that? Well, it's never been done beforrre."

"Oh..."

"So that's why it's in beta, you seeee? We tested it on people heeeere, but let's just say two bottles per day should be your max, all riiight? Drink one in the morning and one in the afternoon... Oh, but if you forget your morrrning dose, don't try making up for it by drinking two in one go."

"...I wouldn't mind asking a few questions about that, Emer, but anyway, I hear you."

"Wonderfulll! Always stick to the proper dosage, okaaay? Bye for nowwww!"

Emeralda ended the call. Emi placed the phone on her low *kotatsu* table, still confused.

The packing slip, with Emeralda's unsteady, childlike Japanese writing on it. The hefty boxes Sasuke Express just delivered to her. The weird way she seemed to soak up Japanese culture and customs, even though her stint in Japan lasted just a few hours.

"Where...*is* she, anyway?"

Still confused, her eyes scrutinized the bottle in her hand.

"Guess I'll give it a shot."

She twisted off the metal cap and was immediately greeted with the unnatural smell of syrupy cold medicine.

Slowly, hesitantly, she tasted a few drops.

"Huh. Yeah, it's just an energy shot, all right. Does this really work?"

It certainly tasted familiar enough—the heavy sweetness that seemed to linger on the tongue for far too long, almost past the cloying medicinal aftertaste.

Emi didn't distrust Emeralda, exactly, but between the packaging, the smell, and the taste, it was no different from the sort of off-brand energy drinks flogged in plastic racks next to the register at seedy twenty-four-hour convenience stores.

It was as if those companies were trying to invent new laws of physics in order to cram just a few more milligrams of taurine into each bottle.

Emi took her time emptying the bottle into her mouth. The liquid burned as it went down her throat, leaving a lingering, metallic, vitamin-y essence that made her twitch her nose. It energized her, yes, but regular usage couldn't be good for her long-term health.

Holy energy or not, it didn't seem like the drink offered any immediate dramatic effects. She was about to toss the bottle into the kitchen trash when she noticed a disheveled mess at the edge of her vision.

"Whoops…"

The packing tape she had pried off the box and tossed haphazardly away was now stuck to the cover of the TV-listings magazine she kept next to her set.

"Aahhhhhhh!"

She squealed in dismay as she ran to the magazine.

"They put *Vice-Shogun Mito* on the cover, too…"

Carefully, she tried to peel the tape off of the photo of her favorite samurai-drama star. The adhesive mercilessly stuck to the cover, ripping the smiling face apart.

Emil looked at the magazine in her right hand, then the ball of tape in her left hand, then sighed. The breath seemed to ferry all the emotion in her body out with it.

"No, no, I can't let this bring me down…!"

She had just promised Emeralda that she'd go behind enemy lines and stake out Devil's Castle. A soldier's mental outlook always had a disproportionate effect on her performance. Venturing past no-man's-land in her current state of gloom might cost her everything she held dear.

Rallying her spirits, she tossed both tape wad and magazine into the trash.

"…I don't have any energy to cook. Curry works, I guess."

Despite her rebellious sneer of resolve as she rose, her steps were slow and clunky as she plodded toward the kitchen and took out her favorite New Hampshire curry mix and Auntie Nan's instant rice packet.

Tossing the curry block on a plate, Emi put it in her microwave and set it on high for two minutes.

With a low, exhausted groan, she watched listlessly as the plate happily spun around, and around, and around inside.

Something about the upcoming visit to the Devil King's precariously flimsy apartment tomorrow made her feel inescapably despondent.

"I…*am* the Hero, right? Zapping a plate of expired curry for dinner doesn't *not* make me the Hero, does it?"

Beep, replied the microwave. She responded with a sharp glare.

Next came the instant rice. Opening the packet just a bit, Emi shoved it back in and tapped out another two-minute order.

"That journey across Ente Isla would've been a lot easier with a microwave and some instant rice, though. Maybe I could take some kitchen appliances home with me, at least. I bet we could harness some lightning alchemy or something to power it with… Oh, wait, would a Divine Thunder spell generate AC or DC power?"

The gap between ideal and reality that began to trouble her long ago had ballooned since she defeated the Devil King—something that Emi herself was less than aware of.

Her expression loosened softly at the smell of the curry plate, a hot meal brought to her in four minutes by the mighty triumphs of her adopted civilization.

"Ooh, I'm almost out of shampoo. Better grab some soon..."

After dinner, she thought over her shower plans while glancing at her wall calendar.

"Is there anything good on TV yet? Oh, wait, *Vice-Shogun Mito* airs tonight!"

The recent rise in moments spent talking to herself was another change that escaped Emi's notice.

✳

Emi sighed as she stared at the passcard the ticket machine spat at her, beeping its annoying tune the whole time.

"At least Sasazuka and Hatagaya are within range of my commuter pass. Got that going for me, anyway."

Emi, whose work commute ferried her between Eifukucho and Shinjuku stations, had a commuter pass that her company paid for. That allowed her to get off at places like Sasazuka and Hatagaya along the line, but looking at it that way, it made it seem like her life-and-death struggle against the Devil King was being funded by the HR department at her job with Dokodemo.

She had taken advantage of the stop at Sasazuka to update her pass. Placing the receipt in her wallet, she wearily lumbered away from the shade of the station roof.

"Every single day, why's it got to be so *hot*...?"

Stepping out of the station's entrance, positioned underneath the elevated rail line, Emi was blinded by the sun's rays, already pounding down in the early morning hours.

Any fervor that remained for the Devil's Castle surveillance mission she promised Emeralda was in grave danger of being burned to a crisp by something even hotter.

Every day was getting to be like this.

In order to defeat Malacoda, supreme commander of the Devil

King's Southern Island expeditionary force, Emi had to slog from one end of the island's tropical desert clime to the other on foot. Here, meanwhile, 120 yen was all it took to score a cold drink, and a quick stop at any nearby café would provide instant air-conditioned comfort. But, still, summer is summer, one of the universe's few truly universal tenets.

Emi took out a flower-print umbrella from her shoulder bag, suited both for the rain and for keeping the sunlight off the back of her neck. Dabbing her forehead with a handkerchief, she set off down the perilous road to Devil's Castle.

This was day four of her drive to keep daily tabs on the Devil King, something she resolved to do upon receipt of her 5-Holy Energy β shipment. Continuing with this thankless, unrewarding job underneath the punishing summer heat required a remarkable amount of endurance.

On the first day, she staked out a position in the bookstore across from Maou's workplace near Hatagaya station, reading through all the nearby magazines on the rack as she kept constant vigil over her target. On the second, she made it to Devil's Castle, but apart from the quiet sounds of normal life, the only unusual thing she saw was a fatigued-looking Ashiya purchasing scallions, dashi soup stock, instant barley-tea packets, and a new drain filter for his kitchen sink. On the third, work obligations kept her away.

"I'm...a total stalker right now, aren't I?"

Emi chided herself as she quenched her thirst with a small plastic bottle of mineral water.

Standing guard over someone's personal life and workplace on a daily basis without any actual purpose would be the textbook definition of a stalker, yes.

Outside of the one day she was too busy to sustain her stalker duties, this was the most concerted effort she made to keep tabs on Sasazuka ever since she first discovered the Devil King two months ago.

And today, on day four, she was butting against the weekend with absolutely nothing to show for it.

Fridays were always busy at work. Instead of staggering over after a long day dealing with calls, she opted for an early-morning spy run, even though the rate at which the sunlight was sapping her will to live was a crucial miscalculation.

"Nngh! I need to be reasonable here! If the Devil King and his gang are just working, eating, and sleeping every day, then great! Hooray for peace!"

Emi tried her best to inspire herself as she walked down a road alongside an irrigation canal that crossed north-south through Sasazuka's residential area.

"…And here I am, hanging around these guys, who are just trying to mind their own business. I'm *totally* a stalker."

It didn't take long for her brain to work against her again.

Once the apartment building that housed the Devil's Castle was in sight, Emi stopped to check on the bottle of 5-Holy Energy β in her shoulder bag.

She hadn't felt any need for it up to now. She had her doubts she ever would.

And if she did, she was even *more* doubtful that the liquid inside would have any effect on her at all.

"Let's just check up on things and get to work… The Devil King's probably sleeping anyway, this early in the morning."

Emi, demonstrating a clear lack of enthusiasm for her chosen duty even before arriving, folded up her umbrella and placed it in her bag to avoid being too conspicuous. Sneaking past the simple concrete-block wall that delineated the Villa Rosa Sasazuka property from its neighbors, she looked up at Room 201, the one closest to her on the other side.

The Devil's Castle lacked air-conditioning, so the windows were constantly left open, letting her hear the castle's denizens conversing with each other. It's not like they were screaming at each other every day, though, so Emi wasn't privy to exactly what they were saying.

Only once had she picked up on Ashiya, the human version of the

Great Demon General Alciel, lecturing Urushihara, the human version of Lucifer, about wasting money on something or other. It demonstrated all too well the pointlessness of keeping such close tabs on them.

"They must've done the laundry today. Nice job hanging all of it. Did they just throw it wherever it'd stay up, or what?"

The clothing and washcloths hanging off the window frames were hanging haphazardly in the wind, hopelessly wrinkled. Time passed by slowly as she contemplated this, until she had finally emptied her water bottle.

"...Well, nothing, I guess. I'm still a little early, but maybe I should head for work."

Just as she muttered it to herself:

"My goodness, can't you handle the laundry with at least a modicum of gentleness? I had no idea you knew so little of housekeeping, Hanzou."

"?!"

Quickly, Emi flattened herself against the apartment's outer wall to stay unnoticed, praising her fast reflexes as she did.

She froze at the sudden voice, her body instinctively carrying her to safety as she assessed the situation.

"If you hang this in such a wrinkled state, it will lose its shape! And you'll see the most ghastly of crinkles once it dries. You should at least be aware of *that* much."

Taking out a hand mirror, Emi extended it past the corner of the wall to examine the upstairs corridor.

It was a girl.

A girl, one she had never seen before, was evening out the wrinkles in the Devil's Castle's laundry, piece by piece.

"Right. Now, do it again. These summer blankets, as well. Spread them out wide, then use these clothespins to keep them in place. And if they fall down, back into the wash they go!"

"Yeah, yeah. Sorry."

The sheepish voice that responded to her was undoubtedly Urushihara's.

This was no mirage, no case of mistaken identity. The hand mirror didn't give her a clear view, but there was definitely a girl there, wearing a triangular head scarf, inside Devil's Castle.

"...I doubt anyone's living on the first floor."

Slowly, Emi edged along the wall, checking that no one was looking down before hiding under a tree directly beneath Room 201. She was now totally concealed from the second floor above.

"Jeez. It's like Ashiya cloned himself or something."

"You have nothing to blame but your own laziness, Hanzou. If you intend to stay indoors like a hibernating mouse all day, the least you could do is assist with the daily chores."

"I swear to...want...say it, too..."

Emi could hear someone that sounded like Ashiya as the girl and Urushihara spoke to each other, but—perhaps because he was on the opposite end of the window—he was difficult to make out.

She focused, trying to decipher the muffled voice, but soon the other two grew too quiet to understand. And even worse:

"Ugh...not now! Jeez, pipe *down*, you bastards!"

The countless thousands of cicadas that called Emi's tree home were crying out the plaintive summer call, simultaneously, at full volume.

Jii jii rhee rhee jkk jkk jkk cht cht cht rheeeeeooouuuuuhhh... The cacophony of calls from this single tree seemed to morph into a single wall of noise, symbolizing the ardent, all-encompassing urges that drove these chatty beasts as they staked their lives upon the only summer they'd ever experience.

Something light bounced off Emi's head. She brought a hand up, only to find it was a discarded cicada skin.

"...They *have* to be trying to mess with me. There's more than one species in there, too."

Emi discarded the skin as she grumbled at no one in particular. But even the Hero of Ente Isla, gifted in all the languages of the world, had trouble getting her point across to the cicada race.

Resigning herself to the futility of trying to shut them all up, Emi shifted her thoughts to her next move.

This was the first major change in four days. She couldn't leave until she got to the bottom of this. The girl from before might be some new visitor from the demon realm, someone Emi didn't know about.

Judging by their laundry-themed discussion, she could tell this interloper was no immediate threat to the area. Regardless, Emi wasn't going to let this opportunity slip through her fingers.

"This might be risky, but so be it…"

Steeling her resolve, she tiptoed away from the window and toward the front stairway.

Then, slowly, as to avoid making any sound, she climbed the stairs. She had her work heels on, so she kept a careful hand on the guard-rail, ensuring she wouldn't take an embarrassing tumble like before.

By the time she reached the end, breathing shallowly the whole way, she was covered in sweat.

The kitchen window overlooking the outdoor corridor was open as expected, providing what little ventilation the apartment had to offer.

"Honestly, Hanzou, what will we ever do with you? Surely this is not beyond your comprehension."

It was the girl from before. Emi crouched down beneath the iron bars covering the window as she listened.

"Now, then. First, you dice these shallots and grate some ginger, then you use some cold water to dilute the soup stock. Then all you have to do is bring the udon noodles to a boil, and it'll be ready to eat at a moment's notice. You can even serve them chilled, if you like, by immersing them in cold water right after they're done boiling. Add a raw egg, and it will be simply perfect."

"Oh, man, you want me to boil noodles in *this* heat?"

"That is exactly what Ashiya does for you, every day and every meal. It would be only proper to offer him some gratitude in return."

It sounded like the girl's diatribe against Urushihara was still underway. At least the topic had shifted from laundry, thankfully.

"Don't let up on him, Ms. Kamazuki. I yell, and yell, and yell at him, and he never listens…"

Finally, Ashiya came in loud and clear. "Ms. Kamazuki" must be the girl's name. The listlessness in Ashiya's voice gave Emi more than a bit of pause.

"I will take care of preparations today, so watch me carefully, lest Shiro chides your performance on the morrow. Here, grate the ginger for me. You know how to use a grater, I trust."

"All right... Hmm? Hey, Ashiya, we didn't use up all the ginger, did we?"

Emi heard the refrigerator open, followed by Urushihara's voice as he peered inside. Then, Ashiya's weak, wavering voice continued.

"Ah... Last night's was the last of it. Sorry, Ms. Kamazuki. We'll have to make do with shallots alone today... Urushihara, shut the damned fridge door behind you!"

The strength popped right back into his voice at the end.

"Hmm, no ginger? It'll be quite lacking in nutrition otherwise. I think I have some ginger amongst the vegetables I brought along. Perhaps I could fetch some?"

Emi could tell this Kamazuki girl was cooking inside Devil's Castle. It raised the question of how she and the demons of that stronghold came to know each other in the first place.

She was never granted the time to calmly think it over.

"Let me look inside my room. I'm quite sure I had a healthy supply left."

The woman's voice began to shift from the kitchen to the front door. Was she going outside? Emi's head swiveled around in a panic. There was no place to hide safely.

"Hanzou, while I'm gone, I want you to unravel the noodles for me with those kitchen chopsticks. Slowly, now. Make sure none of the strands stick to each other."

"Right, right, right."

"One *right* is quite enough! I will return shortly."

The front door rattled. She was coming out! There was no time to guess which "room" she was headed for. Emi had to get away.

Her panic had caused her to lose track of her feet.

"Ah..."

The next thing she knew, Emi was midair, her feet slipping right off the top step of the staircase. The bright blue morning sky sparkled before her, the cicadas providing the ideal background music for her upcoming journey downward.

Off the corner of her eye, she saw her phone, her wallet, her commuter-pass holder, her folded umbrella, her half-read paperback novel, her makeup case, her hand mirror, her handkerchief, her memo pad, her bottle of 5-Holy Energy β, her toothpick case, a tissue packet with an advertisement for some loan-sharking firm printed on it, her pen case, her lip balm (which, for some reason, was unscrewed all the way out), and everything else in her shoulder bag disperse in all directions into the air.

"Yaaaaaagghhhhh!!"

After a moment to take all of that in, Emi herself began to fall in majestic fashion. She didn't know exactly how much force she applied to the foot that slipped, but depending on how she landed, there was the potential for some serious injury. She braced for impact, unable to find a way to soften the blow in midair, when:

"Oof...?!"

With a dull, soft *thud*, the falling stopped without warning.

Emi closed her eyes out of instinct, but the pain was nothing like what she pictured. Instead, all she heard was the pitter-pat of assorted small objects falling around her, and:

"Owwwwwwwww..."

A familiar groaning voice right next to her.

Timidly, she dared to open her eyes.

"...Can't you go up and down the stairs *quietly* at least once in your life?"

The dejected-looking face of the Devil King—well, Sadao Maou, really—was right in front of hers.

"Man, I sure picked the wrong girl to rescue. Not like you're gonna reward me or anything."

"D-Devil King!!"

Emi shouted it out, then quickly shook her head, still unable to grasp the situation.

The assorted possessions in her bag were now littered around her on the ground, the packet of tissues perfectly perched on top of Maou's head. Emi herself, however, was in a more precarious position.

"L-l-let me down! What...what are you *doing*...?!"

Emi felt her blood boil from head to toe. Her body was was currently scooped up into Maou's arms.

Maou must have grabbed her midfall, but the way he was cradling her body like a baby was adding insult to injury for the Hero, one she could barely stand.

The summer heat and the sense of shame at involving Maou in this sordid scene were about to make her burst into flames.

"Put...put me down right now! Wh-what're you trying to do to me?!"

Emi began to flail her arms and legs, her face glowing red despite herself.

"Well, *you're* the one falling off my stairs! Stop...stop squirming like that! We're really gonna... *Erngh!*"

Before he could finish the thought, one of Emi's toes landed a clean hit on Maou's temple.

With a groan, Maou's arms loosened their grip, sending Emi tumbling downward.

"Agh!"

It was a textbook landing—on her butt, right on the paving stones at the bottom of the stairs. She winced as she rubbed her tailbone.

"Oooogh..."

"Don't 'oooogh' me! Eesh! No good deed ever goes unpunished with you, huh?!"

Maou glared down at the wincing Emi, eyes tearing up a bit as he held a hand to his temple.

"Good deed, my ass! You, you, you didn't do anything weird to me while my eyes were closed, did you?!"

Emi held her arms close to her in a defensive posture as Maou continued to rant and rave above her, eyes still lolling around.

"Nothing happened while your eyes were closed! Nothing besides all of your crap bouncing off my head! Did you *aim* at me, or what?!"

DEVIL'S CASTLE FLOOR PLAN
SUZUNO'S ROOM
I WELCOME YOU, MY NEIGHBORS.
ROOM 202
CLOSET (NO SHELVES)
TOILET
READING MATERIAL
OUTDOOR CORRIDOR
N
PLEASE KEEP THIS AREA ORGANIZED.
HOUSEHUSBAND SANCTUARY
URUSHIHARA'S COMPUTER DESK
KOTATSU'S TABLE (PUT AWAY WHEN SLEEPING)
SINK
FRIDGE
WASHER
ROOM 201
SHOES
THIS IS SUCH A PIT.
KIND OF CRAMPED, HUH?
BOOKSHELF
SHOE CASE
THESE STAIRS HAVE TO BE CURSED!
EMI'S 13 STEPS OF HELL

"Well, that's what you get for all the evil deeds you've perpetrated on a daily basis!"

"I'm a law-abiding citizen! A lot more than *you* are right now, I'm guessing!"

"What right do you have to say that?! Apologize to all the law-abiding citizens of this nation at once!"

"Look, don't even get me started, okay? Or how about I toss *you* down the stairs one more time? Maybe *then* you'll show me some gratitude!"

"I'd sooner go bungee jumping without a rope than thank you! What're you even *doing* down here, anyway? I thought you slept past noon every day!"

Taking another look at Maou, Emi realized he was wearing cotton work gloves. An old broom was lying on the ground alongside the dust balls and the contents of her shoulder bag.

How *dare* the Devil King even *think* of doing something like sweeping around his apartment building!

"I'm allowed to be wherever I want, all right? What's so bad about getting up early?! I'm trying to stick to a healthy schedule so I don't get sick this summer!"

"You? Healthy? You're practically the poster child for MgRonald!"

"What're *you* two doing...?"

Urushihara, picking up on the pointless argument unfolding below, picked that exact moment to venture outside.

"I simply must apologize. This would not have happened if I hadn't thrown open the door so quickly."

The girl in the kimono bowed deeply toward Emi. She must have thought this was simply a wrong-place-at-the-right-time accident.

"No, no, not at all!"

Emi violently shook her head in response.

"I just kind of lost track of my footing when I wasn't paying attention."

Maou watched on, a sullen look on his face as he slurped up his cold udon in soup stock.

A wholly unexpected sight unfolded before Emi's eyes in the Devil's Castle.

First, there was Ashiya, lying down with a blanket over him, looking strangely gaunt.

Then there was the gigantic box in the kitchen. Next to it, a girl in a kimono, apron, and head scarf busily slaved away at the counter.

Beyond the udon she had heard about, Emi noticed a surprisingly healthy selection of dishes laid out in the kitchen—cold blocks of tofu sprinkled with *myoga* ginger and sesame leaves, accompanied by a salad of mustard spinach steeped in a dashi-based sauce.

"I picked up most of the stuff you dropped outside, Yusa."

"Oh, thanks. Could you put it over there for me, please?"

Emi wasn't thrilled at Urushihara pawing her personal possessions, but something stopped her from erupting in front of Suzuno. She turned to pick them up.

"Ugh. I *hate* the way you talk. All high and mighty like that."

In Urushihara's mind, she was unsuccessful at hiding her disdain toward the denizens of this tiny square dot of a castle. But she shrugged, uninterested in providing an excuse.

"And what's with *this* thing? It's like an oven outside, and you're still doing energy shots?"

Emi should have expected no less from Urushihara. He had the small bottle of 5-Holy Energy β in hand, dangling it in front of her like a grade school bully as she tried to retrieve her bag.

Her internal reaction was less furious rage and more a light sense of panic. Small flasks of holy energy were not the kind of thing she wanted bandied around Devil's Castle.

"Hey! Give that back!"

With a swipe, she snatched the bottle out of Urushihara's hand, stuffing it deep into her bag. A bead of cold sweat ran down her back as she glared at him.

"If you drink that stuff, you're gonna wind up crashing like Ashiya."

"Crashing? What, don't tell me the heat's made you sick…"

Emi flashed an honestly surprised look at Ashiya, lying on the floor.

He clicked his tongue like an insolent child before turning over to his side, away from her.

"So what if it did? I don't feel too well sometimes, either, you know."

They may have lost all of their demonic energy, but to Emi and Ente Isla, the discovery that extreme heat was detrimental to demons' health was nothing short of groundbreaking.

"Not feeling too well? Like, what happens to you, exactly?"

"I dunno, I kind of lose my appetite. It's like my stomach starts bothering me and stuff."

Urushihara was overjoyed to explain, "I wouldn't find that enjoyable."

Emi shrugged, not finding the topic enjoyable enough to pursue.

"I am not doing this to make you 'enjoy' anything, you..." Ashiya, his drained voice leaping upon Emi, seemed to be having the least enjoyment of all.

Given how Ashiya was always the one demon to constantly treat Emi as a hostile invader, this was a sight she wished she could record and use to blackmail him in the future.

"It would seem my attempt at charity was the unfortunate cause."

Emi turned toward the girl.

Her kimono truly brought the best out of her well-defined, beautiful face. It was such a perfect package, Emi could have easily confused her for a samurai-drama actress. That was how dignified the aura around Suzuno was, like she wasn't even of this world.

Emi found her eyes subconsciously attracted to her chest area.

About the same as me, maybe...?

She sighed. There was an odd sense of relief.

Suzuno may have been the perfect Japanese beauty, but at least one aspect of her differed little from Emi.

The girl, for her part, had a frozen look of anguish or regret on her face, blissfully unaware of Emi's pointless self-comparison.

"I feel terribly remorseful about it. Perhaps I should have chosen something more nutritious to repay these fine men with."

"No, no, Ms. Kamazuki, it isn't your fault. I am enjoying every bit of these udon noodles."

From within his blanket cocoon, Ashiya placated Suzuno, his voice a far cry from the one he addressed Emi with.

"Yeah. The problem's the menu, really. I mean, yeah, it's easy to cook and it tastes okay, but eating chilled udon day in, day out in this heat would make anyone keel over after a while."

The observation from Urushihara, who had yet to lift a finger to contribute to the Castle food supply, drew cold stares from the rest of the room.

Just then, Suzuno stretched her body and turned toward Emi, as if remembering something.

"But I see I've forgotten the most important matter! My name is Suzuno Kamazuki. I have only just settled my belongings down next door in Room 202 last week. I come from a well-known family in a very remote place, one not exposed to the modern trappings of the world, so I remain rather unaccustomed to day-to-day life here. I do hope you'll help a simple country girl make her way in this grand city."

"Uh…yeahh… I'm Emi Yusa. Good to meet you."

The unexpectedly stiff and polite greeting from the woman meekly kneeling before her made Emi feel obliged to arch her back straight upward as well.

"But…and I don't mean any offense…I'm amazed you chose a place like this."

Emi pointed a finger at the dusty, dry tatami mats that lined the Devil's Castle floor, more than a trace of doubt in her speech.

Before she found the condo she currently lived in, Emi's rental agent went into great detail about the things a single woman needed to be aware of living by herself.

Her apartment was on the fifth floor, but even now, she did things like purchase a couple of men's boxers and such just so she could hang them up alongside the rest of her laundry. The buzzer intercom on the ground floor was another plus in her mind.

Villa Rosa Sasazuka, meanwhile, was cheap and close to the rail station, but from the eyes of an impartial observer, it was not at all suited for a young girl living alone.

It was constructed in the Stone Age; there was no bath or air conditioner or balcony; the doors had nothing but simple cylinder locks on them; most of the rooms were completely empty; and the only other tenants were a pack of sadistic monsters from another world.

Judging by the careful exactitude with which she dressed herself—kimonos can be such a pain to keep in good condition—and the apparent food charity she was giving to her destitute neighbors, the cut-rate rent couldn't have been the attraction for her.

And judging by how familiar she'd already become with the group of grown men living next to her in the space of just over a week, she had absolutely no sense of the modern precautions any urban resident would take.

"As long as I have a roof to block the rain, four walls to block the wind, and a sturdy floor under my feet, I ask for nothing else."

Suzuno seemed to read Emi's mind as she silently worried.

"I have no interest in worldly luxury. I simply thought that being near the city would make finding suitable work a simpler task."

Then she fell silent, her eyes fixed upon Emi.

"I wish to find a vocation here that will make my homeland proud."

"A wonderful ambition! You could stand to learn from her, Urushihara."

Ashiya heaped praise upon Suzuno from his sickbed.

Urushihara ignored it as he returned to his computer desk.

"Regardless, I am sure it is fate that brought the two of us together, in the same city within this vast country. I hope we will provide each other with warm support and goodwill toward our fellow human beings."

Suzuno turned toward Emi and bowed deeply once more.

"Um, yeah. You, too."

At a loss, Emi leaned forward to match her conversational partner.

"Whew! Thanks for the noodles. That was great!"

Maou, passing by as he polished off the remainder of his breakfast, let out a cheek-stretching yawn as he brought his utensils to the sink.

"Man, though…I've got so much to do, and remember, and stuff. It's wrecking my mind."

"What do you mean? You're just manning the grill like always, right?"

Emi's brows furrowed as she asked. Maou responded with an out-of-place grin.

"Oho! Well, that's where you're wrong. While you were off wasting away your life, I've made some serious advances as a member of human society."

Human? Emi resisted the urge to lunge at the obvious bait.

"Yeah, that's right, Emi! Get a load of this! Starting on Saturday—tomorrow—I'm going to be the afternoon associate manager at the Hatagaya station MgRonald!"

Maou cocked his head back, hand on hip, the morning sun pouring in through the window behind him. Emi could feel her strength draining.

"Yeah, woo, congrats."

She rewarded the show with a sarcastic nod and the world's least enthusiastic round of applause.

"Hah! You don't even believe me, do you? Well, it's true! My first bona fide managerial role! And an hourly wage hike to match, too!"

"What I'm not believing is that you're seriously trying to brag about it. But, hey, that's great, I guess? Why don't you just keep focusing on your career if you like it so much?"

Emi flapped a hand aimlessly at Maou as he fervently tried to fish for compliments.

"Pfft. So, what, you've got no aspirations whatsoever? Well, fine. Someday, I'm going to be way up high, and you'll be gritting your teeth in anger while you're still stuck here, falling down my stairs all the damn time!"

Maou stuck his tongue out at her, putting a final exclamation point on his manifesto. Emi countered by silently tossing a nearby tissue box at him. Maou easily dodged it, causing the box to land upon Ashiya beside him.

She was expecting some kind of verbal rebuke, but instead Ashiya grumpily flicked it aside and wriggled back into his blanket.

He didn't look well at all, but Emi held little sympathy. She turned her eyes away, no longer desiring the triumphant-looking Maou in her sight.

"……"

"Wh-what…?"

Instead her eyes locked with Suzuno, still kneeling politely, dourly looking up at her.

"Emi…"

She stopped, stole a glance at Maou—still cheerfully grinning as he washed the dishes, comfortable in his conviction that he finally lorded it over Emi for a change—then brought her lips to Emi's ear.

"Are you in a close relationship, perhaps, with Sadao?"

"Haaahhhh?!"

The cry of shock was genuine, enough to make even the resting Ashiya and the earphoned Urushihara turn around.

"Wh-what did you just say?!"

"Well, I merely noticed that your conversation was quite, shall we say, confrontational? Or perhaps *frank* is a more suitable word. There is certainly no sense of reserve between the two of you."

"Yeah…I suppose it's easy to get that impression, but…"

As Emi began, she noticed Urushihara staring at her, chuckling to himself.

"*You* stay out of this!"

A single glare was all it took to silence him.

They certainly didn't hold anything back against each other, and Emi never had any intention to. Having that interpreted as the two of them being close companions was never something that occurred to her.

"Maybe there's no reserve, but more than that, there's no trust, no faith, no friendship, and no other kind of positive human emotion between us, either. Nothing! In fact, if he died in an accident on the way home from work today, I honestly wouldn't mind much at all. So let's just make sure we have *that* straight, all right?"

She made sure she was heard across the room, so she could already feel Ashiya's grimaced gaze and Maou's easygoing grin pointed toward her.

"I—I see…"

Suzuno, meanwhile, had dropped the inscrutable, statuelike expression she seemed to prefer the most. In some ways, it seemed like a sense of relief crossed her eyes.

What would put her at ease about Emi and Maou not being together?

Thinking it over, Emi's eyebrows arched downward. This had already happened before. There was another woman—the only one who still remembered Maou and Emi's battle two months ago.

"I don't want to pry…"

Now it was Emi's turn to whisper into Suzuno's ear.

"But are *you* aiming for that stupid Devil King, too?"

The reaction Suzuno showed at that moment was nothing short of seismic.

Her face, normally willful and resolute, turned white as a sheet. Without a word, she grabbed Emi's arm, pulling her outside of the room.

"Uh? Ah! Wait a…!"

Slamming the door behind her and sneaking a quick look inside, she turned toward Emi and spoke in a hushed, slightly frazzled voice.

"What…what will we do if he hears you?"

Emi was quizzical at first, wondering what about her observation had made Suzuno turn ghostlike so rapidly. But it made sense. If she had hit it on the nose, then perhaps it wasn't the most delicate thing to say, in a whisper or not.

Observing her strong will, dignified presence, and oddly hardened face, she assumed that Suzuno wasn't the sort of girl to wear her emotions on her kimono sleeve. But women are women, she concluded.

"I'm sorry! I didn't think you really…"

Emi meekly apologized, her voice similarly hushed. A sheen of cold sweat appeared on Suzuno's usually marblelike face.

"I…I must say, I am quite impressed."

She put a hand to her heart, taking a deep breath to calm her nerves. "How did you ever know?"

"How did I know? Well…I dunno, I just kind of thought so…"

That was the best explanation Emi had to offer. The namby-pamby response seemed to convince Suzuno well enough.

"I…see. Very well done…"

She couldn't guess what was "well done" about that, but regardless, Suzuno seemed honestly impressed at Emi's clairvoyant skills.

Watching her, Emi couldn't help but regret hurting her feelings just a tad. Still, she had to say it, sooner or later.

This was a girl, after all, who appeared out of nowhere to become a core presence in the Devil's Castle. Not asking would have made Emi wonder if she was an assassin from another world, or—even worse—an apprentice demon in Maou's bloodstained service.

But think it over logically, Emi told herself. An assassin wouldn't move in, then sit there doing nothing for a whole week. And Suzuno was far too prim and proper to be from the demon realm.

"Listen, Suzuno. I'm sorry if I'm being too intrusive, but there's something I want to tell you."

"…What is that?"

If this was just a regular woman, Emi would prefer to keep her out of their angel-and-demon struggle as much as possible.

"I think you better keep your distance from him. Otherwise, it's just gonna make you unhappy."

"Unhappy…? In what way?"

Suzuno looked up at Emi, her face confused.

Lambasting Maou too much to her face would have the opposite effect. Emi knew that much from previous experience.

"That's…not the kind of guy any regular person can handle. I'm just saying, it's best if you don't get too close to him."

"…! B-but, but, I may not seem that way, but I've been through a great deal of trials and tribulations in my life!"

Suzuno seemed to be awfully hard on herself as she shot back.

Emi had little interest in this girl baring her entire life's story to her, but Suzuno gave her no time to speak.

"But...all right. If that is what you say, I will keep a respectful distance away. I am sure there is something between you and he that I am not aware of."

She had an odd sort of sixth sense about what Emi was thinking at any given moment. Emi had no idea why she was so in tune with her mind, but in the very short time they'd known each other, the amount of trust this girl had thrown upon her feet was wholly novel to her.

"But no matter what you may say, I am in no position to leave at this point. I know this is terribly audacious of me, but I hope you will provide me with whatever assistance you deem appropriate."

The beauty had returned to her face as she gave a respectful standing bow.

Emi felt at fault here as well. Here was this poor girl, unwittingly caught up in the intrigues of Ente Isla, and Emi's inability to vanquish the Devil King once and for all had left the door wide open for her.

"Certainly. If I can."

She smiled and nodded.

On the condition, of course, that it didn't involve playing matchmaker for Maou.

"Very well... Thank you. My mind is at ease now, a little."

The stone wall that was her usual facial expression seemed to relax itself slightly.

Not even Emi suspected that Maou and his cohorts had forced anything upon Suzuno. But the experience of being the sole woman in their "household" must have put her on pins and needles.

Speaking with Emi, the first female companion she'd ever had in Tokyo, must have been just the release valve she needed.

"Oh! Hang on a moment."

Emi gently pushed Suzuno aside and ventured back into the room.

"You guys didn't do anything weird while I was gone, did you?" Emi glared at Urushihara as she groped around inside her shoulder bag.

"I ain't in *that* much of a hurry to die."

Keeping one eye on Urushihara as he sullenly replied, Emi took out her memo pad and pen, ripping off a piece of paper. Jotting something down, she handed the sheet to Suzuno.

"This is my address, my phone number, and my e-mail. If these guys do anything to you, you can call me for help anytime."

"Very well. I owe you a great debt."

Suzuno nodded as she delicately placed the paper into her kimono. Emi had no idea until now that women stuffed things under their kimonos like that.

"Look, who do you think we are, anyway?" Maou, wiping off the morning's dishes, finally had to speak up.

"I think you're a bunch of hideous monsters that I'd put even a cockroach above, that's what. I doubt you'd do it now, but if you do anything weird to Suzuno, I'm gonna rip your head off and hang it out that window, all right?"

"What are you, Dracula?"

Emi paid the comeback no mind. "...Well. I better push off. But don't worry. They may not look it, but they've got every reason not to break any laws right now."

Emi aimed the last part at Suzuno as she draped the shoulder bag over her body. Then she turned toward Maou.

"Be good to her, all right? I'm serious here. Men and women run on *real* different wavelengths!"

"Yeah, I don't need to be reminded. But at least I'm not gonna ignore the help she gives me, unlike *certain* people I know. Get out already!"

Emi accepted that response, although she knew a Hero placing too much trust on that was undebatably shirking her duty.

"Right. See you."

She was kind enough to shut the door behind her.

Suzuno stared at the door for a moment.

"Y-y-yaaaagghhhhh!!"

Then, at the sound of Emi's scream, she lunged for it. On the outside corridor, still in her two-toed socks, she was greeted with the sight of Emi halfway downstairs, sweating profusely, her hands balled tightly around both handrails.

"I-I-I'm fine. I'm fine this time, okay? Really."

She let out a hoarse chuckle, then ever-so-slowly sidled down the second half before briskly walking off in very apparent shame.

"She bite it again?" she heard Maou call out from inside.

"No, she regained control of herself halfway."

"...Yeah, looked that way. She's sure going fast, though. Like she's trying to run away from us."

Urushihara mumbled his agreement, eyes fixated on the PC screen.

✳

"Okay, Marko! The fate of tomorrow's afternoon shift rests upon your shoulders. Stay diligent! Don't let that new Sentucky Fried Chicken get the jump on us!"

Kisaki laid the pressure down hard on Maou that Friday evening, several hours after Emi blundered her way into his apartment.

Starting tomorrow, for the next week, Maou would be the shift supervisor for the afternoon hours. In other words, his career as assistant manager was just about to kick off. When he reported in for the lunch rush, Kisaki rewarded him with a custom name tag reading SADAO MAOU in shiny lettering, indicating that he was the man in charge for that shift.

His old SADAO (A) sticker tag seemed like a relic from his ancient minimum-wage days now. Starting today, his tag gave his *full name*. It made him proud, somehow.

Thanks to the careful tutelage Kisaki instilled in him up to this day, he was ready in mind and body, a fairly comprehensive understanding of store management practices drummed into this brain.

"I'll make sure to have my phone on me in case any emergencies come up, but unless it's something really catastrophic, you can go ahead and make any decisions that need to be made yourself. This is meant to help you grow, after all."

"Absolutely."

"Good. I like to hear that. Do your best out there, okay? Don't make me have to send you to Trinidad and Tobago."

"I thought you were joking."

Maou pulled at his face nervously.

"The only time I tell jokes is when I want people to laugh."

He got the message.

"We don't have much staff on hand this shift, so you better brace yourself. Think of it as getting a head start on your shift-supervisor job."

"Huh?"

Maou took a glance at the shift schedule posted on the wall. The only lines extending all the way to closing time at midnight belonged to Maou and Kisaki.

Between five and ten PM, another line joined them down the grid.

"Ooh. Chi, huh...?"

Maou whispered it to himself. Kisaki keenly picked up on it as she peered at the schedule.

"You aren't still having a tiff with her or anything, are you?"

"Not a tiff, no..."

His voice trailed off before he could finish the sentence.

Chiho Sasaki, "Chi" to her workmates, was a crew member Maou had more or less personally raised from her first day forward. She was one of those rare teenage girls with a real talent for customer service. A career in the hospitality industry may well be waiting for her someday.

What she *also* was, was the only girl in Japan who knew that Maou was the demonic overlord of another planet, and that Emi was the Hero who looked forward to violently murdering him.

Not that Chiho's knowledge of these events particularly bothered either party. They made no special effort to ensure the girl kept it a secret, and they didn't expend any magic attempting to erase her memory.

Chiho, for her part, wasn't the kind of modern Japanese citizen who'd go around shouting, *That guy's the demonic overlord of another planet!* No one would believe her, and she knew any efforts along those lines were futile.

A more relevant concern was that, two months after the battle against Lucifer—where Chiho stumbled upon all these unbelievable truths—she was still being oddly standoffish around Maou.

She wasn't terrorized by working at MgRonald alongside a blood-thirsty alien monster. Even Maou was starting to twig to the fact that the cause lay elsewhere.

Kisaki, gauging Maou's response, squinted coldly at him.

"Well, if whatever it is starts affecting our daily sales, you'll *wish* you were in Trinidad and Tobago."

The aura she projected instantly flipped itself into Northern Arctic Blizzard mode.

"You'd probably wind up somewhere like Greenland instead."

"What, above the Arctic Circle?! Does anyone even *live* there?"

"Well, that's pretty rude to the Greenlanders, don't you think? Greenland's part of the kingdom of Denmark; it's got its own parliament and everything. Over one hundred thousand people live there! There's even a movement to make it independent from…"

"I didn't ask for geographical trivia, and besides, I'm not going anywhere *near* there! What do you mean by 'whatever it is'…?"

"I *mean*, if some young new manager can do the work but has trouble dealing with a teenage girl taking a fancy to him, then fine. That, I can laugh off. But if that trouble starts affecting my bottom line…don't expect any mercy."

The very definition of straight talk. A palpable dizziness swayed Maou's mind, forcing him to lean against the front counter for balance.

Indeed, Maou may not have realized it, but Chiho had fostered some real feelings for him as they worked together on the front lines of fast food. And even now, when she knew he was the Devil King, it was still the case.

"I mean, you know, am I going to have to bar female employees from working with you, or what?"

Kisaki continued her rant, unaware or simply uninterested in Maou's emotions.

The clock inexorably wore on, and before he realized it, it was almost five PM. He had trouble staying calm, but nevertheless bellowed a hearty "Welcome to MgRonald!" when the automatic door opened in front of him.

"Oh, um, h-hello."

Chiho Sasaki was reporting to work, still dressed in a summer outfit. She clumsily greeted Maou at the counter.

"Uh…mm…hey."

They spoke to each other the bare minimum amount necessary to perform their work duties, but otherwise, the amount of daily chitchat had plummeted. Even today, Maou had no idea where to even begin mending the fences.

"Oh, hey there, Chi."

A voice sounded out to his side.

"Uh… Oh! Um, good afternoon, Ms. Kisaki!"

The look Kisaki gave Chiho was one of delighted interest, a complete 180 from what she had for Maou.

"Go get changed, okay? Maou's gonna have a lot of work to do starting tomorrow, so he'll probably have a lot to discuss with you, too."

"Ah…uh, yeah. Sorry."

Chiho nodded, then walked past Maou's side and into the staff room behind the counter. She was mere inches from him, and they didn't even make eye contact.

"Heh. Looks like a terminal case."

Kisaki grinned to herself as she saw Chiho off.

"I have to admit, this *is* leaving me ever-so-slightly worried as I leave the store in your capable hands."

"Ever so slightly…? I know Chi and I are a little awkward with each other right now, but it's not like we're fighting or anything. It's not going to affect our work at all," Maou half whined, half defended himself as he stared at the staff-room door.

"Well, even if *you're* fine with it, Chi might not be so much."

The words breezed out of Kisaki's mouth. Maou looked at her, surprised.

"We may all just be cogs in the huge machine that we call the MgRonald Corporation, but before that, we're human beings. You can't get a bead on how people interact with each other from a single viewpoint. Even if you try to, it's not going to improve things around the workplace."

"You…think? I suppose so."

Maou cast his eyes downward. The observation made him realize exactly how shallow he was being. Then, with consummate timing, Kisaki lightened the mood.

"Ahh, you'll be fine. Chi's still young. Inexperienced. She just needs a little while longer to get herself together. Once the right spark comes along, she'll be back to normal in no time."

In terms of life experience, Maou had an advantage of several centuries over both Chiho and Kisaki. On paper, at least. Unfortunately, the sort of experience he'd gained over those many years was nothing he could apply to *this* thorny affair.

But, as he soon realized, Kisaki's advice, while not solving the problem, did help relieve the load on his mind a little. He took a long, hard look at his boss, like he suddenly knew everything about her.

"I have to hand it to you, Ms. Kisaki. You're really something."

"Hey, it's just work drama. Get as old as I am, and it starts to come naturally."

Still a bit lost in the fog, Maou tried his hardest to focus on the predinner rush checklist. Kisaki stopped him.

"Let's have Chi handle that, shall we? I want to take a close look at how she works while we're not busy."

"Um, sure…"

Kisaki plucked the check sheet from Maou's hands.

"Better take your break while you still can, Marko. You can go out and have dinner as long as you're back by six…unless you wanted to eat here?"

Maou shook his head at the invite.

"Thanks, but I'll take my break in the staff room. I brought a bento box along today."

"A bento, huh? Starting to cook for yourself a little? Well, just make sure whatever you cook doesn't start rotting in this heat before you can eat it. That goes double in a food-service job like this. Keep your bento in a cool, dark place, and don't forget to stick a dried *umeboshi* plum in there to absorb the moisture."

Maou nodded. This was all common sense.

"I'm all squared away there. I'd be in trouble if I couldn't work, after all. Anyway, see you after my break."

Maou set his time-clock code to BREAK, then ventured into the staff room.

Immediately he ran into Chiho, who had just stepped out of the women's changing area.

"Oh…"

Chiho, realizing Maou was there, swallowed nervously, averting her eyes.

"Uh…so, I'm going on break for a second. Ms. Kisaki said she wanted to check out your, like, work ethic or whatever before we got busy."

"A-all right…"

She nodded, hands held forward as if holding a hot potato in front of her chest, then started to pass by Maou's side when:

"…?"

Noticing Maou take a package out of his messenger bag, wrapped in a bandanna he purchased at the local one-hundred-yen shop, Chiho stopped for a moment.

"Maou, is that…?"

It was one of the rare occasions in the past two months when Chiho actually initiated conversation with him.

Maou unwrapped the bandanna, revealing a dual-tier bento box, both on the large side and featuring a design that was just a little too gaudy for a man to comfortably sport around.

Then he brought it up to face level.

"This? Just a bento meal."

"A bento…? That's kind of a cute pattern on it. Did Ashiya buy it on sale or something?"

Being aware of Maou's true colors, Chiho had naturally met Ashiya before. She was also aware of his demonic origins, as well as his role tending to the household chores and Maou's self-centered demands.

It was a harmless enough question, but Maou, blessed with the first chance at a decent conversation in two months, put little thought into it before giving his honest answer.

"Nah, I borrowed it from my neighbor. Did I mention that? Someone moved in next door a little while ago."

"Someone moved in? …Into *that* apartment?"

Chiho's eyes opened wide in innocent surprise. She knew the state of squalor he lived in, of course. But his next few words were enough to make her entire body freeze.

"Yeah. It's this girl, actually…"

"This *girl*?!"

"Whoa! You don't have to yell like that."

Chiho's bloodcurdling scream was enough to make Maou jump. Chiho ignored the rebuke.

"Y-you, you borrowed a bento box from, from this young girl? What on earth is—"

"Hey, Chi, stop shaking me!"

Before he knew it, Chiho had grabbed the collar of Maou's work uniform, pulling it to and fro.

"S-so, so, so, this *girl*…this girl lent it to *you*, Maou…"

"Y-y-y-yeah. Yeah, so please stop shaking me, Chi…"

The Devil King was physically helpless against a teenage girl.

"I…I really don't want to imagine this…like, *really, really* don't want to! But…but did *she* make it?"

The whites of her eyes shone as she glared at Maou, hands still firmly gripping his shirt. The look of desperation on her face was nothing like the standoffishness he'd had to deal with these past two months.

The girl he was talking about was Suzuno Kamazuki, and with Ashiya still bedridden—okay, floor-ridden—and incapable of much physically, it was none other than Suzuno who'd obediently volunteered to whip up a bento for Maou instead.

Between the udon she lugged over on moving day and the ginger and whatnot she had today, Suzuno had no qualms with bringing her own ingredients into Devil's Castle and whipping up meals for them on the spot.

The demons, of course, had no room to complain. The ice was firmly broken with their new neighbor, and the savings in their food budget were proving to be substantial. But Maou had never even dreamed that this arrangement would prove to be such a minefield later on.

"I...I...I guess she did, probably. I think."

Chiho was no longer in any mood to accept Maou's feeble attempts at muddling the bare truth.

"C-c-can, can, can, can..."

"Can?"

"Can, can I take a look at, at what's inside?"

"Yes! Yes, so stop shaking me! Please!"

Finally removing her hands from Maou's collar, Chiho warily peered into Maou's open bento box, almost scared to see what was inside.

The topmost tier of the box was packed to the gills with little side dishes in a dazzling array of colors. Chiho's face stiffened at first sight of the deluxe spread before her, but the next thing she noticed made her blink in confusion.

It was the braised burdock root that caught her attention first. Followed by the *chikuzenni*—braised chicken and vegetables. Then the *kikka-kabu*, the baby turnips steeped in salt water and cut into flowery shapes. Then the vinegar-marinated sliced carrots and daikon radish. Then the *kuri kinton* sweets made of chestnut paste.

"*Osechi...?*"

"*Osechi?* Which?"

KIND OF A CUTE
PATTERN ON THEM.
DID ASHIYA BUY IT
A SALE OR
BUT, DID
SO THIS
THIS GIRL,
LENT IT TO YOU,

Maou asked reluctantly, not having had any past experience with the traditional Japanese New Year's cuisine, which is often the most money a family spends on a single meal all year. Chiho shook her head.

"Let me see the bottom tier!"

She whisked away the topmost box.

What unfolded before her was all too expected, which made it all the more horrifying for her to see.

Atop a bed of white rice was an enormous heart-shaped design made of seaweed, bordered by an enclosed row of fresh dried plums.

✳

Even after night fell, the heat wave dominating Tokyo showed no signs of dissipating.

"'Lo…"

As Emi stepped into Friend Market, the convenience store on Nano-hana Street nearest to her home in Eifukucho, she was greeted by a clerk whose passion for customer service was a far cry from Maou's.

Emi, the only customer in the store, breathed a blissful sigh upon feeling the AC on her forehead, then made a beeline for the bento corner.

"…I always wind up buying the same thing, don't I?"

Emi muttered it to herself as she reached for a plastic-wrapped curry meal with the improbably long title HEALTHY FILL-UPS—SUMMER VEGETABLE CURRY! ALL THIS AND ONLY 1500 CALORIES! Figuring this wouldn't be quite enough, she also picked up a small package of coleslaw, a cup of instant soup, and an éclair for dessert, stacking all of it above the curry package.

With any of her curry dinner's alleged health benefits now thoroughly neutralized, Emi strode to the cash register.

Working at a call center guaranteed that she never had to worry about unscheduled overtime, but thanks to her earlier stop at Hatagaya for the purposes of her Hero duties, she was coming home quite late tonight.

Out of the four days she had kept her vigil going, this was undoubtedly the most tumultuous. Thus Emi decided that a stop by Maou's workplace would be in order. Boarding the Keio New Line, she disembarked at Hatagaya station and took up her favored position at the magazine rack in the bookstore opposite MgRonald, the ideal location for her stakeout.

But—and she had a feeling this would be the case—all this earned her was the right to stare at Maou, his manager, and Chiho Sasaki, the only Japanese person who knew the truth about him, as they dutifully carried out their shifts. The full stalker experience, in other words.

"'Eat it up 'ere?"

She nodded at the clerk, who had the enigmatic habit of omitting syllables here and there, as her purchases were totaled up.

Something seemed unfair about all this. Thanks to a generous neighbor, Maou was eating like a king, and meanwhile Emi was wasting time and energy and being rewarded for it with artery-clogging convenience-store food.

"'nk youuu. Come back soooon."

Emi picked up the plastic bag housing the warm curry, turning toward the exit, when:

"!!"

She flinched and looked upward, feeling a clear and present murderous rage fixated upon her.

Summer or not, going home from work or not, no longer able to live without air-conditioning or not, Emi had a trained sixth sense for this that had never left her.

Especially when her own life was involved.

So by the time the black shadow which suddenly appeared lunged at her like an enraged murderer, at a speed no Japanese person could ever manage to top, Emi was already positioned for battle.

And when, thanks to this excessive speed on the shadow's part, her assailant failed to notice the automatic door slowly lumbering open between it and Emi, crashing straight into the clear glass door and falling down with a *thud*, Emi didn't move an inch from her fighting stance.

"Nn? Whuzzat?"

The clerk, apparently a native speaker of mole-people language, shot a glance toward Emi.

Beyond the glass door, still lumbering open but now cracked, Emi's diminutive assailant lay on the ground, dressed in a shiny plastic rain poncho, camouflage pants, and a black ski mask, looking the part of a bank robber who'd just darted out of the barber after a quick haircut to hide his identity.

The weight of his body kept the sensor activated, allowing the door to remain open and the cold air inside to swarm out of the entrance.

Emi tossed her bag on the floor and slinked toward the register to put her purchases down, wanting to be rid of her luggage as soon as possible.

"Sssir, y'all right?"

The clerk leaped out from behind the counter, mistaking this new guest for someone who just had an unfortunate accident. It wasn't until he approached the door when the assailant's out-of-place clothing gave him pause.

"Get away!"

From the side, Emi pushed the frozen clerk out of the way. He barreled into the rack of free help-wanted magazines, surprised at this sudden attack, but the effort ultimately saved his life.

A blade of light ripped through the space where the clerk once stood. Emi felt a large, weighted mass fly by, scraping her shoulder, reducing the sleeve of her shirt to ribbons, and worst of all, cleaving the bag with her just-purchased bento cleanly in half.

Emi, checking to ensure the clerk was still on the ground, was quick to react.

"Heavenly Wind Blade!!"

Without a moment's hesitation, Emi launched her holy sword, the Better Half, at the bizarrely dressed burglar who'd just destroyed her sleeve and dinner.

The guided shock wave released by the sword in her right hand slammed against the assailant, sending him flying outside of the store with a loud *crash*.

"Stay in here and call the police!"

She didn't know if the clerk was listening, but Emi shot out of the store before he could have an opportunity to see her sword, pursuing the plainly suspicious-looking suspect.

But another flash of cleaving light was waiting for her from the side as she exited.

Emi deflected the bolt with a deft turn of her holy sword. The clang of metal against metal echoed. She leaped, attempting to get above the head of this ambusher.

"Heavenly Fleet Feet!!"

Focusing the powers of the Cloth of the Dispeller that lurked within her squarely upon her legs, Emi jumped forward and landed cleanly on the roof of the house across the street.

It was no physical feat any regular person could have managed, but the ski-masked burglar's eyes never turned away from her.

Emi went through the effort of summoning her holy sword and Cloth without hesitation because she realized that, apart from his crazy garb, this was no ordinary thug she was dealing with.

No mere burglar, for one, would have an enormous scythe in hand.

It was the kind of scythe most people only see on the Death tarot card, one just as tall as the masked assailant wielding it, easily capable of cutting in half three or so human beings in a single swipe.

The stylistically mismatched burglar had nothing like that in hand during that first headlong lunge into the convenience-store door.

Unlike the sort of weapons most would-be felons tend to prefer, this was nothing one could easily hide in a pocket or violin case.

Considering the *clang* of metal when that scythe met Emi's holy sword, and considering the scythe was solid enough to withstand Emi's blade in the first place, and considering how this maniac seemingly produced it from thin air, there was no way this fashion disaster was from Earth.

"I don't know if you're human or a demon or whatever, but why are you attacking me in public like this?!"

Emi began by giving her attacker her honest opinion.

"I don't care about myself, but if you're going to hurt the people of Japan, don't expect any mercy from me!"

Bringing Better Half level with her body, she kept it high as she leaped off the roof.

"Rrnnnngh!"

The fall was driven by more than just momentum. It was an all-out bullrush toward her foe, powered by the maximum amount of force the Cloth covering her legs allowed.

But her assailant remained still, scythe at the ready, before swiping it downward in a grand arc.

Emi had predicted the move; her sword was deflected, but she used the momentum to twist her body around and unleash a rear kick with her left foot.

The Cloth-powered kick, stabbing with Emi's full strength, rammed into her opponent's left shoulder.

Even though she had this foe off guard, simply flailing away wouldn't end the battle. Aiming for a KO, Emi prepared to rush at the dazed burglar, targeting the solar plexus.

Then, at just that moment, the scythe-wielder released a flash of light from beneath the ski mask.

The purple, beamlike flash would have seemed like a terrible '80s direct-to-video special effect to the casual observer, but Emi, feeling a cold rush down her spine, cut through the blast with her sword.

Something within Emi said that under absolutely no circumstances should she let that beam touch her.

But what happened next was far beyond anything Emi could imagine.

"Huh…?!"

The holy sword was robbed of its light.

Better Half, the sword that resonated with the holy force inside of Emi, began to flicker like an almost-spent lightbulb, shrinking down to the size of a long dagger.

Emi brought the sword back, trying to return it to its original "phase one" size, but the scythe-wielder continued with the barrage of purple light, all too ready to overwhelm her.

"Wh-what the hell *is* this?!"

The blasts were not that rapid in succession, but Emi had never heard of a force powerful enough to literally shrink her holy sword. She was at a loss to imagine what a direct hit would do to her body, but she was no longer able to brush the attacks off with her sword. In a moment, the tables had turned.

Emi found herself in a panic at this unexpected attacker, someone who she surmised must have been an assassin from Ente Isla. But the battle against this light-emitting, scythe-slashing maniac ended in equally unexpected fashion.

"Ngh!"

Suddenly, the scythe-wielder groaned as the barrage of purple light ceased.

Surprised, Emi looked over to find that the assailant's drab-colored ski mask had transformed into a fluorescent orange, right down to the eyes themselves.

"No!"

Now it was a round, orange blast of…something that crossed Emi's line of view, accompanied by a male voice.

The ball struck the scythe-wielder on the shoulder, spreading bright orange across most of the assailant's Windbreaker.

Emi flashed a quizzical look back at the convenience store.

There stood the clerk in his full glory, now outside of his shop and throwing antitheft paintballs at the assailant.

Emi's assailant was unflinchingly on the offensive during this entire battle, but now was lying on the ground in agony, face covered by a hand. Some of the paint must have seeped through the ski mask.

"Hey…"

This show of brute courage threw Emi. Having pride in one's work duties is fine and all, but those paintballs were meant to help pursue fleeing criminals. Apart from the special scent agents they were laced with, they couldn't have packed that powerful a punch.

If the scythe-wielder decided to lash out against this new attacker, Emi had little means to stop the attack. Emi turned toward her assailant—

"Huh...?"

—only to find her powerful opponent fleeing, back turned, stumbling wildly back and forth across the street.

"...Uhhhh." Emi groaned to herself.

"N-no! Get back 'ere!!" The clerk, meanwhile, was unfazed, continuing the paintball assault as his downed foe lurched off.

All they could hear was a ball or two splattering against something a bit away in the darkness. It was hard to tell if any of them hit home.

Emi dissipated her sword back within her body as quickly as she could. The only thought in her mind was: *Come on, really?*

Here was this obvious assassin from Ente Isla, first bashing straight into an automatic door, then summoning this gigantic scythe before tasting shameful defeat by a cashier with some paintballs? How did *that* happen?

Avoiding pointless conflict was something to be celebrated, of course, but this climax was enough to make any Hero lose their enthusiasm for the whole Hero gig.

"Oh! Yer aright, ma'am?!"

The clerk finally noticed Emi, still caught up in the heat of the moment. Emi had silently sheathed her sword and Cloth of the Dispeller within her while the scythe-wielding maniac fled, but it could easily have been noticed if the clerk had kept a cooler head.

"Are *you* okay? I'm sorry I pushed you away like that."

"Ah, no biggie. Jus' kinda hit my 'ead a little."

There was a red mark on his forehead from where he no doubt plunged headfirst into the help-wanted-magazine rack. That beat being freed of his intestines if he had run straight for that freaky burglar, of course.

"Should we call the police or something?"

"Oh, yeah, the silent 'larm shoulda already called the security dudes 'n the cops for us!"

Then the clerk picked up Emi's hand, suddenly remembering something.

"Oh, 'n, uh, so the 'mployee manual sezzat I needa keep alla customers 'nside. You mind waitin' a sec 'til the cops show up?"

"Uh."

Emi groaned. The police had a crime scene to inspect, after all, and at least a couple of witnesses to speak with. This wasn't what she'd expected.

How long would the cops need to complete their investigation?

"...Umm, sure, no problem."

It occurred to her that she could leave her cell phone and ID and ask to take a quick trip back to her apartment. She vetoed the idea at once. It wasn't in her best interest to further interrupt her private time with yet another visit to her neighborhood convenience store later on.

It wasn't a matter of whether she trusted the clerk or not; it was just the sort of self-defense mechanism any single woman in Tokyo was equipped with.

Dejectedly, she went back inside to her shredded shopping bag. Inside, the curry, coleslaw, and éclair were mixed together in a pulp, like a particularly whimsical pizza.

Emi plucked out the lone survivor in the bag before turning toward the clerk.

"Can I get some hot water? I'm hungry, so I'm hoping I could at least have the soup while I'm waiting."

Turning to a water kettle in the corner, the clerk filled up the crushed soup container with steaming liquid before inviting Emi into a seat in the back office.

Looking around the one place in the convenience store she'd never seen before, Emi found herself muttering.

"Well, *that* fight sure cost me."

The Better Half sword she manifested this time was restricted to its phase one form, but contained a level of force that was incomparable to what she had handy against Lucifer two months ago. At this rate, she had no doubt that phase two would be accessible to her, even with her Cloth of the Dispeller fully deployed.

That made it all the more urgent that she found out what that purple light *was*, exactly. She had never run into a foe capable of essentially annulling her holy powers.

Sipping at the soup after letting it seep in water for a minute, Emi gritted her teeth in frustration. It was already shaping up to be a lonely night, and the events carried out by that weirdo scythe-wielding burglar maniac only served to make her feel smaller.

The next time they met, she swore she would slash this mystery assailant in half before any more strange, otherworldly abilities became involved.

"Uh, ma'am, this's yers?"

The clerk stepped back in, carrying the shoulder bag Emi tossed away the moment all this began.

"Oh, sorry. Thanks."

It had completely escaped her mind. The clerk pointed at it as she took it from him.

"Uhh, I think th' phone's goin' off 'r something..."

"Huh? Oh. Ah!"

Blushing instinctively, Emi plucked the vibrating phone out from the bag.

She must have forgotten to put it on mute. It was playing a sonorous rendition of the theme from *Maniac Shogun*, one of her favorite samurai dramas, at max volume.

"Uh...ha-ha-ha-ha! You'd, uh, you'd be surprised how addictive that show is."

Making excuses she had no reason to make, Emi brought the phone up against her face.

"Yusa! Yusa, something's up with Maou!"

The frenzied scream from the phone made Emi move her head away.

Chiho Sasaki's name and phone number were displayed on-screen. Almost spilling her soup in surprise, Emi flashed a confused look at the girl's chosen way to start the conversation before reluctantly bringing the phone back to her ear.

"Ch-Chiho? What's going on?"

"Maou! Maou, Maou…"

"What about him? Is he dead?"

Emi, far too depressed at the moment to want to think about anything even resembling Maou, let the rather extreme question form on her lips.

She knew full well that Chiho had feelings for Maou.

After the battle two months ago, she'd given her contact information to Chiho, partly to ensure her safety and partly to keep tabs on what Maou got up to during work hours. They'd enjoyed the occasional rambling text- or voice-based conversation about nothing in particular since.

Nothing seemed out of the ordinary between them at MgRonald earlier today, making Emi wonder what could possibly make her so hysterical, when:

"No, he brought a bento in! A homemade bento!"

The voice was tear-laced as it reported the awful truth.

Swallowing a mouthful of soup, Emi tried to figure out why this would make anyone want to cry.

"A bento? So what? The food at MgRonald isn't free. Ashiya's probably needling him to cook at home more often. What's so unusual about…"

"It's not Ashiya! It's a big heart mark with a bento—*girl*, homemade, two tiers!!"

"All right, could you calm down a little and get your nouns and verbs and stuff in the right order?"

Emi smirked to herself. Now she knew why Chiho was so worked up.

That thoughtless Maou must've done something to hurt a woman's feelings again.

"So who's it from? That girl who moved in next to them?"

"You *knew* about that, Yusa?! And you're willing to put up with that?!"

"Huh? Put up with what?"

Where did *that* question come from? It's not like Emi cared whose cooking Maou decided to shovel into his mouth. Besides, she'd kind of just had her own dinner scythed.

"I...don't see why I wouldn't. I mean, sure, if the Devil King gets in better shape, that might put the entire world in danger someday in the long term, but I can't watch over every single decision in his life."

Suzuno Kamazuki was certainly a girl with a boundless reserve of naïveté, but Japan's a big country. It may be hard for a dyed-in-the-wool Tokyoite to imagine, but the daughter of an old, traditional family from out in the boonies may just live that sort of lifestyle, even today.

And if Maou was going to do anything that'd put her in danger, he would have done it long ago, during the several-days-long period when Emi wasn't aware of Suzuno's existence.

Emi mulled over this while sipping another mouthful.

"And you still call yourself a Hero, Yusa?!"

The indignant rebuke made Emi hold the phone away for a moment again.

"What if that next-door neighbor is some bad guy or assassin who's thinking up ways to kill Maou and his pals? What then?"

"......"

Not even Emi was expecting *that* from Chiho's mouth. It stunned her into silence.

"And besides, don't you think it's all just a little too *weird*? These three guys, all living in a cramped, decrepit apartment—they've plainly got no money, and they're not particularly cool or whatever anyway, and this girl just moves right in and gets that close to them? That just doesn't happen! Maou told me it was just a neighborly gift, but what kind of girl would do that for a neighbor, a complete stranger she just met a few days ago?!"

"...I know I'm not in any position to ask, but you *do* like him, right, Chiho?"

The amount of abuse Chiho was laying upon Maou's feet was harsh enough that Emi somehow felt obliged to check.

"Well, I'm just *saying*, I'm about the only girl who would even *think* about doing something like that!"

She thought she was the only exception in the world. Young love can be blind like that sometimes.

Even so, Emi had seen for herself how deeply Suzuno had ingratiated herself with the denizens of Devil's Castle. She'd heard the woman herself express a keen interest in the Devil King.

Along those lines, Chiho plainly had larger threats to her life than some box lunch.

But, recalling the events at the Devil's Castle this morning, Emi suddenly realized something else.

She had given Suzuno her contact information. In great detail, no less.

Emi reasoned the girl could use some other female friends in Tokyo, but on the very day the Devil's Castle changed before her eyes and she gave her contact info to a girl upon their first meeting, she was attacked by a scythe-wielding maniac.

Was that related somehow?

But it was hard to imagine such a prim, proper woman, so stately in her traditional kimono, going around in that hilariously unstylish outfit. The only thing the two shared in common were their relatively small frames.

Still... thought Emi as she collected herself.

Was it ever *truly* a coincidence if huge events befell the Hero and the Devil King...at the same time?

The battle against Lucifer and Olba two months ago flashed across her mind.

"Yusa? Hey, Yusa?"

Emi's self-immersion was ruined by Chiho calling her name.

"Oh! Sorry. I was just thinking about something."

"Well, look, Yusa. You're the Hero, right? So you're gonna have to defeat Maou sometime, right?!"

Emi swallowed. It was like Chiho had her physically cornered in the back office.

"I… Well, yeah, pretty much, but…"

"So, you know, if you wanted to help me out…"

Emi, who had no idea how her plan to mercilessly slay Maou would help out his would-be girlfriend, waited for Chiho to continue.

THE HERO
OWES A
FAVOR
FOLLOWING
A WILD
CHAIN OF
MISUNDER-
STANDINGS

The first report of Olba Meiyer's disappearance sent shock waves across the All Bishops' Sanctuary, the meeting place shared by the six archbishops that led the Church.

Olba was an important figure in this cabal, not just one of their number but one of the intrepid adventurers who joined the Hero on her quest to dispatch the Devil King.

But the Reconciliation Panel, the self-policing group within the Church that handled the investigation into his disappearance, released a report just as shocking after completing their search of Olba's office, which lay in the Church's headquarters within Sankt Ignoreido.

"The Hero Emilia is alive and well in another world?!"

As the report was read to the remaining five archbishops in their sanctuary, Robertio Igua Valentia, the eldest of their flock and the one among them that served as chief canon of the Church, was the first to react, almost falling out of his chair.

"But Olba himself stated to me that Emilia Justina and her Better Half sword disappeared into nothing at the end of the pitched battle against the Devil King Satan!"

"It would appear that was a total fabrication, sir."

The female inquisitor submitting the report spoke coldly toward the five, all but striking down the oldest among them with her words.

"We have discovered traces of multiple sonar transmissions that he aimed at this other world. The recent capture and holding of Emeralda Etuva and Albert Ende was also perpetrated by Archbishop Olba's underlings."

"What...what on...!"

Robertio, whose health had been the subject of recent rumors itself, glowed red in the face at this cascade of unbelievable news.

"Regarding Emeralda Etuva, we have confirmation that she has returned to her home, the Holy Empire of Saint Aile. Other reports state she is publicly avowing Emilia's safety and spreading the word of Olba's apostasy far and wide."

"A-a-apostasy...! Apostasy, by an archbishop...!"

"Canon Robertio! Please, take a breath and calm down!"

Cervantes Reberiz, archbishop and administrator of the Church's agricultural policy, rose to place a reassuring hand on Robertio's back as he shot back against the Reconciliation Panel representative.

"My dear lady, please refrain from overly inciting our order with your—"

"If I may, Archbishop, I am merely stating the truth."

The inquisitor gave them no quarter.

"But...but how we can simply avow that Olba was lying to us...? Perhaps he himself learned that Emilia was alive and set off to help her..."

"I'm afraid that is not possible, Canon. A dead Hero was found to be alive. Why would a lone man not spread this cataclysmic news far and wide, instead keeping it to himself for whatever reasons he deemed fit? It is only natural to conclude that Archbishop Olba had a motive to ensure that Emilia's 'death' was as true as he himself reported earlier."

The inquisitor sighed, face stern upon continuance.

"And if Saint Aile's most well-known court alchemist is officially declaring that Emilia is alive, we cannot ignore the impact this will have. It directly conflicts with the Church's public position that Emilia is dead. I request a well-considered decision."

"A well...considered..."

Robertio hyperventilated slightly, his anger threatening to make his heart beat its last at any moment.

The inquisitor was not ready to relent, standing firm while facing the panic-stricken canon.

"Will you recognize the mistakes Archbishop Olba has made, or will you continue to push the Church's decisions upon its people?"

All Bishops' Sanctuary was plunged into a profound silence.

"Or, to be more exact, will you affirm and condemn the apostasy committed by the archbishop against the Church, or will you instead decide to murder Emeralda, Albert, and finally Emilia herself?"

"This is ridiculous... Emilia and Albert are one thing, but what could we do against Saint Aile's court alchemist...?"

Cervantes seemed to suffocate on the words. The inquisitor continued, wholly unfazed.

"It is something the Church has always done, ever since the days when the Devil King's armies freely roamed the land, in order to solidify the Western Island as a monolith under the name of the Church. And when I say 'the Church,' I mean myself and the other members of the former Council of Inquisitors."

The statement made the already-heavy atmosphere around the Sanctuary seem to sag even more painfully upon the council.

But nothing would stop the barrage.

"No matter which option you select, the Church will have to pay a great sacrifice. But if we leave the problem unattended like this, the sun will set for good upon the Church's infallibility and authority. I doubt many people would choose to place their faith upon a Church so willing to throw away the Hero, the hope of the people, the woman who dispatched the Devil King."

The inquisitor's glare pelted like a storm of stones against the shaken Sanctuary. Heavily, Cervantes opened his mouth.

"You are part of the Council of…that is, the Reconciliation Panel, yes? How would you handle this question?"

The woman's answer was curt.

"I am sure, Archbishop Cervantes, that you understand the import of the Council of Inquisitors transforming itself into the Reconciliation Panel, at least in name."

Cervantes quickly averted his gaze away from the woman's eyes.

"In the past, it was the goal of defeating the Devil King that united us. But now, when everyone believes that threat to be gone, it would be a grave mistake to believe that simply any act in the name of the gods shall be forgiven."

"Wh-what are you saying?"

Robertio did not fail to notice the point the woman danced around.

"I was hoping that the initial shock would subside before I continued."

She chose her words gingerly as she sized up the five archbishops before her, one by one.

"But Satan, the Devil King, is also alive and well on this other world."

Robertio fell away senseless, foam dribbling from the corner of his mouth.

✳

"So you're having trouble drumming up the confidence?"

Saturday morning, the following day. Early in the morning, with the early-summer sun just beginning to make its full presence known, Emi and Chiho found themselves standing in front of the door to the Devil's Castle.

"Well, I mean…you know."

Chiho, hiding herself behind Emi as she peeked furtively at the door, was carrying a bulky tote bag. Emi could easily imagine what was inside.

"If I fail here, I don't know if I can recover from that by myself…"

Fail at *what*, exactly? It seemed silly to even bother asking.

"I'm just saying, it wasn't really right for the summer season, but it was, like, a *really* well-made bento box! Plus, you know, if it's got poison or something in it, Maou and his friends could be in big trouble..."

"If an Ente Isla assassin was going to poison him, they would've done it ages ago."

Even Emi could be sure of that.

Chiho felt like either potentially disastrous conclusion would be a huge blow to her, but the matter of her own true feelings at the moment was by far the more urgent issue to tackle.

"Well, standing there and blaming us for all of this isn't going to accomplish anything. Just be yourself. Take the bull by the horns."

"...All right!"

Emi pushed Chiho out from behind her, giving her a reassuring pat on the shoulder.

After a moment, Chiho turned back around, the nervousness still writ large upon her face.

"Uhm, Yusa? I'm sorry. Thank you."

Behind the terse statement was a full understanding of both *Yusa* and *Maou*.

Even if Chiho may already have one foot firmly planted in the events sweeping Ente Isla, from Emi's point of view, it would not be the most laudable of tactical decisions to allow her any closer to Maou than she already was.

Right now, in full control of her holy energy, there was no longer any obstacle between her and obliterating the Devil King.

She could wipe clean the memories of everyone in Japan who ever interacted with him—there weren't *that* many of them—massacre the rest of the Devil's Castle, call for Emeralda and Albert to zip on over, and make a triumphant return to Ente Isla. That was all there was to it.

But, after a smile with a whirlpool of emotion behind it, Emi responded.

"No problem. I don't care about them at all, but I want to still be friends with you, Chiho, so..."

That, too, was an honest, earnest slice of Emi's heart in verbal form.

Whether that heart came across or not, Chiho took another deep, emboldening breath and rang the Devil's Castle doorbell.

The reward was instant.

"Ah, yes, welcome back."

"…!"

Chiho was frozen, unbreathing, at the sound of an unfamiliar female voice. Even Emi could clearly see the resolve she spent so much time building up begin to crack and wobble.

Thus, it was not Maou, the master of the house, who opened the door, nor was it his faithful househusband Ashiya. And it certainly wasn't Urushihara the unemployed shut-in. It was Suzuno Kamazuki, the refreshing morning-glory pattern on her aqua-blue kimono framed by her familiar apron.

Even with her hair put up, the morning sun still shone brilliantly through it. It was already growing humid, but not a drop of sweat betrayed itself on her skin, the milky white of skin which so brilliantly matched her kimono. She was drying her hands off with a towel as she opened the door, indicating her presence in the kitchen until this very moment.

She seemed younger than either of her visitors at first glance, but her firm, refined countenance had an air of maturity that Chiho's still lacked.

"Ah, good morning, Emi…and may I ask who you are?"

"I-I-I…"

Her voice was calm and collected. Chiho, meanwhile, sounded like someone had superglued her throat shut.

"Sadao, there is a visitor at the door."

Chiho was struck dumb once more at this unknown Japanese beauty's words.

She had referred to Maou by his given name. It was a sign of intimate familiarity in Japanese. As far as she knew, nobody else in Maou's life used it.

Chiho never had, of course, being younger than him and more or less his apprentice at MgRonald. She doubted she could even if asked to.

And yet here was this woman out of nowhere, expressing honest, homespun warmth as she called him *Sadao*.

Chiho began to find it hard to remain standing—not because of dizziness, but from the sheer hopelessness of it all.

Emi, watching from behind, had no lifeboat to give her. This was Chiho's battle. Only Chiho had the power to change anything.

"Uh? Is Emi back around again?"

"No, not merely Emi."

"Huh?"

It was Sadao Maou, the only man in Chiho's eyes.

"Whoa, Chi?! What're *you* doing here? It's pretty early, isn't it?"

And his first reaction to Chiho was, at best, indifferent.

"M-Maou…"

Even before the battle began, Chiho's eyes had already begun to tear up.

Emi brought a hand to her forehead in exasperation. *This is pointless. He doesn't even realize what's unfolding right now.*

"Um, ah, well, um, I, uh, if you'd, uh, like, uh, to eat…"

She bravely attempted to piece a few words together, her voice like a mosquito's cry, but having the wind knocked out of her so early on made the process painfully difficult.

"Uh, is something up, Chi?"

Even Maou noticed Chiho's odd behavior by now, but all he did was watch on, warily, as her face quivered.

The lifeboat arrived from inside Devil's Castle.

"Oh… Is Ms. Sasaki out there…?"

It took the form of Ashiya's listless voice, one that still managed to boom audibly out the door.

"I hate to bother you, Ms. Kamazuki, but I have some teabags inside the shelf under the sink…"

"Ashiya?"

Chiho noticed that, on the other side of Maou and this unknown woman, Ashiya was lying on the floor, covered by something resembling a blanket.

"Oh, no, are you sick, Ashiya?"

"Yeah, I dunno whether to call it that or not, actually." Maou scratched his head as his eyes darted between Chiho and Ashiya. "But, like, this is the story behind that bento yesterday, I guess."

"Huh?"

Chiho, tears still in her eyes, now flashed a look of utter bewilderment.

"Oh, my, look at how finely you chopped these *shiso* herbs! It's so beautiful…"

"Yes! And a well-sharpened knife performs half of the work for you. After that, take a leaf, cut it in half, place the halves on top of each other, crumple them up, then cut it into strips, and it could hardly be easier."

"So how did you get that red-leaf lettuce all crisp like that?"

"Well, first you wash it thoroughly in cold water, then just shake the excess water off. Remove the core and set it aside first. That will help you remove the sand and other bits of dirt you wouldn't normally see. Much more effective than simply running it under the tap."

"Don't you need any soy sauce on this *hiyayakko* tofu?"

"Oh, no. I use a solution of white soup stock diluted in water. That way, the taste of the tofu won't clash so harshly against the saltiness. It results in a much softer, smoother flavor."

Chiho and Suzuno were deep in conversation.

Emi faithfully listened on, a tad nonplussed by this turn of events.

Chiho, learning that Suzuno had come to help Maou keep his home affairs in order after the summer heat got the best of Ashiya's health (and that she simply had the habit of referring to people by their first names), had finally shooed away the tears from her eyes.

After taking a disdainful look at Urushihara, idly wasting away the morning as he let his neighbor handle all the hard work, Chiho reintroduced herself to Suzuno.

"Well! I should say that the variety of food Chiho brought for us will result in quite a lovely breakfast."

The dining table was already largely filled by the time Chiho added her own fried chicken breasts and potato salad to it. For breakfast, it was almost too extensive of a buffet.

"Uh...well, hey, thanks a lot, Chi. This is kind of a surprise. Can't wait to tuck into it."

Maou thanked her as his hand wavered over the table, belying his total inability to decide on his first dish.

"Of...of course!"

"Thanks a lot, Ms. Kamazuki..."

Ashiya, sitting up, looked almost emaciated as he bowed his head.

"Hmm. We've got a lot of people here. Do we have enough teacups and chopsticks?"

Maou began a quick head count.

"Oh, I brought my own."

Chiho cheerfully took a small box out from her bag.

"Very well. In that case, Emi, I do hope you will sit next to me. I am afraid I have nothing but disposable chopsticks to offer, but..."

Suzuno invited Emi, who had been all but tossed aside by now, by offering a set of wooden chopsticks.

It was a remarkably lively morning meal, a scene that made Emi wonder if this was really the Devil's Castle after all. By the time everyone had cups and chopsticks, Urushihara finally drummed up the energy to sleepily lurch over.

"Huh. Breakfast already?"

He brushed off the dirty looks all of the other diners flashed him.

"I don't see any seat or chopsticks or teacup for me, man."

Maou, Ashiya, and Chiho each occupied one side of the *kotatsu* table, with Emi and Suzuno sharing the fourth. There was no room left for Urushihara to sit.

Instead, there was a plastic container and fork on the computer desk.

"Our guests come first. And the person who contributed the least to the meal comes last."

Ashiya was cold as ice.

"...Dude, you're gonna so regret this. Like, isn't that the container my Sugiya dinner came in?"

Urushihara half muttered it to himself, dejectedly looking at the disposable plastic bowl as he forked some rice into it.

It was what he deserved, given that even Chiho, who treated nearly everyone she met with kindness, couldn't conjure any sympathy for him.

"So...how are you, anyway, Ashiya? Are you feeling okay?"

"Thank you for your concern, Ms. Sasaki. Thanks to Ms. Kamazuki's kindness, I have been given ample opportunity to rest my weary bones. I hardly wish to be any more of a burden to our Devil's Castle, so I plan to return to my regular routine beginning today."

"And we have Chiho to thank for that. Such a cornucopia of rejuvenating ingredients she brought along! Nothing like some good meat to revitalize a man's appetite."

"Well, thank you! I wish I could cook like you, though, Suzuno."

The breakfast conversation couldn't have been friendlier. Emi gauged Suzuno carefully as it unfolded.

The words they exchanged yesterday plainly weren't enough to dissuade her away from Maou, but judging by her cooking and her friendly demeanor toward Chiho, there wasn't anything suspicious about her.

And think about this: The maniac burglar from last night took a paintball right on the ski mask. That paint, and the smell, isn't the sort of thing that comes off in a day or two. It seemed fair to conclude that Suzuno couldn't have been Emi's scythe-wielding attacker.

"Ah, experience has a way of making anyone a veteran over time, Chiho. I am sure the day will come when you surpass even me in the kitchen."

"Yeah, but Mom cooks for the family at my place, so I don't really get much of an opportunity to practice."

"Oh, the opportunity will come, trust me on that. I, too, was fed very well by my family through all my life, but in many ways, it was more a matter of them continually pushing food in my direction. Why, when I moved away, they made me bring a virtual larder filled with supplies!"

That solved another lingering mystery in Emi's mind. Given her experience with the inside of the Devil's Castle's cabinets, she was wondering who was footing the bill for all these ingredients.

"They were kindly hoping to aid me with my finances until I found useful employment in the city, but having such an enormous quantity will only lead to it all spoiling in the summer heat. So, if I may say so in front of all of you, having three hale young men with healthy appetites next door has been a great help to me."

It was hard to tell if Suzuno was trying to relieve Chiho or prove to Emi that she took her advice to give up on Maou. Or neither.

She mentioned she wanted to find a decent job yesterday, come to think of it. Emi, tossing her doubts and worries to the wind, picked up the conversational thread.

"What kind of work are you thinking of, by the way?"

Suzuno, for reasons only she was aware of, gave Emi a strange look.

Emi was a bit thrown by being stared at from point-blank range, but Suzuno took a look at Maou and Ashiya before nodding to herself, seemingly convinced to herself about something.

"I will not ask for a salaried position. As long as the proceeds allow me a bare pittance to live on, I have no complaints."

The response was crisp and clear. The use of the word *pittance* was perhaps a bit behind the times, but given her location in Sasazuka, right near the heart of Tokyo, she had a wealth of options to choose from. And given it was toward the start of the month, if she hurried, she would have a decent-sized paycheck waiting for her in just a few weeks.

"A job to make my homeland proud" was setting the bar rather low, but given that she and Emi had only just met, it was the sort of noncommittal response she expected.

Emi didn't have long to chew on this.

"Well, why don't you come work at my place?" Maou, as unthinkingly as always, completely failing to read the atmosphere around him and just blurted it out.

"‼"

"‼"

"?"

"……"

"…Ah, jeez."

Chiho froze in place, Emi's eyebrows furrowed, Suzuno tilted her head to the side, Ashiya's eyes turned toward the ceiling, and Urushihara verbally expressed his disgust.

"We're kinda low on staff for a lot of shifts right now, so I don't think we'd have a problem taking someone else on. Because, Chi'll be there, so you'll have someone familiar around while you're learning the ropes."

Did Maou ever stop to think that familiarity with the staff was far from the problem here? Or, for that matter, did it even occur to him why Chiho was on his doorstep this morning in the first place?

Urushihara, sitting away from the dining table, could see the whirlpool of awkward emotions whirling around the center of the room.

"Well, you can't really make her answer that question right on the spot, can you?"

Emi, finding no other way out of this, tried to extend a lifeline to Chiho.

"You can think of her as a potential applicant, of course, but…you know, there are good things and bad things about having personal acquaintances as your coworkers. So maybe you should, you know, think about it a little more first?"

Chiho looked at Emi, eyes held helplessly open.

"True… You do have a point." Suzuno nodded her agreement. "Thank you very much for the offer, Sadao. I will give it due consideration. And who knows? Perhaps I will ask you for a formal introduction at a later time."

"Yeah, uh, sure thing."

"And if I do, I do hope you will put in a good word for me, Chiho."

"A-all right."

Chiho stole a glance at Emi for a moment before bowing her head at Suzuno. Emi's eyes darted back slightly as she noticed this.

There was no pretense. No hidden meaning. Just a simple exchange of words. A dining table filled with honest devotion and skill. A direct, to-the-point personality to match her direct, to-the-point speech.

To both Chiho and Emi, there was absolutely nothing they could seize upon to make them suspicious of Suzuno Kamazuki.

"Would you like me to maybe show you around Shinjuku and so on?"

Emi decided to bite the bullet first.

Neither Emi nor Maou was willing to let this woman remain content with living in abject poverty and starvation. Emi knew they had to get her introduced to modern society to some extent, even as she knew it would be pointless to expand the circle too much further.

If Suzuno really was just a typical Japanese woman, Emi wanted her life as distant from Maou's as possible.

"It'll be easier to pick up on things if it's just us women together. Let these guys take you, and who knows what kind of weirdo things they'll teach you."

"Hey, that's just being mean!"

Maou spoke up, dissatisfied with this appraisal. Emi paid him no mind.

"Well, even if it is, I'm confident I could do a better job of it than *you* could."

Emi snorted haughtily at Maou. He shrugged in response, but declined to take it further.

"And how 'bout maybe you lend her some clothing or something? You know, for work and stuff. I think she looks cute in a kimono, but she's, like, gonna need a suit and a bag, right? Like, office casual, like you've got on, Emi. You could be a secretary or something, right?"

For once, Urushihara said something Emi could agree with, which she appreciated. She was not, however, as much a fan of how he picked up her shoulder bag and bandied it around without permission.

"Hey! You can't just touch that! You'll infect me with your unemployed-itis!"

"It's not a disease! I was just looking at it! Jeez!"

Urushihara bit back at this (in his mind) uncalled-for assault. Chiho gave a cold rebuttal.

"I'm amazed you can just *do* stuff like that, Urushihara."

"Aw, quit it already! You're all treating me like some sort of idiot!"

He retreated back to his lair, howling in anger along the way.

"Indeed, however, my chest of drawers is lacking in such things. I have little in the way of purses or footwear. Perhaps I had best atone for that, if necessary."

"You've got more than just…kimonos, right?"

Emi asked the question casually. She had never seen Suzuno in anything else.

"I do not. I have kimonos, and sandals, and these socks, but none of the pairings that you or Chiho are sporting so dashingly."

The confession was as shocking as it was so breezily given. Her audience exchanged glances with one another.

"Is that…strange, in some way?"

Suzuno looked around, a slight twinge of concern on her face. Even she noticed how this seemed to surprise everyone.

"No, nothing strange about it, exactly, but…"

Ashiya trailed off midway.

"Damn, Suzuno, you're like some kind of samurai princess."

Even Urushihara seemed thrown by this revelation. The other two women in the room were less forthright with their amazement.

"…Yusa, if you could perhaps introduce me to a clothing store as well…"

"Umm, sure! If we have the time."

Chiho and Emi nodded to each other, the nervousness painted on their faces.

Maou interjected between them.

"I dunno, as long as you don't come out looking all weird…"

He nodded to himself.

✳

"Well, thanks again for letting me visit so early in the morning. Get well soon, Ashiya."

"Not at all. Thank you for all the lovely things you brought over. Now, no funny business before you take Ms. Sasaki back home, Your Demonic Highness."

Maou and Chiho left the apartment, Ashiya seeing them off. Chiho blushed a bit in response, a smile on her face.

"What are you, my wife?"

Maou flashed a glare back at his roommate.

"She has loyally served you, my liege, in both personal and business matters. It is only right that you repay the debt with equal kindness."

"Pfft…yeah. Anyway, see you."

Maou wore a hangdog look on his face as he went downstairs, Chiho following behind. Ashiya watched for a few moments before shutting the door.

The two of them weren't due back at work until the afternoon. But it was Ashiya who pushed Maou into seeing Chiho back home, reasoning, "How could you allow Ms. Sasaki to merely wander off after she just brought this sumptuous feast to our door?"

Ashiya did not always have such a rosy opinion of Chiho's advances on Maou in the past, but apparently he was willing to loosen the reins with anyone willing to help the demons break even on their monthly budget.

Much of this also stemmed from the aggravation at the living vegetable called Urushihara taking root in the corner with no end in sight, although neither Maou nor Ashiya himself had consciously realized this yet.

Emi and Suzuno had left the Devil's Castle in advance, Emi

expressing a wish to show Suzuno some spots around town before work began.

Maou, meanwhile, walked next to Chiho down the sidewalk, the bag containing the assorted plastic containers Chiho had brought along safely ensconced inside the front basket of Dullahan, the Devil King's trusty steed, as he wheeled it along.

"...Too bad you don't have a seat or a carrier on the back of your bicycle, Maou."

"Dullahan, you mean. But, hey, you can't expect that much from a used fixie, right?"

"Well, it's still too bad."

Chiho flashed a chiding smile. Maou was nonplussed.

"Yeah, but if you sat on the back of this thing, I could be cited for upward of twenty thousand yen, you know? I'm skirting the law already when I use an umbrella in the rain."

Maou was only aware of this thanks to Ashiya having given him an extensive rundown of the fines and penalties involved with Tokyo bicycle law, as well as the potentially disastrous effects this would have on their finances.

Chiho rolled her eyes, giving Maou an exasperated look.

"I know *that*. I didn't say I wanted to do it or anything. I kind of meant something else."

"Mm?"

"Oh, nothing. But anyway, once we reach Sasazuka station, we can just take Koshu-Kaido Road toward Hatagaya."

With that, Chiho slowly began walking half a step ahead of Maou. He obediently walked behind, still pushing Dullahan. Glimpsing her back, it dawned upon Maou that Chiho lived in a freestanding house. With her family, no doubt. If he kept going, he'd wind up being face-to-face with her folks.

"H-hey, uh, Chi?"

"Mm? What is it?"

Chiho swiveled her face behind her.

"So, uh...thanks for giving me such a lavish breakfast. It was great."

"Oh, it's nothing compared to Suzuno. But I appreciate the compliment."

He could tell there was more than a trace of doubt in her voice, but Maou decided to press on with the question in his mind.

"Listen, uh, are your parents cool with this?"

"With what?"

The weirdly diffident response was enough to stop Maou dead for a moment.

"Oh, uh...I mean, you know, Chi. A girl like you, hanging out in a place like we've got? Did your parents mind much?"

"Oh, that?"

Chiho put a finger to her chin as she thought over her answer. The question seemed to faze her little.

"Well, they didn't say anything, anyway. I told them exactly where I was going, and my mom gave me a bunch of pointers while I cooked, too. Mother-approved, I guess you could say!"

The reply far exceeded expectations.

"Wh-what about your dad?"

Two months ago, when Maou and Chiho were caught up together in a collapse inside an underground mall in Shinjuku, Chiho's policeman father was one of the first responders. Back there, she seemed less than willing to be seen together with Maou, but...

"Well, I kinda didn't tell him where I was going last time. It's fine today, though."

"Oh. Just fine, huh?"

"Mm-hmm. He actually kinda cried this morning, too, like 'Oh, you've finally got someone you want to give a home-cooked meal to' and stuff."

Mother- *and* father-approved. Even more unbelievable.

"Oh, that reminds me. What're you gonna do for your lunch bento today? Suzuno's out with Emi right now, right?"

"What am I gonna do...? Well, I didn't really think about it."

He had little reason to. The bento that so violently jostled Chiho's world was the very first Suzuno had made for him; it was hardly a regular custom yet. So Maou gave the honest truth, a response Chiho replied to without turning around.

"Well…if you'd like, would you like me to make one?"

"…For me?"

That was the most intelligent response Maou was capable of. Chiho stared at him sourly.

"Would I have asked you if I was making it for someone else?"

"Well, no, but…hey, why not? I'm sure Ashiya would be happier with me eating whatever you make instead of living off junk food all the time."

His formal permission granted, Chiho's sulky glare immediately transformed into a bright flower blossom of a smile as she skipped into the air.

"Ooh, great! I'll make sure it's nutritious and stuff, then. Wouldn't want Ashiya to worry too much about you!"

Maou may have been slow on the uptake in certain ways, but he still had over a year's worth of experience living in Japan under his belt. Even he saw the meaning behind a teenage girl going out of her way to cook for some guy she wasn't even related to.

But there was still something bothering him.

"Well, about that, Chi…"

"Yes?"

"Don't we…you know, worry you at all?"

"Oh…you mean, you guys?"

Chiho scoped out their surroundings.

"You mean about how you're demon aliens and stuff?"

The lack of anyone nearby had apparently made her comfortable enough to blurt it out. Her summer skirt rustled in the breeze as she turned around.

"Yeah, kinda…"

Maou was speechless, not expecting it to come out so easily after she'd danced around it at first.

"Well…I guess I'd be lying if I said it didn't. Maybe you guessed it when you saw me with Emi this morning, but we like to text each other every now and then. So I know a little bit about what you were up to back on Ente Isla or whatever."

Chiho took a light breath, breaking a sweat under the pre-noon sunlight.

"But before I knew that, Maou, I kinda started liking you, so..."

The words just seemed to pour right out. Maou's eyes shot upward. Watching them, Chiho laughed nervously.

"Oh, you don't have to look at me like that. You must've understood what Albert told you, right?"

"Uh, no, uh..."

Chiho prompted him along, albeit without much forcefulness.

"Don't just stand in the middle of the street like that. There's a car coming."

Scurrying back to the edge of the street, Maou watched as a Nekoto Transport shipping truck whirred by.

"But did you notice yet, Maou? The reason why I've been so distant these past two months?"

"Not...really, no."

"When we went to work, right after you fought Urushihara, you asked me if I wanted my memories erased."

"Y-yeah..."

Chiho took a deep breath, then turned back around. The early-summer sunlight traced across the edges of her billowing skirt, along with the corners of her warm, soft smile.

"Well, I don't want to forget about the people I like. Ever. No matter what."

The wind lapped against her ever-so-slightly reddened cheeks as Chiho let her hair blow freely.

"...!"

Maou swallowed. Chiho giggled a bit in response.

"You don't have to act all shocked to death every time, Maou. Are you really trying to conquer the world, or what?"

"Uh...well, I mean..."

"At least keep walking!"

Chiho had completely taken over the conversation.

"Yusa tried to stop me at first. She said she didn't want me to regret anything, falling in love with you. But this was all my doing in the first place, you know? I started liking you, and if I want to stop, I'll do that on my own terms."

A steel rod plunged straight into the fluffy, cotton candy–like feelings that surrounded them, one that even Maou was defenseless against.

Every iota of her resolve was now revealed, embedded in her smile. Maou had no way to respond.

"Chi…"

"So, you know, even if you see me as nothing but the new girl at work, that's all right. That, and me liking you… Those are two different things."

The sunbeams from above told Maou that there was not a single trace of guile within Chiho's smile.

The Devil King, rendered silent and frozen thanks to a few simple words from a human girl, not even two decades of age, would certainly not be a good role model for his minions back home to follow.

"…This is exactly why you humans can be so scary sometimes."

"Exactly. And you should be particularly careful around women. Men get the wrong idea a lot about this, but if you mess with us, you'll pay for it. Big-time."

"I'll make a note of that."

Maou chuckled to himself as he nodded. It was apparently enough for Chiho.

"Well, today's your first day as shift supervisor, right? Good luck with that."

With that somewhat forced attempt at changing the subject and lightening the mood, Chiho confidently strode forward.

"Yeah, right. I'll try my best not to have my entire paycheck garnished."

He was quick to accept the gesture.

"You are a proud artisan, Sadao. Taking on such heavy responsibility…and blessed with such a loyal, respectful crew, no less."

"Exactly! I'll have to try my best not to drag you down! ...Um..."

"Hmm?"

"Mm."

"Huh?"

Maou completely failed to notice that someone else was walking next to him.

"You are truly loved, Sadao."

"S-S-Su..."

"Suzuno?!"

Maou and Chiho leaped back in unison.

"S-S-S-Suzuno! Wh-when were *you* over there?!"

Chiho confronted Suzuno, her previously cherry blossom–tinted cheeks now the shade of an overripe apple.

Suzuno was supposed to be out with Emi, but now, out of the blue, she was right alongside Maou and Chiho.

She had a faintly elegant air about her, clad in her kimono and lacquer-coated sandals, carrying a large, traditional *kinchaku* drawstring bag. But how did she, and the rhythmic clacking of her wooden sandals, escape their attention?

"Wh-when did you show up, how much did you hear, why didn't you say anything, why are you here, didn't you leave *before* us?!"

Chiho, nose bright as a Christmas reindeer's, furiously blazed away at Suzuno.

"I caught up to you barely a minute ago. My ears picked up the conversation beginning with 'even if you see me as nothing but the new girl at work.' I hesitated to speak up because even from afar, I could tell this was an intimate conversation. We did indeed leave early, but I realized I had left my belongings at home, so Emi proceeded on ahead while I returned to fetch them."

Coolly and dutifully, Suzuno answered each of Chiho's emotionally charged questions.

"Nnnnhh!!!!"

Chiho's entire body now shone dark red. Steam began to blow out of her nostrils.

In other words, someone had just overheard her confessing her deepest emotions for Maou.

"Worry not. Witnessing the way you treated Sadao this morning, it was plain to surmise your feelings, Chiho."

"S-S-S-S-Suzuno?! You're saying that on purpose! In front of *him*!"

"On purpose how? Any why is your face such a bright shade of crimson?"

"That's what happens when you *say* stuff like that, I'm really embarrassed, what are you even *thinking*?!"

"That may be, but it would be an even queerer thing if I failed to surmise as much. Besides, your feelings are already quite clear. It does not bother me to hear them out loud once more…"

"I'm not talking about that! Maybe you're right, but it's still embarrassing to me! Ugh! I mean… Ugh!"

"Chi, Chi, calm down a little…"

"In fact, Chiho, I find it quite virtuous and attractive, how clearly and blissfully honest you are with your own heart…no matter who it may be pointed toward."

"Um, that wasn't a knock on me just now, was it?"

Suzuno remained forthright and honest as she spoke. Chiho, meanwhile, was almost at the boiling point.

"……!!!!"

She let out a voiceless scream, her face resembling the top third of a stoplight.

"Agh! Hey! Wait! Chi!"

Without a word, Chiho snatched Dullahan away from Maou, stomped on the pedals with astonishing force, and was off at full speed.

Maou, left behind, extended a helpless hand toward Chiho as she executed a tailslide around the corner and out of sight. Then he glared at Suzuno.

"Mm. Quite loved indeed."

"Eesh. You didn't have to prod her like that. She's going through a lot at her age."

Maou hung his head in disappointment, scratching his forehead.

"Ughh… Hopefully Chi won't get in an accident, zooming off like that."

Suzuno's eyes flew open in response.

"…That is a surprise."

"What is? The fact I'm actually worried about someone else?"

"If I may be so rude as to say so."

"Yeah, well, I don't think you're the first to say that. Man, do the folks I know really have *that* little trust in me?"

The Devil King was now in full-on crabby mode as Suzuno suddenly asked a question.

"What do you think it means to be loved by someone?"

Maou wiped the sweat off his forehead with a sleeve—whether it was the heat or something else, he couldn't say—before knitting his brows.

"What, are you running a survey or something?"

"No… I meant nothing particularly profound by it."

"And you expect me to believe *that* after what you saw? …Well, it's hard to say, just having it asked like that. I don't want to just brush it off or whatever, but if Chi trusts in me that much…and, more to the point, if her parents do…then I guess I'll have to be just as sincere with them. Not that I know what to *say* to anyone yet. Why're you looking at me like that?"

He had given an honest reply to this goofball question, and yet Suzuno was now looking back at him like some exotic animal she had never laid eyes on before.

"…Did I say something weird, or…?"

"Huh? Ah, ah…ah, no, n-not at all. It was merely a touch surprising to me."

"*What* is?! And, look, shouldn't you go regroup with Emi anyway?"

"…Ah. Yes. Right."

Suzuno shook her head, as if shaking the cobwebs out of her brain. Maou took another sleeve swipe at his forehead.

"I'm sure she's over at Sasazuka station. Lemme show you a shortcut."

"A…?"

Suzuno once again seemed caught off guard. Maou ignored it.

"You see that alleyway? Walk a little ways down and you'll reach the Bosatsu Street shopping area. Make a left there and follow the line of shops down, and you'll wind up right in front of the station."

"Er…yes. Certainly. Thank you."

"Also, if you wanna find a job, you're probably gonna need a phone for people to contact you with. I know you don't have much scratch to work with right now, but you better buy a cell phone ASAP. There's a shop or two by the station, but if you don't see anything you like, I'm sure Emi knows where you could go downtown. Anyway, have a good one."

"…Yes. Thank you."

Taking another look down the path Chiho took, Maou breathed a dejected sigh before turning his back to Suzuno and heading back toward his apartment.

Suzuno couldn't help but watch him go. As she did, Maou suddenly turned back around after a few steps.

"Good luck finding a decent job! Try not to let all the crowds freak you out downtown."

And then he walked off, not bothering to wait for Suzuno's response.

She stood there for a few moments, finding herself unable to move.

"Did you find your bag?"

Emi, waiting in front of the Sasazuka station turnstile, walked up to Suzuno upon spotting her. Suzuno nodded, still in a slight haze.

"Yes…yes, safe and sound. I apologize for making you wait."

"Not at all. Is something up? You look a little off."

"No…but…are we boarding the…um, train? Right now?"

Emi didn't know why she added a question mark after the word *train*, but paid it no mind as she nodded.

"Yep. It's only one station from Sasazuka to Shinjuku, but it's still kind of far to walk. Oh, and watch you don't take the train to Motoyawata, either. That's two extra stops, and it puts you way at the far edge of Shinjuku, too. Do you have a passcard or anything? You'll have to buy a regular ticket if you don't, but setting up a fare card now will make it a lot easier in the future."

"Um...yes. About that."

Suzuno took a look around her surroundings, plainly a tad confused.

"If I may be honest with you, I have yet to board a train in my life."

She had a knack for making these jaw-dropping revelations in the plainest, most everyday tone of voice possible.

"...What?"

Emi had no idea how old Suzuno was, but eyed her suspiciously regardless. What kind of far-off forbidden kingdom did she live in if she was old enough to live alone, but still hadn't seen the inside of a train car?

"And what is this *fair card* I keep hearing about? Is it used to gain access to the market fair?"

"What?"

"Hmm?"

There was something odd about how Suzuno just pronounced that.

"I...apologize if I said something strange."

"Uh, *strange* isn't the... Um. Well. Anyway, let's just buy a ticket, all right? I'll explain what a passcard is later. Tickets are..."

She stopped once she noticed Suzuno standing statuelike in front of a ticket vending machine.

"...Um, can I ask an honest question? How the heck did you make it to Sasazuka?"

This was starting to get silly. She didn't even know how to purchase a ticket? Whether she was born in Japan or Mars, she had made her own way to Tokyo. It wouldn't have been impossible for her to completely avoid public transit the entire way, but it certainly would be inconvenient.

Suzuno, meanwhile, was unable to hide her perplexed mood next to the doubtful Emi.

"Well, I apologize if I am somewhat lacking in local knowledge. I used a Gate to come right down upon Sasazuka."

"Oh, right, that makes..."

The sheer matter-of-fact way she put it made Emi almost fail to pick up on it at first.

"...What was that?"

Her face tensed up. Something told her she had just heard one seriously important confession.

"I said, I came down directly upon Sasazuka through the use of a Gate and have been busy assembling my new identity in the city, so until I grow more familiar with city life here, I'm afraid that I..."

"W-wait! Wait!"

Emi's pulse surged. She brought a hand to her chest, as if trying to suppress it, and gave her surroundings a close look before bringing her darkened face closer to Suzuno's.

"A-are you from Ente Isla?!"

This had come almost immediately after Emi concluded Suzuno was harmless. A tad off-kilter, but harmless. Emi's mind was already plunged halfway into panic mode.

Even Suzuno reacted with surprise at the question, her eyes wide and pointed toward Emi.

"Had you not noticed?!"

How could I have been expected to? Emi thought as she pressed on.

"You never breathed a *word* of it to me!"

"But you said it yourself! You said you were after the Devil King!"

"What?!"

"I was a tad surprised, as I never thought you would use that name in front of the man himself. But then you advised me not to take any rash action. That I should 'keep my distance' from him, or I would be unhappy!"

"Whaaaaat?!"

"I have been through a great number of trials and tribulations in my life, but if it is the Hero advising me to stand down, then stand down I shall. However, even if I pulled up stakes at that very moment, I had no place left to go. Thus I asked you for assistance—assistance you promised to give. Along with your contact information, no?"

"Whaaaaaaaat?!"

Emi was awash in a sea of confusion, but the truth behind Suzuno's explanation was starting to dawn on her.

Then, the full truth finally hit home. That conversation, just outside of the Devil King's doorstep, was the result of Emi and Suzuno gravely misunderstanding each other.

"So you did *not* say that because you knew of my true colors?!"

"How the hell was *that* going to show me who you really were?!"

Emi felt she had the right to be angry.

"You found nothing at all strange about it?! This dainty young girl, freshly moved into her new apartment, briskly meddling with the lives of the three men who live next door? You thought it was a perfectly everyday occurrence?!"

"Yes! I did! And having you act like I didn't is really pissing me off!"

This was her reward for preoccupying herself with keeping this strange young girl from getting wrapped up in her destiny. Nobody was "getting wrapped up" in anything. She was involved from the start.

"Then what did you possibly mean when you asked if I was 'aiming for' the Devil King?!"

"Huh? That… I mean…"

There was no way Emi could tell the truth. That she'd mistakenly thought Suzuno was attracted to him. She thought the embarrassment would overwhelm her for a moment, but it was really Suzuno's fault she made the mistake in the first place.

"W-well, why did *you* ask me if I was 'in a close relationship' with him?!"

The reply came clear as day.

"Because I had word that you fought alongside the Devil King!"

Emi's eyes shot open.

Besides the residents of Devil's Castle, the only people who knew that Emilia the Hero teamed up with Satan, the Devil King, in battle were Chiho, Emeralda, Albert, and Olba.

There was no way Emeralda and Albert would spread stories that would put the Hero's name in question. The only alternative was that Olba, still in custody of the Japanese authorities, had found a way to transmit the news to Ente Isla.

And, from there, it was easy to surmise the sort of Ente Islans who could receive that sort of news.

Emi decided to start by declaring her innocence.

"You have *got* to be kidding me! We had a common enemy! There was nothing I could do about it besides defeat him while the Devil King was in the same location! And anyone who calls it 'fighting alongside' him is making a terrible, terrible mistake!"

It was the very definition of splitting hairs, but to Emi, said hair was as long, wide, and visible as a brick wall.

In terms of her intentions, at least, the Devil King remained Emi's foe during that battle, even as she fought against Lucifer and Olba.

As for how *other* people interpreted it…that, even she had to admit, was a different story.

It was clear how an external observer could have believed he was watching the Hero and Devil King tag-teaming against an archbishop of the Church. And then she was attacked on the very day she handed over her address and phone number.

"So, what, you thought I joined sides with the Devil King so I could get revenge against the Church?! Is that why you dressed up all funny and attacked me at the convenience store yesterday?!"

Someone closely allied with Olba would no doubt step up to fulfill his most fervent of wishes. That was easy enough to surmise.

And there was every chance that someone would simply want vengeance against the archbishop's nemesis, completely unaware of his crimes.

But Suzuno, suddenly looking quite a bit more suspicious than a few minutes ago, stared quizzically at Emi as she crossed her arms in thought, acting for all the world like Emi's accusation was out of left field.

"A 'convenience store'? How does one sell convenience, exactly? I am not sure what you mean."

"Oh, if *you* don't, how do you think *I'm* handling this right now, huh?! Are you pulling that act on purpose, or are you really that stupid?!"

Emi used a hand to cup her face.

"I was attacked, all right? At the store! On the day I gave you my info! By someone from Ente Isla! And not to defend the Devil King, but it wasn't a demon, because whoever it was had the power to cancel out my holy sword! Which means it had to be you…!"

Emi stopped cold. Now everything was out in the open, on the laundry rope of confrontation.

"W-wait a moment, please. Me, attacking you? I have done no such thing! I knew full well that you were Emilia, the Hero! I knew the strength you possessed as a knight of the Church! And while I am not wholly useless in battle, I was hardly so foolish as to wage a duel I had but little chance of winning!"

Emi watched the surprised Suzuno carefully as she defended herself.

That scythe-wielding maniac had taken a paintball point-blank to the face.

Her well-defined features and supple skin made it difficult to notice at first, but up close like this, Suzuno was clearly wearing no makeup.

Those antitheft paintballs were made with a compound you couldn't rub off with household cleaners. But if Suzuno were last night's assailant, she would resemble a fluorescent-orange panda right now.

And when they sat next to each other this morning, Emi didn't smell anything off—neither the telltale scent of the paintball, nor any unusual perfumes that could have hidden it.

Resisting the urge to further shout Suzuno down, Emi gave the dourest face she could muster while hissing angrily:

"…Well, look, I'm sorry if I'm a little slow on the uptake. Can you clue me in? Who are you, and what're you trying to do, just waltzing into the Devil's Castle like that?!"

Her voice had grown desperate. And loud, although it wasn't the sort of conversation any passersby had the courage to butt into. Still, Emi made a point of looking around to ensure Maou or Ashiya weren't spying on them.

"…My true name is Crestia Bell, chief inquisitor of the Reconciliation Panel."

Emi did a double take. The term *Reconciliation Panel* was not one she was expecting here.

"I apologize if we experienced a breakdown in communications earlier. So, once again, I ask you. Could I ask for your help, and your cooperation, Emilia Justina, as the Hero of Ente Isla? I promise I have not come here to hurt you."

Suzuno bowed her head. It was a sincere gesture, Emi thought. She sighed, noticing the bright red hairpin with the four-petaled flower entangled in a whorl. It was modeled after the Cruciferae family of budding plants—the "cross-bearing" flowers. She looked up at the station clock.

"Let's save this for after we reach Shinjuku. I don't want to be late for work."

With that, she set off for the turnstile.

"Ah…um, what?"

Suzuno stared goggle-eyed at Emi's back, perhaps surprised that the Hero would put her Japanese employer ahead of her true identity.

"Look, this is the kind of country Japan is, okay? Let's get moving."

Emi, feeling a tad victorious, placed her fare card on the sensor and walked through the turnstile.

"W-wait a—*ngh!*"

She turned around at the sound of Suzuno's odd groan.

"L-let me go! I—I cannot afford to be stymied here…"

"......"

She looked at Suzuno, the tip of her kimono's belt caught by the closing gate as she tried to follow Emi through the turnstile.

The thought of the yawning culture gap they would have to traverse, and all the associated trouble they'd have to navigate on the way to Shinjuku, threw Emi into a deep depression.

✳

The true fate of Emilia the Hero and Satan, the Devil King, was discovered within the papers Olba left behind.

From there, she used the Church's sonar to track down traces of the waves emitted by the Holy Silver of Evolution, the divine tool instilled within Emilia that formed the core of her holy sword. She found what she was looking for from another world.

She also found a shard from the single horn Emilia had reportedly sliced off the Devil King's head in their final battle. Using it to weave a special sonar pulse that could pick up on the pattern of his demonic magic, she spread signals far and wide across the universe.

The results showed a concentrated presence of demonic force focused in a certain area. But even before she learned of those results, she already had more incontrovertible evidence at hand.

This evidence, however, was not something she reported to the sanctuary. If she did, it was easy to picture the entire panel of archbishops falling dead on the spot.

It came into her hands via a completely unexpected coincidence.

As she pored over the papers in Olba's study, a transmission arrived on the Link Crystal she used to form idea links across worlds. It had come from Olba himself.

The link was laden with noise, but she could still tell that he was alive, confined in an alien planet with no ability to open a Gate, and seeking help.

And while it sounded too good to be true, she had also taken full note of what he said next:

"Emilia the Hero formed a team with, and fought alongside, the Devil King."

✳

"I served the Church in its missionary arm…and now it pains me to think I considered myself an expert at analyzing the ways of foreign lands. This nation, Japan, is far beyond my feeble understanding… There is not a single city similar to this on Ente Isla…"

Suzuno was nothing short of shattered.

The uproar within her mind began the moment she was stopped by the turnstile gate at Sasazuka station. She successfully purchased a ticket afterward, but—still unable to tell the difference between a paper ticket and a chip-embedded fare card—she was ruthlessly blocked once more after trying to wave the ticket over the touch sensor.

"You still dare to interfere with me?!"

After screaming at the machine, she tripped over herself at the top of the escalator, sending a wooden sandal flying. This was followed by her politely replying to an station intercom announcement, raising eyebrows across the platform, then losing her footing inside the train during the maze of rail junctions that preceded the final stop at Shinjuku.

Once at her destination, she was awed by the great crowds of people, mistook the red cross in front of the blood donation center for a Church outpost, and—once safely up on the surface—gaped in abject amazement at the innumerable high-rises and cars and human beings that surrounded her.

By the time they finally arrived at Sully's, a café nearby Emi's workplace, her face had been drained of all vigor. The sensory overload had quickly proven too much for her.

Sully, by the way, was the name of the man who first founded the chain, in a faraway realm known as "Washington." Emi avoided mentioning this, figuring it wiser to keep the scope of Suzuno's terminal culture shock to one nation at a time.

"So…what were we talking about, then…?"

"I know you haven't seen a TV before, but I didn't think you'd seriously shout out, 'Ohhhh. There's a man inside that thin board on the…'"

"Please, stop talking about that!"

Suzuno clapped a hand on the table to make her point, cheeks already blushing a tinge.

If she was to be believed, she had conducted research into such modern Japanese trappings as computers, mobile phones, and television sets. But the shock of seeing all of this in person was something she just couldn't control, judging by the barrage of comical exclamations she was making to no one in particular.

"The documentation I had at hand indicated something larger and box-shaped! Then I wouldn't have been taken so aback! One can hide a person inside a box easily enough!"

"The shape of it doesn't really matter…and, just so we're on the same page here, there isn't a guy inside."

Picking up the glass of iced coffee delivered to their table, Emi took a sip to quench her thirst.

Suzuno ordered a cup of tea, but had no idea how to use the little cup of nondairy creamer it came with, ultimately rocketing its contents straight onto the adjacent floor.

"What kind of 'documentation' did you have, anyway?"

The question had been wiggling around Emi's mind all morning. Given her claims of having studied the local culture beforehand, her behavior was a poor fit for modern Japan.

"I learned that the kimono was a traditional Japanese garment, so I studied the resources where they appeared the most often. I think you call them 'samurai dramas'? I also viewed several long-running documentaries depicting modern Japanese life. I thought I could trust them! Some dated from this era that I understand people call 'the fifties'!"

Suzuno turned her eyes upward as she tried to recall her primary sources.

"Well, that explains all the goofy anachronisms, I guess." Emi smiled wryly to herself.

"Hey, but which samurai drama did you like the best?"

There was more than a hint of curiosity to the way Emi asked the question.

She was a fan of the genre, after all, but nobody around her expressed even the slightest interest in her fandom. Now, she hoped, she finally had a fellow woman to share her personal tastes with.

"Well...I do like the ones that star wandering *ronin*, like *Oarashi Montaro* or *Lone Lion and Cub* or *Three for the Slash!* Things like *Vice-Shogun Mito*, or *Maniac Shogun*... They did not quite touch the same chord with me."

"...Oh."

In nearly every way, they seemed to have nothing in common. Emi sighed as she returned to the main topic at hand.

"So...if we can go back to Sasazuka for a moment... What does the head inquisitor of the Reconciliation Panel want with me? What could possibly possess you to live next door to the Devil King?"

Despite her position in the Reconciliation Panel, it had to be said that Suzuno demonstrated no sign of being a Church assassin after Emi's life. So far.

But what other reason did she have for taking a Gate trip on over, then? Emi studiously watched over Suzuno, lending an attentive ear to whatever she had to say.

"Well, if I could summarize it for you..."

Suzuno leaned forward, her face betraying her tension.

"My first goal was to ascertain whether you were alive or not. As I followed Olba Meiyer's trail, however, the only clues I unearthed were related to the Devil King, and his activities in this world. Thus, I reasoned that if I kept a close watch on the Devil King himself..."

"The Hero would show up before long. I sure walked into *that* mousetrap."

Emi shrugged. There was no other way to put it. Hook, line, and sinker.

"There is no way for me to express my sorrow for the deplorable crimes Olba Meiyer committed. Judging by the way you acted around him before knowing I, too, was Ente Islan, I can only conclude that his tale of you forging a pact with the Devil King was a complete fabrication. His actions do not reflect the collective position of the Church. I, at least, hope to serve as your humble ally."

Suzuno leaned several inches closer.

"Now, allow me to dance around the topic no longer. I want you to defeat Satan, the Devil King, and return to Ente Isla with me. I want you to prove you are alive, expose Olba's crimes, and guide the Church back to the path it must traverse."

"No."

"...That was rather fast!"

Suzuno almost spilled her tea as her elbows lost traction on the table.

"You could at least give it a modicum of thought!"

"No. I'm not working with anyone from the Church any longer."

Emi poured a packet of sugar into her iced coffee, calmly stirring it with her straw.

"But you promised to work alongside me!"

"That doesn't count. I made that promise before I knew who you were."

"You care so little about your position, about your honorable reputation within Ente Isla? Why not bring it back to what it *should* be?!"

"Oh, like *I* care about what the Church and all the other kingdoms think."

Emi stared out the café window as she calmly brushed Suzuno off. Suzuno followed her gaze.

"What is...?"

Suzuno scowled as she began the question. Emi halted her, pointing out the subway entrance facing the window with her eyes.

"Could you understand that I'm not exactly welcoming you with open arms, if you consider that you work for a group whose boss triggered a collapse in an underground tunnel packed with innocent people, just to kill me and the Devil King? You know Olba's here, right?"

"......"

Speechlessly, Suzuno looked at Emi, then the view outside. She nodded, even though her face had *I cannot believe this* written all over it.

"I had no idea he had gone so far..."

"Olba teamed up with Lucifer to wreck this nation, just for the sake of killing me. Emeralda and Albert know, too. They were there. In fact, you could ask Lucifer yourself later. You know that's who Urushihara is, right?"

Emi placed her glass down as she turned toward Suzuno.

"That's why I thought you were that attacker yesterday, too. But even if you weren't, I have zero intention to work in tandem with someone from the Reconciliation Panel."

"...Why?"

Emi was all too quick to respond.

"Because the Hero is charged with slaying the Devil King."

It sounded like the most obvious of truths, coming from Emi's mouth. It seemed to rally Suzuno's spirits.

"Then let me join you! I traveled here with the intention of slaying him myself, if I had to."

"That is my job, and mine alone. Don't meddle in this."

"How you could say such things...?"

"Do I really have to spell it out for you? You *are* a higher-up in the Reconci—well, really, the Council of Inquisitors, right?"

Emi made a point of correcting herself midway. Suzuno fell silent, feeling her blood pressure plummet.

"Listen, I don't know what you've done up to this point. So I do apologize if this is hurting your feelings."

Noticing Suzuno falling into an awkward confusion, Emi attempted to lighten the mood a little. But, "I don't want anyone taking me defeating the Devil King and using it for their own gain. That, at least, I hope you understand."

With that, Emi looked at a clock on the wall. It was getting close to her work shift.

"That, and I don't know why you're keeping them fed, but I just want to warn you—if you keep trying to mess around with them in your cute little ways like that, they're gonna spot you out. He's *still* the Devil King, you know."

"...I appreciate the warning."

"I'm going to kill the Devil King for my *own* sake. So just stay away from him, all right? Go back to Ente Isla. And rest assured, I'm never going to let any of them set foot on our homeland again."

Picking up the check, Emi stood up, took out a wadded-up magazine from her shoulder bag, and handed it to Suzuno.

"Of course, I'm sure you're still working on your own itinerary. So take this. It's a free help-wanted magazine. I picked up a copy at the station just now, but there's a lot of others just like it, so try looking around a bit."

Suzuno looked blankly at Emi, then at the cutesy pig logo on the corner of the magazine's cover.

"You'll want to read that if you plan on staying here a while. Learn a bit about what people do to earn a living in this world. Your speech and your clothing are just too much of a mismatch, you know? Try researching fashion a little. Watch the people around you. I need to go to work. You can get back home yourself, right?"

Leaving the openmouthed Suzuno behind her, Emi paid the café bill and left the building.

Then she put a hand to her forehead and heaved a heavy sigh.

"I *hope* that brought the message across."

She had already survived here in Japan for at least a week. Emi doubted this harsh rejection would be enough to drive her to despair.

Unlike Olba, she had already expressed a desire to bring Emi back home. That was enough to convince Emi she wouldn't do anything to earn further disapproval.

It had been a packed morning. Emi wondered if her spirit could hold out for the entire shift. Perhaps an energy drink was in order. Not 5-Holy Energy β. A *real* one.

"Oh! Hey, Emi!"

Emi turned toward the voice.

"...Oh. Morning, Rika."

Rika Suzuki, her coworker, had just reported in for work. For now, she was the one person in Japan Emi had the frankest relationship with.

"A little morning coffee? That's a rarity."

"Yeah, pretty much. I had to meet up with someone I know."

"Ooh! A man, maybe? You pretty much never talk about your personal life, so..."

"Oh, come on. It was just a girl."

The two friends walked off toward work, exchanging another weekday's worth of idle conversation.

✳

"I...I'm really sorry about this!"

Upon reporting to work, Maou was greeted with Dullahan, safe and sound, and Chiho bowing her head down to him like a praying mantis.

Maou laughed it off, but even now she was red in the face, hesitating to lock eyes with him.

Parking Dullahan out back, he joined Chiho inside, searching for a way to soothe her bruised ego.

"...Huh?"

He scowled as he looked around the dining area. Even Chiho, still blazing with crimson shame and embarrassment, noticed something was wrong.

Maou generally reported to work at noon sharp. Thanks to this Mag location—just off Hatagaya station, sandwiched between a residential area and an office-lined street—the lunch rush should already have been under way. Today, though, there wasn't even the hint of a rush.

Kisaki stood behind a register, beaming. Behind her, one of the college students handling the morning shift kept a respectable distance, his face white as a ghost. That was enough to tell Maou the whole story.

His manager always saved that plastered-on smile for days when sales were down.

"Um, good—"

"It's been dead."

"—morning... Pardon?"

If Maou was hesitant to speak up, he was even less ready to continue after hearing Kisaki's hardened voice.

"Six hours since we opened, and we're eating Sentucky's traffic dust."

"Huh?"

"Our customer numbers are down eighty percent from yesterday. I'm starting to think those bastards at SFC are conspiring against us."

Even considering the circumstances, a rival franchise opening up right nearby, this was a pretty wild accusation. That 80-percent drop wasn't unheard of—an "off" day or the wrong weather outside could make all the difference—but Kisaki was absolutely convinced Sentucky was behind it.

"Why...? Why do I have to go back to the office for training starting today?!"

Kisaki bellowed at the empty dining space in front of her, her smile unflagging. The morning part-timers shook in fear.

"It gives me nightmares to even imagine it, but if our customer stats keep up this pace the entire day..."

Kisaki's death stare swept its way across Maou, Chiho, and then the rest of the crew. Never before had a beautiful woman's smile sent such frigid waves of fear down their spines.

"You want to be sent to Greenland? Hmm? Are you listening, Shift Supervisor Sadao Maou?"

"No, ma'am."

The Devil King never imagined what a frog felt like while being eyed by a pit viper. Now he did.

Grabbing Maou's shoulders from across the counter, Kisaki's eyes glinted like a predator out for blood.

"Then you have my full permission to do *whatever it takes. Destroy SFC.*"

"Yes, ma'am!"

Chiho and the rest of the crew joined Maou in a stiff military salute.

"Whatever it takes," of course, meant whatever common sense allowed in terms of ways to improve MgRonald sales, not to physically wipe SFC off the map.

Even at the peak of lunch, traffic still failed to reach what anyone could truthfully call a "rush." The new Sentucky Fried Chicken, meanwhile, was running a roaring business. Even from the opposite end of the street, that much was obvious.

Even the cheerful smile emanating from the statue of Major Fyres, the friendly old man that decorated the doorstep of every Sentucky franchise in statue form, seemed like a gnarled, ghastly sneer to him.

Once Kisaki left the building, the enraged look in her eyes living up to her unofficial nickname, "The Sales Demon," Maou tried to fight back with whatever means he had at hand.

More intimate service, without getting too pushy with customers. A shake booth outside, powered by an external cooler. Finally, an employee out front talking up the current free-refill offer on MgRonald coffee. Maou ordered all that and more on Chiho and the rest of the crew. He even ventured out the door himself at times, shouting himself hoarse as he tried to coax customers inside.

But the effort was all for naught. The two PM register check revealed customer numbers down about 70 percent from the day before.

"Well, great. If this is what we get on day one…"

Maou stated out loud what Chiho and the staff were already thinking.

The dining space wasn't completely devoid of customers, but there was no way these numbers would appease Kisaki's passionate grudge against Sentucky Fried Chicken.

The chill provided by the slightly overactive AC was enough to remind the entire staff of Greenland once again. It didn't help warm their hearts.

"Welcome!!"

Maou was the first to speak as the automatic door shuffled open, revealing a new customer. He made a beeline for the counter.

"Hello. I apologize for interrupting you, but could I speak to the manager?"

It was a small, thin man in slightly oversized sunglasses, well-defined lines framing his face. The suitcase in his hand indicated he was a businessman, but between his compact stature and the comparatively novelty-sized glasses, he looked more like a child dressed up as a mob boss from a '70s yakuza movie.

Maou had already memorized the names and faces of all the top management that dealt with the Hatagaya location. This must be some kind of external business.

With the manager away, it was up to assistant manager and shift supervisor Maou to handle this. He walked up to the man in front of the counter, the crewman next to him stealing furtive stares at this unexpected customer and his request.

"I apologize, sir, but our manager isn't here today. My name is Maou, and I'm the current shift supervisor. If I'm able to, I'd be happy to handle any questions you may have."

The man lifted his eyebrows up high.

"Ah, Sadao Maou? Superb. I've heard the rumors about you."

He may have been below Maou's line of sight physically, but there was something about the man's demeanor that made Maou feel like he was suddenly below even that.

"Despite the name, they say you are a diligent worker, a superior talent, a thoughtful leader, and above all, a font of human kindness."

"Er, yes… I appreciate that, sir."

What did he mean by "despite the name"? People occasionally told Maou that his name seemed a tad old-fashioned for a young man in the twenty-first century, but having this man he'd never met before make such a frank observation rattled Maou a bit.

What also rattled him was the oddly strong scent of mint he noticed surrounding the man as he stood there. It must have been some kind of deodorant or cologne, but such an intense man-made scent was enough to seriously impede kitchen work around here.

"I apologize, but have we met somewhere before?"

And before that, where would he have even heard about Maou, just another fast-food part-timer?

"No, we haven't."

The small man cracked a broad smile.

"However, I have been aware of you for a very long time before now."

This is one of *those* customers, isn't it? Maou had trouble shooing the impolite thought from his mind.

Then the man brightened up, suddenly remembering something.

"Ah, but look at me. Here, allow me to introduce myself."

He took out a small metal holder from an inside pocket, removed a business card, and presented it. Maou nodded to him, accepted it with both hands, and then froze once he saw the position printed on it.

"The...manager of Sentucky Fried Chicken?"

A wave of nervous murmuring erupted across the MgRonald crew members.

"My name is Mitsuki Sarue. I thought I would introduce myself to our new neighbors."

The man who called himself Sarue smiled lightly as he scratched his head.

"I apologize that I failed to pay a visit earlier. We've just been so busy with everything, you know."

Maou could feel a spark fly from his mind's tangled wiring.

"Hatagaya is such a wonderful neighborhood, isn't it? Nestled right between a business and residential zone. Great crowds of potential customers. Lovely women everywhere. I must praise MgRonald's great foresight in establishing a foothold here first!"

"...Huh?"

Chiho, standing behind Maou, had trouble believing this sight.

"But regardless, I finally found a spare moment just now during our thriving opening-day business to pay a visit. And a good thing, too, since it seems I am not intruding at all at the moment!"

Listening to this backhanded stab at MgRonald's current emptiness, Maou felt a lightning crack of agitation echo across his mind like nothing experienced before in this world.

"...Yes, we are a tad slow at the moment. But all the more opportunity to get to know our neighbors better, of course."

Maou was not the sort of Hatagaya station MgRonald afternoon shift supervisor/assistant manager to let his customer service–driven smile crumble at such an affront. Though it *was* starting to toe the line.

"Oh, not at all! Our shared customer base is always looking for the next novelty, you know. I'm sure things will be back to normal in no time."

The smile was rewarded with another taunting declaration of their superiority, this one camouflaged in the mask of modesty.

If Kisaki were dealing with this, Maou could easily imagine her losing her cool and sledgehammering Sarue through the door. But with the location in Maou's able hands, there was no way that would be forgiven. Kisaki was ultimately the one responsible for his actions, after all.

Maou praised himself for retaining his cool and refusing to take the bait.

"I would certainly hope so, sir. In fact, I look forward to great success for the both of us here by the station. And I'm sure that, when she comes back, our manager would be delighted to repay your visit with one of her own."

So would you kindly get the hell out of here? Maou politely weaved in between the lines.

The response seemed to take Sarue by surprise, but he nonetheless flashed an ironic grin.

"Well...! I suppose you certainly aren't the person I know after all." He bowed his head down as he continued.

"It is a shame I couldn't meet the beautiful manager I've heard so much about, but while I'm here, could I perhaps order a value meal to go? ...Mm?"

His eyes stopped on Chiho, looking on with the rest of the crew members behind Maou.

"My, how pretty."

"Huh?"

Within the instant Maou noticed where Sarue's eyes were pointed, Sarue had all but teleported himself into position, right in front of her.

"Such a bright future this fetching young lady must have. It would simply delight me to purchase a meal prepared by you. You and those dainty hands of yours!"

The grimace on Chiho's face was clear to everyone.

It didn't take a genius to tell that Sarue was here to rile up his new competition. As if that weren't enough, he was far overstepping his bounds with the crew on duty. Chiho began to open her mouth.

"Sasaki?"

Maou's sharp, supervisor-accented voice was enough to close it.

"Would you mind taking this customer's order, please?"

"...Certainly."

Maou gestured to Sarue to come toward the register. Sarue took one more look at him before keeping his eyes squarely fixated upon Chiho until she accepted his order and left.

"*Someone's* looking kinda peeved."

Chiho was still sulking long after Sarue left.

"Why shouldn't I be? That Sarue guy obviously came in here to pick on us. Doesn't all that junk he said bother you at all, Maou?"

"Well, if it bothered you that much, that just shows you've grown to the point where you take real pride in your work. You're not just here for the pay, in other words. I'm a lot happier about that, myself."

"...Ugh."

Chiho attempted to tighten her pout even further. The effect twisted her face instead, as if she was trying to avoid yawning.

"...You're so dense all the time, but whenever something like this happens, it's always like *this* with you."

She muttered it to herself, too inaudible for Maou to hear, before turning her face away. She didn't want him seeing her twisted expression, the result of being complimented when she wanted to get all riled up instead.

"If you let yourself stay angry at a difficult customer, that's just bringing yourself down to his level. We just have to stick to our guns, you know? That's what makes it all work out, and it lets you keep your pride, too. As long as they're paying us, a customer's a customer."

Maou rubbed the bottom of his nose, a contrived attempt at an air of authority.

"How was that? Kinda assistant manager–like of me, huh?"

"Yeah, until you said *that*." Chiho giggled.

"I guess I should apologize for not stepping in when he got all flirty, though. That must've sucked."

"Like I care what that ankle-biter had to say to me." Chiho shook her head as he bowed lightly toward her.

"Ankle-biter! That's a good one."

Maou clapped his approval as the rest of the crew nodded and laughed.

"Man, I'd really hate to work for a manager like that, though. Is he even treating this business seriously? With *that* kind of cologne, he's probably gonna get a pile of complaints."

The rousing pep talk belied an honest concern Maou had for his new rival. Retailers in the same shopping area had a way of influencing each other's reputations, both for better and for worse. It wasn't something he could revel in without pause.

"Do you think he deals with customers with those glasses on, too?" Chiho interjected.

"Yeah, well, maybe he's trying to avoid UV rays. Ashiya mentioned something like that to me once. Or maybe he's got eye problems. Kinda hard to tell these days."

Maou was more concerned about the weird...whatever it was

Sarue was trying to say, without actually saying it. But that had to wait. For now, they needed to get sales back to normal before closing.

"Right. Let's get back to some serious selling."

"You got it! I am *not* gonna let 'em win!"

The episode seemed to be behind them now, as Chiho led the surprisingly raucous round of cheering.

"Okay! Bring 'em on! One hundred, two hundred, I don't care! It's time to do some *work*!!"

"That's the spirit, Chi. We'll get some more concrete intel on SFC later on today, so let's keep this machine running."

"Concrete intel?"

Maou puffed out his chest and nodded at Chiho.

"Yep. Gotta make use of the tools at hand. Or your faithful generals, anyway. Besides, when I told him my salary was in jeopardy, he had no choice but to say yes."

❋

Even by evening, the waves of heat that lapped over Tokyo's summer skies showed no sign of relenting.

As they left the office together, Rika asked Emi what her plans were for the evening. Emi hesitated before briskly dodging the question.

"I kinda have someplace to go."

She was terribly harsh on Suzuno earlier in the morning, but there was every chance the girl decided to take action after all, despite her stern rebuke.

"Oh? That's too bad. Something with your friend from this morning, maybe? Well, lemme know when you're free, 'cause I still have this Takano Fruit Bar coupon to use, okay?"

"...Sure, I'll find a free day pretty soon. Sorry."

Visions of the colorful all-you-can-eat fruit paradise flashed across Emi's mind. It took all of her willpower, alongside her sense of duty, to quell the thought.

It was understandable, then, that the disbelief was written clearly on Emi's face as they found Suzuno just outside the building, looking very different from the way she had in the morning.

"Hmm? Hey, isn't that the girl you were with?"

For a second, Emi considered denying everything and dashing off.

"Emi! Have you finally completed your duties?"

Well, scratch that, Emi thought as she ran up. Forced to accept the cards dealt, she dejectedly turned toward Suzuno.

She was sporting a refreshing water-print kimono, the kind one would expect to see in Kyoto travel pamphlets, along with a cross-shaped glass hairpin. In her hand were two bags—one paper bag from a store inside the Kakui Fashion Square building, the other one plastic, bearing a DEF Mart logo and apparently holding a pair of sandals.

A balloon was tied to her tote bag, which featured a Japanese-style print of a goldfish. Inside, Emi spotted a plastic mineral-water bottle and a Moonbucks Coffee tumbler.

"You bought all that, and you *still* couldn't pick anything besides a kimono?"

Emi felt perfectly justified in saying that ahead of anything else. What on earth had happened to this poor girl, the girl who'd asked the Hero to slay the Devil King just half a day ago?

"As a member of the Church missionary force, it is part of my duty to examine the economic trends in our areas of operation. Besides, I noticed multiple women in similar kimonos passing by."

"...You had that much money on you?"

"I did bring a sizable number of, ah, financial instruments along with me. I sold several examples to a store known as Mugi-hyo."

That was that name of a well-known Tokyo pawnshop. But what would a high-ranking Church figure be doing with "financial instruments," whatever those were? Emi doubted she had much idea of the yen's value in modern Japan. Hopefully she didn't flog off precious Ente Isla relics at bargain-basement prices.

Suzuno continued by taking a pass holder out from her bag, one with yet another fetching Japanese-themed pattern on it.

"And look! I purchased one of your 'fare cards'! I, er, 'charged'? Yes! I did that! All by myself!"

In a rare bout of excitement, she flashed the penguin logo on the card at Emi.

"...Well, good job."

It was like congratulating your baby sister upon completing her first errand for Mom and Dad. Emi had to resist the urge to pat Suzuno on the head as Rika intervened.

"Is this your friend, Emi?"

"Uhm..."

She paused for a moment.

"Yeah, pretty much, I suppose."

"Well, you don't sound too sure."

A selection of excuses flashed through her brain, all of which involved conjuring up more lies about her upbringing. As she pondered, Suzuno suddenly began introducing herself to Rika.

"How wonderful to meet you. I am Suzuno Kamazuki. I have lived in Tokyo for only a short period of time, but Emi has been an enormous help to me."

"Oh. Neat! My name's Rika Suzuki. I work with her, as you probably guessed."

Emi remained silent, unable to grasp Suzuno's intent.

"So, Kamazuki, did you move to Eifukucho?"

Rika asked the obvious question. If she and Emi were interrelated, it'd be natural to think they lived nearby each other.

But the query was enough to fill Emi with an impending sense of doom.

"No, my residence is in Sasazuka."

"Sasazuka? Really? But you're in Eifukucho, right, Emi?"

"Y-yeah, but..."

Emi tried to signal to Suzuno her trepidation, via her eyes. Suzuno's were elsewhere.

"Emi struck up a conversation with me not long after I moved here. She was visiting the neighbors next door."

"Oh, I see...but, wait, what were you doin' in Sasazuka, Emi?"

Rika almost seemed ready to drop the topic before something caught her attention. Suzuno chose that exact moment to turn her eyes toward Emi. Noticing this, Rika made a face like a chicken bone was stuck in her windpipe. Now the focus of the conversation was somewhere wholly different.

"So, the reason I waited here, Emi, is because I had another request."

"...What are you going on about?"

After the all-but-final snub she gave her this morning, Emi was not expecting Suzuno to come begging to her yet again. In front of a total stranger, no less. She could tell Suzuno was up to something, but without knowing what, there wasn't much way to combat her.

Trying to push Rika away at this point in the encounter would raise far too many suspicions. That was why Emi was a bit sharper than usual in her response a moment prior.

"...Oh, uh, sorry if I'm being a buttinsky or whatever. Should I get going?" Rika, at least, was a good enough friend to read the tea leaves for her. But Suzuno was too quick to respond.

"No, not at all. It is a simple enough request. I was hoping, Emi, that we could go and visit Sadao's workplace together."

"Sadao? Have I heard that name somewhere before?"

"No, really, what are you...?"

Suzuno was more than happy to blurt out Maou's name in front of Rika. Now Emi knew what she wanted. But it was already too late.

"I want to see this man, this Sadao Maou, at work. I know you bade me not to approach him, but I am not the sort of woman to acquiesce so readily to that."

"......"

Emi grabbed her head. The sheer arbitrary looniness of her vocabulary was what galled her the most.

Rika, suddenly finding herself an unwilling spectator to the verbal joust, butted in once more.

"Oh, right! Sadao Maou's the guy you're friends with, right?"

"See...? Now you've done it..." Emi groaned.

"You talked about him when you stayed at my place, remember? Ooh, this isn't some kind of competition I'm listenin' in on, is it?!"

"Rika, no, hang on a..."

On the face of it, that seemed the only logical interpretation. Two women were at physical odds over the heart of one Sadao Maou. That was how *she* wanted to frame it.

Rika cracked a muddled smile as she waved her hands in front of her.

"Well, hang on, hang on! Listen, if you don't mind me speaking up as a woman witnessing all of this…and I know I'm being a *total* buttinsky at this point…but something like this isn't going to be solved by just one of you alone. So if you want to really nip this in the bud for good, then I think we need to get this Maou guy in the same room. And yes, I know it'll be awkward at first, but it'll save everyone a lot of grief later, you know?"

"No, Rika, it's nothing like…"

Emi frantically tried to stop Rika's bubbly imagination from fizzing over the lip.

"…Indeed. Perhaps you are correct."

Suzuno smoothly turned the conversation back toward Rika, all too ready to consider her suggestion.

"Hey!"

"So where is he, huh?"

"I understand he works at the MgRonald in Hatagaya."

"Heeeyyyyy!!!"

"Ah, chill out, Emi. Hatagaya's right by here, isn't it? Well, the sooner the better, I say!"

"I, I *am* chill! Rika, there's really no need for…"

"It'll be fine, okay? Just calm down. Remember, I'm on your side here!"

Yeah, maybe she *thinks* so. That's the whole damn problem. Emi began to reconsider the value of having friends at all.

"Oh, and don't you worry, either! A good judge needs to be fair and impartial, you know."

Rika smiled at Suzuno. As if that girl needed any more goading.

Suzuno, the deceiver, and Rika, the deceived, warmly shook hands. A decent solution failed to find Emi's brain.

"Hey, stop doing this without any input from me! I'm not going anywhere!"

It was her last resort. But the Japanese coworker and Ente Islan chief inquisitor in front of her chose, by coincidence, the same words to counter her, even though they had very different meanings behind them.

"...Are you sure?"

"...You are *sure* of that?"

There was a twinge of sadness to Rika's eyes. There was a *mind if I continue steamrolling all over you?* leer to Suzuno's. Total victory was hers.

"Nnnn...!"

She must have taken Emi's groan as her admission.

"...Well! Shall we, then? I'll step aside during the actual proceedings, of course. But now that I'm a total buttinsky, I gotta make up for it as much as I can, right? Besides, I'm an expert at this kinda thing."

Rika began to walk on ahead.

Now that Rika's back was turned, Emi flashed Suzuno the basest, most predatorial glare she could. In response, the normally calm and collected Suzuno crumpled her face a bit, as if silently apologizing to her.

"If I asked you to come along myself, I was afraid you would turn a deaf ear."

"Come along for *what*?!"

Emi lashed out in a hissing whisper to keep Rika from listening in.

"Today, the Devil King is in a position to rule over other humans, no? In a small, infinitesimal way, yes, but..."

It was true. Emi remembered Maou's pathetic bragging about being promoted to assistant manager.

"So what?!"

It was Saturday evening, but the sun was still high and the city filled with people. It was easy enough to keep their conversation away from Rika's prying ears as they proceeded.

"So, I am concerned that you are undertaking your mission of slaying the Devil King in a rather...leisurely manner."

Suzuno's eyes were sharply pointed toward Rika's back, looming ahead of them.

"He may seem harmless enough as he goes about his daily business, but once a Devil King, always a Devil King. Once he gains the power to lead and control humans, there is no telling how this leopard may change its spots. I want to avoid disaster before it happens, but I am all too aware that I, alone, am not up to the task."

Emi wondered what kind of disaster Maou could engineer as a temporary overlord tyrant carrying out a reign of terror against a single MgRonald franchise. Having borne frequent witness to his work attitude, she knew Suzuno's fears were beyond unfounded.

"I wished to avoid stoking the flames needlessly by taking action on my own, but I knew that if I simply asked you, Emi, you would rebuke me once more. So, I opted to take a different..."

"All right! I get it, I get it!"

Emi heaved a defeated sigh.

There was a time, not too long ago, when she was on pins and needles over when the Devil King might finally emerge from this namby-pamby burger-chef shell.

But now, although she wasn't ready to forgive Maou for all his past atrocities, she was all but convinced that the demons of Devil's Castle were harmless to Japan, as long as you didn't prod them too much.

The idea of advocating for the Devil King still made her queasy, but perhaps watching Maou at work would help assuage some of Suzuno's fears as well.

"And remember, you were attacked by a masked interloper just the other day. My mission does not end with the Devil King's defeat—I must also bring you back to Ente Isla, so we may finally learn the truth. Working together will help dispel any doubts that linger in my mind...and, besides, I may even come to your aid if the need arises."

Were it not for her Church duties, Suzuno would've made a killer saleswoman. Emi had to laugh at the full-court press she was delivering.

"Well, right now, the biggest issue is how we stop Rika from going all nuts like this."

"Stop me from what?"

Rika turned around at the sound of her name.

"...Nothing. Sorry. Let's get going. I want to get this over with."

"Ooh, *someone* likes her chances!"

Nothing in the world is scarier than goodwill run amok.

Climbing up the stairs to the Keio New Line Hatagaya station exit, Rika took a good look around her, hand defiantly on hip.

"Well, we're here...but the MgRonald's looking pretty dead. Maybe now isn't the right time for an intervention after all. If it ain't busy in there, it's gonna get reeeeeal awkward if this whole thing goes south. Having other people around helps keep things more restrained, you know?"

Perhaps Emi was overthinking it, but something in Rika's cool, calculating analysis indicated that there was nothing she'd relish more than a total lack of restraint in upcoming events.

"We don't want to mess up his work environment too much if it gets weird, either... Well, good thing there's a packed Sentucky Fried Chicken just across the street. How 'bout we head there and formulate a plan first?"

"I know you're loving every minute of this, Rika."

The only choice left was going with the flow. Emi could, perhaps, use her holy power to control Rika's mind from the rear. But she felt ashamed to take such drastic steps against a friend simply trying to help...no matter how far off the mark she was.

Taking a glance at the MgRonald, it was clear Rika was right. The place was far from crowded. If they stepped in right now, Maou and Chiho would no doubt be standing right at the counter, mouths agape.

"All right. First off, tell me a bit more about this Maou guy. Maybe that'll give us a clue to solving this mess."

How could it possibly do that? Especially given the roles of the people involved. Emi couldn't guess how Suzuno intended to explain her way around this.

Or did she seriously intend to lie about all this and claim she and Emi were in a knock-down, drag-out for Maou's heart and soul?

Pushing the ponderous door open, the trio entered the lavishly decorated, three-story Sentucky Fried Chicken Hatagaya franchise. It was just as crowded as Rika described it. Emi hoped against hope there were no free seats left.

"Hello and welcome to SFC! We just had a table for four clear out. If you could just make your way to the register..."

The attending employee's small gesture of kindness quashed the hope within ten seconds.

"Here. We have an easy-to-read menu available to peruse right here."

The counter was a bit too cramped to have three people peer at the menu simultaneously, so the employee, short in stature and wearing a strikingly out-of-place pair of sunglasses, handed Suzuno and Emi an extra copy.

Emi accepted it without question, not that it was any easier to read than the menu sitting on the counter.

"I'll have an iced coffee. How 'bout you two?"

"I think I shall order a maple cookie and iced tea value set. With milk, please."

"...Iced coffee."

"Sweet! I'll cover it this time, okay? Oh, and that'll be all for us."

The pint-sized employee she spoke to nodded with a smile.

"Perfect. We will have that out in just a moment. If you're interested, I have a grand-opening coupon here for you to use..."

Rika accepted the colorful flyer offered to her as she brusquely presented a one-thousand-yen bill.

"Right. We will begin preparing your order at once. I am sure our food and drink would be overjoyed at the thought of being consumed by such a beautiful trio of women. Let me give you your change."

"Okay… Hyuh?"

Her attention turned toward the coupon, Rika extended a hand out without giving the employee a glance. The small grunt of surprise was the result of him cupping her hand before placing her change and receipt in it.

Instinctively, she shot a glance back at him. His back was already turned as he prepared their drinks on a tray, blissfully unaware of Rika's response.

"Huh. One of those 'hands-on' customer service things, maybe?"

Thinking nothing particularly unusual about it, Rika turned her eyes back toward the coupon. After a few moments:

"Well, my apologies for making a group of fine women such as yourself wait for so long. Here is your order."

It couldn't have been longer than a minute's wait, but Rika gave the employee a vague nod as she accepted the tray and met up with Emi and Suzuno downstairs.

"Man…It's always men like that, you know? They act all nice, but take 'em out on a date, and *you'll* wind up having to do all the heavy lifting. And that cologne, jeez!"

"Who're you talking about?"

"Oh, no one in particular. Let's go upstairs."

Emi and Suzuno followed Rika back to the stairway. Rika gave a passing glance to the employee from before as she passed by, but he was already concealed by the line of customers who were waiting behind her.

"All right. Now that we're all settled down, how 'bout we cover the events that led us to this point? This guy…Sadao Maou, right?"

Rika sat Emi and Suzuno down on the sofa side of the four-seat table the employee pointed out to her, then gave them both a serious look, like a judge calling court into session.

"I know you talked a little to me about him before, Emi, but I'd like to get both of your opinions here, while you're together. How 'bout it?"

"Well, to me, he is the neighbor of the dwelling into which I recently moved…a kind one."

Emi gave Suzuno a side glance. All gung-ho fervor about slaying the Devil King just a moment ago, and now she was back to *this*.

"And to me, if it were possible, I'd like to kill him right now."

Emi wasn't lying about it, but Rika hardly took her words literally.

"Ooh, kind of a big difference of opinion, huh? Sounds like you're hiding something here, Emi."

Emi, intending to hide nothing at all, glowered in surprise.

"Listen, Rika, I should really make this clear: There is nothing at all between Maou and me. I don't want her getting involved with him for completely different reasons. It's not like we're fighting over his love or anything."

"Oh, really? But when you stayed over with me, didn't you say something about how 'Maou is all mine' or something?"

"I did *not*! Quit putting words in my mouth!"

Two months ago, Emi stayed overnight at Rika's apartment following the tunnel collapse. When the topic turned to Maou, whom Rika spied with Emi at the disaster site, Emi didn't recall saying anything further than "we just came to know each other, we aren't even acquaintances, someday I'm gonna give him what he deserves," etc., etc.

"Besides, why are you so hell-bent on matching me and Maou together anyway? Just thinking about the idea makes me sick! Hanging out with that cruel, wicked, stubborn, thoughtless, bummy freak, someone who thinks he did you a favor just because he lent you a piece-of-crap umbrella…" When it came to criticizing Maou, Emi was full of material to bring up.

She let it pour out of her like a bursting dam, hoping to keep Suzuno from stealing all the momentum.

"You will *not* berate him like that, Yusa!"

She was stopped by an interloper.

Suzuno looked up as Rika spun around in her chair.

They were met by a man standing tall as he stared down at them, still holding a tray full of the remnants of a recently eaten meal.

It was Shiro Ashiya, denizen of Devil's Castle, a man who, until this morning, was put into a state of half delirium by the summer heat.

"What are *you* doing in here?! Where *were* you until now, anyway?" Emi pointed a panicked finger at him.

Ashiya pointed out a barstool on the far end of the dining area with his eyes.

"I noticed you when you first came in here! I had deliberately avoided you because I didn't want any more trouble today. I was hoping to slip out of here unnoticed, but I am *not* the sort of monster to stand by idly while you spread all these horrid lies and falsehoods about that great man!"

Given his admission that he was ready to slink out without a word, Ashiya's lofty morals rang hollow in Emi's mind. Still, internally, she had to praise him for not letting any *His Demonic Highness*es slip.

Suddenly, Emi thought of a way to both avoid a verbal conflict with Ashiya and use him to her best advantage.

"Wait a sec, Ashiya! I could actually use your help here. This has a lot to do with you and Maou, too."

"What? Why would I *ever* even raise a *finger* to…"

"Well, what, you're here to conduct research on this place for your friend, right? I'll be happy to buy whatever you want."

"Hmm. Well, if you insist."

"Whoa!"

It was Rika who let out the amazed squeal. Up to this moment, she had had Ashiya and Emi yelling at each other over her head. Now, even though she never let her eyes off of him, he was suddenly seated next to her.

The laser-quick change of attitude was enough to exasperate Emi. Her plan seemed a tad less airtight now.

"I…I had no idea you were such a greedy pig."

"Hmph. You misunderstand me. Right now, the only thing that takes precedence in my mind is our house's finances. If it will provide us with valuable money savings, I will climb any mountain, wade through any mud bog, withstand any humiliation!"

"Quit acting stupid. You don't have to get all high and mighty over free fast food."

"Quiet, you. Now, I was unable to research SFC's dessert and salad selection on my current budget. Perhaps I will make a secondary order later."

He was shameless.

"Um... Is this a friend of yours or something?" Rika asked.

"Absolutely not!!"

Ashiya and Emi spouted off in an impromptu chorus, loudly enough that the diners nearby flashed them another look.

"I am not exactly sure who you are, but among your companions, I am perhaps best known as Ms. Kamazuki's neighbor. My name is Shiro Ashiya."

"Oh! Well, hello there. I'm Emi's friend Rika Suzuki. So if you're her neighbor...does that mean you live with this Maou guy?"

"Indeed I do. You know of the master of the house?"

Ashiya glanced at Emi, checking with her to see if Rika was aware of their true identity the way Chiho was. Emi shook her head listlessly.

"Yeahhh, kind of. And I'd like to know some more about him, if you don't mind me asking."

Ashiya's sense of danger tingled.

To him, Rika was a complete stranger. What business would she have, inquiring about someone like Maou, who wasn't even part of her culture's demonic royal hierarchy?

"Uh, Ashiya? There's really nothing to be afraid of. I'm pretty sure about *that*, anyway."

Emi's words weren't enough to ease his wariness.

"So basically, the way I understand it, there's this guy that Emi doesn't want other women to hang out with," Rika said.

"Eh?"

Ashiya's eyebrows wrinkled as he gave Emi an honestly concerned look. "Yusa, what is all of this about?"

"...That's what I'd like to know."

Ashiya sized up Rika, Suzuno, and Emi, in that order, before continuing.

"A man who Emi doesn't want other women near, is it...?"

He ruminated over Rika's words.

"And it may involve me, as well? I see. Trying to catch me off guard, are you, Yusa?"

For just a moment, Ashiya flashed a slight grin at Emi, confident in his victory over her mind games.

"Well, indeed, where should I begin, then?"

He pretended to think it over for a moment.

"I…don't think Ms. Kamazuki is aware of this yet, but Maou and I used to manage a company together."

This went beyond Emi's imagination.

"Whaaa? A company?!"

Rika was predictably stunned.

"A-Ashiya?! What're you talking about?!"

Emi's eyes were similarly round and wide.

"What on earth does he mean?" Suzuno, meanwhile, remained subdued as she asked Emi this question, which Emi had no way of answering.

Maou's next-door neighbor had yet to reveal her true self to Ashiya, of course, hence why Ashiya was so intent on giving her this bald-faced lie.

"Like, Maou isn't *that* old, is he?! Is he one of those start-up whiz kids or something?" Rika continued.

"Something of the sort, yes."

"Wowww… Well, this certainly paints things in a new light! So what kind of company was it?"

"Well, our primary business was in real estate management and temporary staffing. There was some construction work, as well. We were called…the Maou Group."

"…Oh, yeah, a lot of architectural firms call themselves 'The Something-Something Group,' don't they?"

Rika was spellbound by the remarkable and no doubt true story of Maou's past.

Emi and Suzuno were not.

"…Temporary staffing? Really?"

"Quite a 'group,' indeed…"

They both whispered it to themselves, Emi having a difficult time figuring out where Ashiya was daring to take the story.

"But, sadly, the venture ended in failure, and now we live in—and I apologize to Ms. Kamazuki; I know you just moved in and such—a dilapidated apartment and scrounge together what part-time work we can. Maou and myself, along with another business partner living with us, are doing our best to struggle against the difficulties we face in rebuilding our good name and fortune. The question for me, then, is how Yusa is involved with this."

Here it comes. Emi gasped slightly. He was all but asking her to screw this up.

Making a mistake here could mean having to rearrange the memories of Rika, her friend—something she preferred to avoid.

It was a thought Ashiya couldn't have understood, but he continued his life story regardless.

"Yusa, you see, worked for a rival firm at the time."

"Huh? Emi? You worked in the construction business?!"

Rika's attention immediately zoomed back toward Emi, but Ashiya kept going before she could defend herself.

"No, you were still a temp employee back then, weren't you?"

"A temp... Um. Well."

The Church was supported by donations from the people of Ente Isla, its knights paid via the taxes collected by the barons they served. Compared to that, Emi—who was rewarded strictly for her actual "work performance" on the demon-slaying battlefields of her homeland—was, if you looked at it a certain way, a temp. Being a Hero wasn't a career most people stayed in, or survived, very long.

"My goodness. You, the Hero of her domain, a temporary worker?"

"Don't *fall* for it, Suzuno!"

Emi elbowed Suzuno under the table lightly.

"We were active in a variety of industries, but we were still a small-scale business, the sort where the top managers were out on the field, every day, directing work sites and so forth. But thanks to her own talents and the backup her company provided her, we often found ourselves scrambling for contracts against Yusa."

"Scrambling for contracts… But why would a big company give that kind of work to a temp?"

"Ah, well…you know, I kind of had some connections. Like, I knew one of the guys on the executive board, so…"

Emi attempted to explain her past in a way that would be acceptable to a modern Japanese person's ears, adding some painfully concocted details to dovetail it with Ashiya's story.

"Ohh. Well, I guess it makes sense you've been around, huh? You're so good with languages, besides. So what happened next?"

"Yusa had a number of powerful coworkers and managers watching over her, but…well, really, we were a bunch of ragtag kids, none of whom were particularly more experienced in the field than any of the rest of us. And when the economic downturn came, smaller firms like ours were the first to crumble."

"Hohh… I guess so, yeah. I've heard about how stingy the banks are with making loans and stuff these days. And with all the cheap imports coming into Japan, a lot of companies are losing out, even if they make better products."

Rika first reacted to this news with surprised curiosity, but now, as she listened to Ashiya go on, her expression was gradually starting to change.

She was born in Kobe, the daughter of a family that ran a small factory workshop. Her parents and relatives were all involved with the firm in one way or another. Rika witnessed that much for herself as a child. Something about Ashiya's ridiculous yarn must have struck a chord with her.

"So, in the end, Yusa was the only one competing with us for contracts…and that wasn't a winnable battle for us. Thus, we closed up shop, and after spending a year-ish in our apartment in Sasazuka, we happened to run into Yusa again. She remembered us from our business dealings, of course, and I'm sure she has our own opinions and such about us, In fact, she occasionally stops by to see how we are faring."

"Oh, that sort of thing…?"

Rika nodded several times to herself, apparently reaching a logical conclusion in her mind.

Emi, meanwhile, could feel the blood draining from her brain. Ashiya had spent the past several minutes painting this broadly positive image of Emi, and Rika was lapping it right up.

She was gonna owe big-time for this. It wasn't the kind of thing she could repay with a couple of dessert items and a salad.

"So, recently, the very kind Ms. Kamazuki here moved in next door. If Yusa would prefer that she stay away from us, I'm sure it's because she doesn't want her caught up in our indigent, hand-to-mouth sort of lifestyle…not in *this* economy."

"…Hand-to-mouth?"

Suzuno repeated the words loud enough for Ashiya to hear. He calmly nodded in response.

To Emi, meanwhile, nothing could be further from the truth. All she wanted was for Suzuno, just a regular girl in Emi's eyes at the time, to keep her distance from the Devil King and his lackeys. But she couldn't find a way to counter Ashiya, whose tale was proving remarkably credible to Rika at this point.

"Maou is still a young man, but he unfortunately doesn't have a college degree or any other higher education. For someone like that, starting a new firm takes a great deal of knowledge, money, and connections…all three of which we regrettably lack, in spades, at the moment. The only work we had a shot at were the kind of contracts that even Emi, at the far fringes of her firm, would be fighting for."

"…You don't have to call it the fringes," Emi whispered back in frustration.

"Instead of taking the sort of vast risks we prefer, I am sure Yusa wants to help Ms. Kamazuki. Guide her into an honest, stable living situation. …And it looks like you've been enjoying the fresh air of the city today, have you not?"

He chuckled as he took in Suzuno's fancy hairpin and kimono, both different from what she'd worn this morning, as well as all the purchases at her side.

"Oh, er, this was simply a matter of studying social customs, and…"
She looked down shyly, face turning red despite herself. The whirlwind of modern Japanese urban living must have been a roller coaster for her.

"Well, there's hardly anything to be ashamed about. A woman like yourself, enjoying the big city… What could be a better way to take in the social scene?"

After this little show of concern for the women in his life—far more than his boss ever demonstrated—Ashiya's face tightened.

"Regardless, Maou still hasn't given up on his goal of building a new and successful firm. Today, he's devoting himself heart and soul to MgRonald as he tries to learn the art of management from the ground up. In a single year, he has already risen to the post of shift supervisor. One day, when the time comes, I look forward to working under him in a new, and healthier, outfit…and, until then, I will do everything I can to support him."

Emi could see Suzuno's face stiffen up from the side. Just now, in front of the Hero and a Church cleric, Ashiya all but declared that the demons had not given up on taking over the world. It would be strange if that *didn't* unnerve Suzuno.

"But, as they say, all of life is a gamble. And I can certainly understand if Yusa has concerns about Ms. Kamazuki becoming deeply involved with us, lest she becomes affected by something unraveling in the future."

"Oh, I am very much involved already."

Suzuno blurted out the words without thinking. Emi began to sweat. No one had heard her, luckily. Ashiya continued after a short pause.

"Maou can be a rather stubborn person at times…or, should I say, he tends to bear a grudge against people. He rather dislikes Yusa's visits, even though she is simply acting out of concern for us. Thus, I think the situation is quite a bit different from what you may be picturing, Ms. Suzuki."

If it wasn't for the others around her, Emi likely would have stamped her feet hard enough to shake the floor.

Ashiya was wording this expertly, well enough to change the

views of the person he aimed them toward. He was in full control of the entire narrative.

Emi *was* concerned about Maou, yes, and she didn't want to have Suzuno involved in their battle. But she was hearing it from the mouth of a demon. A demon who was coming to Emi's aid.

The embarrassment was enough to make her want to disappear, but Rika, lost in the saga of a young entrepreneur's rise and fall, was too enrapt to notice.

"But...well, wow, huh? You guys must be about my age, and you're doing all these crazy things! That's amazing! Boy, now I'm feeling pretty silly for getting all these wacky ideas in my head! You should've just said so earlier, Emi."

"......"

Emi could do nothing but sit in silence, her mind occupied with the rueful observation that Rika wouldn't have listened to her if she had and the painful realization that she'd never come up with an excuse nearly as eloquent as Ashiya's.

"Indeed...but, in the end, we failed. Our president now works part-time at MgRonald, and I serve as his faithful homemaker. And one of us barely even lacks the desire to search for honest work at all. Some 'whiz kids' we are."

"Yeah, but..."

Rika's face transformed from admiration to earnestness as she turned toward Ashiya.

"If you're keeping yourselves going with odd jobs and still staying pretty comfortable, I'd say you guys got out pretty clean."

"Pretty...clean?"

Ashiya failed to grasp the meaning of the term.

"I mean, it sounds like you didn't leave much debt at all when the company shut down. You didn't bounce any checks, you didn't go bankrupt, and you aren't being chased around by creditors or anything, right? If you have the talent to wind things down that neatly, I'm sure you'll get a chance to try again pretty soon."

She had the completely wrong idea. The unexpected encouragement left Ashiya stunned for a moment.

"My family back home runs a small factory, too, and…like, it's just a regular company on paper, but whenever things looked like they were about to go south, it united the whole family. Like, everyone would work together to get over the hump, even if it was just little stuff. Even if didn't have anything to do with the factory's business. So maybe it didn't work out the first time, but Maou and that other guy you mentioned… They're eating your food, sleeping in the bedsheets you washed, wearing the pants you put out to dry, right? You're providing all the bare necessities they need, and you should be proud of that, I think. You're all really looking out for each other. I think you've got a bright future ahead of you."

Rika spoke slowly, chewing over every word as she continued. Ashiya, though surprised at first, nodded lightly. The words hit home somewhere inside.

"Yes…yes, I suppose so."

He took another close look at Rika.

"Thank you very much. You are the first person to ever say anything like that to me."

He smiled softly, guilelessly. In the dying rays of the sun, his somewhat gaunt face evoked an odd sense of longing.

It was just a matter of his having been laid up for the past few days, in fact, but the sight made Rika freeze for just a moment. She could feel her pulse rise.

"Ms. Suzuki?"

Rika came to at the sound of her name. She waved her hands, flustered.

"Oh! Um…yeah. Well, sure. Sorry I was such a buttinsky."

"Not at all. To be honest, I've had a great deal on my mind as of late. I was starting to lose confidence in myself. But hearing you say that…I feel a touch better now."

Everything about Ashiya's voice indicated that he was probably serious. Being a househusband meant that one could never expect a great deal of praise for his performance.

The idea of the Devil King framing his conquest of Earth around the corporate ladder of a worldwide fast-food conglomerate had begun to vaguely disquiet Ashiya. Was this really what they should be doing?

And in that frame of mind, Rika's encouragement soaked deeply into his heart, in a way nobody could have predicted.

"Do you? Well, that's...that's great. Yeah. Really great."

Rika took a sip from her iced coffee, clearly trying to drown her confused emotions.

"Rika?"

The sudden metamorphosis was easily enough to arouse Emi's suspicions.

"Ahhhh! Huh? Emi? What's up?"

She was shocked enough that she almost dropped her cup.

"What do you mean, what's up? I mean...what's going on, all of a sudden?"

"Oh, nothing! Nothing, nothing, nothing!"

"...You said it four times."

Suzuno was kind enough to provide a running count.

"Still, though... I guess everybody has their own story, huh...?"

It sounded like a bold, effusive declaration as it came from Rika's mouth. She sipped up the remainder of her coffee in one go.

"Y'know, I'm starting to think I want to see this Maou guy for myself."

"Huh?"

Emi's response almost seemed too exaggerated.

"Well, I mean, it takes some serious work to make it to shift manager that quickly in a place as big as MgRonald. Maybe he messed up once, but it sounds like he's a pretty hardworking guy, you know?"

"Perhaps... He did receive a hundred-yen raise after two months working there, he said..."

The memory of Maou's broad smile on that day still flushed Ashiya's heart with sadness, but Rika demonstrated amazement yet again.

"Really?! A hundred yen? That's crazy! In two months? 'Cause that's a lot more than you'd normally get for making it through your probationary period. And MgRonald doesn't exactly go easy on

its employees, either. You know, in the right environment, I bet he could really get some things moving!"

"Yes…in the right environment…"

To Ashiya, Japan was the wrong environment from the very start for their brimstone-scarred activities.

"Maybe I better get in on the ground floor with him, huh?"

"Whoa! Rika?!"

Emi could no longer remain silent. Rika stopped her.

"I don't mean in a weird way. I just mean, this is a guy who's definitely gonna be going places in business. I *am* the daughter of a company president, after all, so I've got a sharp eye out for this stuff."

"What do you mean…? I don't quite…"

"When you're running a small workshop, the connections you establish on the front lines become really important. If Maou does another start-up and hits it big, having that connection in place now instead of later definitely wouldn't hurt. 'Cause you'd be surprised, all the links these little companies share with one another across Japan. I don't know if Maou's line of business matches with ours at all, but if it does, I certainly want to know."

"You know, I never asked, Rika, but what does your family make?"

"We make footwear accessories. Mostly shoe soles and stuff."

That was never going to be a match for Maou's despotic aspirations, no matter which world he wound up on, but there was no point popping her balloon now.

"…Well, I will say that Maou certainly does have his sights on upward mobility within the MgRonald empire. And who knows? He might place a shoe order with your family one day, Ms. Suzuki."

And Ashiya was all too ready to keep that balloon inflated.

"Ooh! If he gets involved with staffing, we'd be happy to provide cheap, long-lasting shoes for his company's uniforms. No order too small!"

The balloon now occupied the entire dining area, almost smothering Emi.

"You know, I'm sorry to keep ordering people around, but do you think I could go see him? I know you have to report back to him, Ashiya. Plus, I could help him with his sales a little, too!"

"That was exactly what I was hoping. In that case..."

Ashiya flashed an evil grin, a devilish one dripping with intent, at Emi.

"You'll be joining us, right? I'll expect that you will. I think I'd like to get some cookies and a thousand-island salad to go, if you don't mind. We can head to MgRonald after that."

"You greedy little..." Emi bitterly snapped back at him. But if she didn't follow his orders, there was no telling how this story would unfold.

"I need to repay Ms. Kamazuki for all the favors she's provided for us lately, too. I would be glad to cover for it, so please let me know if you'd like anything."

"Oh, no, I...I plan to make dinner at home, so..."

Ashiya's attitude toward Suzuno was markedly different from how he acted around Emi.

Emi, noticing Rika ever-so-slightly pouting behind Ashiya's back, felt her headache grow ever more painful.

The group headed downstairs, finding the place just as busy as before. A fairly long line snaked out from the cash registers.

"...You three wait outside, okay? I'll be right out once I buy that stuff."

Emi saw them off, then dejectedly joined the line.

The misunderstanding with Rika was solved, but now she had a wholly different type of problem to tackle.

With an adversary as calculating as Ashiya, failing to repay a favor would no doubt lead to endless bickering afterward...not to mention some form of payback.

Unsure how to offer repayment that would fully satisfy Ashiya, Emi ultimately decided that the only thing to do for it would be violently dismembering him in combat. As she settled on this conclusion, she realized she was next in line to order. She scanned the menu, searching for Ashiya's requests.

"Well, hello there, my lady. Making a face like that would spoil anyone's dinner, you know."

Emi looked up, only to find the undersized employee that took Rika's order earlier.

His face was compact and thin, and he was clad in a T-shirt and black apron, setting him apart from the rest of the staff. Judging by the name SARUE written in Chinese characters on his name tag, he must have been the manager or something. He had a pair of sunglasses on, a rarity in face-to-face retail operations like this one, and they couldn't have befitted him less.

"Yeah, sorry about that. One Gourmet Cookie order and one salad with thousand-island dressing to go." Emi didn't appreciate the comment much, but paid it little further mind as she tossed a thousand-yen note on the tray in front of her.

"Absolutely. Ah, there is something distinctively attractive about a young, beautiful woman looking tormented over something..."

Emi flashed the employee a highly dubious look. The complaints were liable to roll in soon if this was his take on customer service.

"But, no matter what it is that concerns you, time has a way of changing everything, whether one wants it to or not. If you find yourself no longer able to change events by your own free will, you may live to regret it."

"...I've never had an SFC employee meddle in my personal life *that* much before."

Emi bunched her eyebrows together. It didn't seem to faze the employee, who nimbly placed her order in a paper bag.

"Indeed. I apologize for my intrusiveness. But allow me to say just one thing."

He likely just wanted to hand Emi her order, but the man with the SARUE name tag seemed to stretch his body halfway across the counter as he presented the bag.

"Men tend to seize upon women when they are at their weakest. I would advise watching your step carefully."

"...What's *that* mean?"

"Oh, nothing profound, certainly. Thank you very much. I hope you'll come back again soon. I'm ready to take the next customer here, please!"

The suspicions raised in Emi's mind at the obviously meaningful advice the employee had for her were blocked by the family waiting behind her.

"Oops!"

A small boy from the group ran forward excitedly, bumping into Emi as he did.

"S-sorry about that! ...You know you shouldn't run off like that! Are you all right?"

The mother, holding a baby in one hand, used the other to grab the child's presumed brother as she bowed her head at Emi.

"Oh, no, I'm fine..."

There was no way she could press the employee any further. Not with all these people in line, and not with Rika and the rest waiting outside. Emi went away from the register.

"...is allergic to...like shrimp, and crab, and certain types of fruit..."

"Give me one moment to check on that, madam."

Emi overhead the fading conversation as she thought to herself.

"More trouble's the last thing I need..." she whispered softly to herself as she left.

She didn't turn around, too weirded out and not wanting to get further involved, but something about Sarue's eyes made it seem like she was still being pursued.

✳

"So they've got a grand-opening sale running and they're giving out coupons. Is that it? Anything else?"

Ashiya was in the midst of giving Maou his reconnaissance report inside MgRonald.

"As far as I could observe, even considering that SFC offers a different main menu from MgRonald, it was hard to tell why there should be such an extreme difference in the crowds. The customer service was perfectly normal as well."

Ashiya went over a piece of paper he had used to jot down his thoughts as he spoke.

"One thing I did notice was that the fried chicken they're famous for certainly does live up to expectations. It depends on the type of piece, of course, but it tasted wonderful, right down to the bone. Quite a surprise!"

"To the bone? Eesh…"

Maou glared accusingly at Ashiya for a moment. Ashiya shook his head in response.

"According to what I had Urushihara dredge up for me, Sentucky uses some kind of unique trick when cooking their fried chicken. Much like the meat we enjoyed at that *yakiniku* restaurant, the flame reaches right into the core of the chicken's cartilage and so forth. The fact that there isn't much residue left on your plate after you're done eating seems like a small detail, but I think that tells the entire story."

Maou crossed his arms and nodded at Ashiya's very homemaker-like opinions.

"Huh. Not exactly the best way to maintain a turnover ratio, but if you're willing to sit and linger for a while, it feels a lot nicer having a clean tray in front of you. If someone took the tray away, it'd feel like they were kicking you out, besides."

"Also, if the signs are to be believed, they grind their coffee fresh for every cup. The beans are supposedly organic, too."

"Organic? What, they make it out of organs?"

Ashiya corrected the very demonlike mistake on Maou's part.

"No. *Organic* means they use beans grown naturally, without any artificial fertilizers and such."

"Right, but if you grind up organs, wouldn't that give you this red gunk? Why do they call it 'Blue Mountain,' then?"

It was hard for Ashiya to tell how serious Maou was being. He decided to brush it off.

"Well, regardless, it certainly does its job from an advertising perspective. Strictly speaking in terms of taste, I imagine it is refreshing enough for coffee at that price range."

"Hmm. Now isn't exactly hot-coffee season, but that could be a problem in a few months."

Maou placed a finger on his forehead, a perplexed look on his face, before motioning at Ashiya to take a look around the dining area.

"But...yeah, you're right. There isn't any real decisive advantage they have over us, I don't think."

With sales targets placed high for Saturday traffic, observers from the home office had been phoning in on an hourly basis to report Sentucky's visitor numbers. Between their numbers and the estimated amount of purchases they made, SFC was ahead of MgRonald by nearly fifty customers and almost thirty thousand yen for the day.

Even worse, MgRonald's numbers had been steadily dwindling ever since morning. Apart from Ashiya, only a single new party had paid a visit during the dinner period.

"You are correct, my liege. But, after having sat inside for two hours or so, there really is little more I can offer. Beyond that, all I can guess is that passersby are having their attention diverted by the novelty."

"Yeah. There's a chance of that...but then, there's a chance of everything."

Maou shrugged.

"Well, we're not just gonna sit here and watch. I'll see what kind of measures we can take to hit back at 'em. Thanks again."

The simple verbal reward for his two hours of sentry work made it difficult for Ashiya to keep from turning around and leaving.

"Not at all. I am happy to be of service to you. Now, if I could be of service to your sales figures, I'd like to order two Big Tuna Burger combos, please. Large fries and drinks on both. I have no doubt Urushihara will whine about it, but that should suffice for dinner tonight."

"If that dead weight in my Devil's Castle whines about the food he's freeloading off us, go ahead and punch him out for me. You've got my permission."

"Yes, my liege."

It was an oddly homespun exchange between the two arch-demons.

"Also…"

Ashiya turned around a nearby table, flashing an ironic smile.

"I do hope you'll treat the ladies well."

"Huh? Uh, yeah. Whatever."

Maou gave a vague nod.

"Once I return home, I intend to take a different approach. I will try to have Urushihara explore more of the company's underside. Perhaps there is some hidden trick to their business that is not so obvious from the outside."

"If there is, I doubt he's gonna find it on the Net. We're kind of in different categories anyway, so it's not like knowing their suppliers or cooking methods is gonna help much. Don't try to overdo it, okay? You're still recovering and stuff."

"Oh, there is no need to worry about me, Your Demonic Highness."

As the two demons muttered to each other in low voices, Chiho briskly assembled the required items together, completed the value meals in a mere minute or so, and handed them to Ashiya.

"Thanks for waiting, Ashiya. And good luck to both of you guys in this fight, okay?"

"Certainly. Thank you very much. I will do my best."

Chiho returned the thanks with a smile.

As Ashiya lugged the heavy bag out of the dining area, Chiho watched him leave before her eyes turned toward the other group in the dining area.

"Wow, they sure are connected to each other, huh? In business, and in private, too, I guess. Always thinking about how to improve their business… Real pros, huh? You sure know a lot of people with talent, Emi. Oh, uh, counting me, too, I hope!"

"Yeah. Sure. You're in."

"These seats are harder than Sentucky's…"

The trio of women were free-flowing with their opinions, despite not having ordered anything. Turning toward them, Maou flashed a taut, uncomfortable smile.

"Um…if…I…may…ladies?"

"…What?"

One of the women grumpily acknowledged Maou's presence.

"Would you mind placing an order before sitting down, if you could?"

"Oh? Huh. Small iced coffee. Bring it over for me."

It was the cheapest possible order on the entire MgRonald menu. Emi, free of Ashiya's prying eyes, was no longer interested in currying favor with demons. Maou's temple throbbed.

"We work on a self-service ordering system over there at the counter…*ma'am!*"

"Okay, will you be nice enough to bring it over if I add an apple pie?"

Emi steadfastly refused to stand up. Barely capable of maintaining his customer-service smile, Maou turned toward Rika instead, sitting across from Emi.

"Ma'am, would…"

"Wow, so you're Maou, huh? Y'know, considering how loyal Ashiya is to you, I can't say you're exactly brimming with charisma. The shift you're supervising looks pretty darn dead to me, too."

"…Would you tell me who the hell you freaks think you are?"

The punishing evaluation of his looks and work ethic, coming from someone he'd never exchanged words with in his life, finally pushed Maou over the cliff.

"Ooh, you better watch your words, huh? The headquarters wouldn't want to get letters about this, would they?"

Rika grinned from ear to ear as she deliberately watched Maou, utterly unfazed.

"Shut up. Even customers have rules they have to follow in here. Who *are* you, anyway?"

One of Emi's friends, no doubt. Which meant this girl was Maou's mortal enemy.

"I'm Rika Suzuki. Emi's coworker. You're Sadao Maou, right? Emi and Suzuno and Ashiya told me about you."

"...I don't know what Ashiya and Suzuno said, but *she* couldn't have said anything good about me."

"Well, Ashiya and Emi had a kinda one-sided view of you, so I thought I'd go and check you out for myself."

"Huh. Great. You must love butting in on people's lives, don't you?"

Maou glared at Emi, who was lazily resting her head on a propped elbow.

"Ugh... I'm getting no customers. I got *Emi* in here... I'm gonna be flat broke by the end of the night."

"Oh, you shouldn't say things like that, Maou..."

Chiho chose that moment to arrive, tray in hand. "My! You certainly seem full of vigor, Chiho."

Suzuno was first to greet her.

"Thanks, Suzuno. Busy day?"

Giving Suzuno a smile, Chiho sidled next to Maou, looking a little peeved.

"Yusa is a valuable customer of ours, you know. What did you say to me earlier? 'As long as they're paying us, a customer's a customer'?"

With that, Chiho placed the tray on the table.

"One iced coffee, and one piping-hot apple pie!"

"Oh! Chiho!"

She must have eavesdropped on Emi's order. Hurriedly, Emi stood up to grab her wallet.

"I'm sorry! You know how I get with Maou, so..."

"Oh, that's all right. I understand. I'm really not allowed to prepare orders until we put it through the register, but we aren't going to be crowded for a little while yet. That'll be three hundred yen."

Sheepishly, Emi handed the coins to Chiho.

"Pah. So *that's* how you treat Chi, huh?"

"Of course that's how I treat her. You think I put you and her on the same level? That's being really rude to Chiho."

"Ooh, zing."

Rika giggled at the exchange.

"So is this your friend, Yusa?"

"Sure am! Rika Suzuki. I work with Emi all day."

"My name is Chiho Sasaki. Yusa's been a big help to me in a lot of ways!"

Chiho bowed politely. Rika studied her face, pondering over something, then beckoned her over with a finger.

"Yes?"

"Chiho, right?"

"Yes... Ahh!"

Without warning, Rika grabbed Chiho, hugging her tightly.

"You're so cuuuuuute! Isn't she? She is just the cutest! I mean, this must be some kind of modern Japanese miracle!"

"Agh, agh, agh!"

Chiho waggled her arms around in a futile effort to escape the sudden attention.

"I can't believe all these amazing people you hang out with, Emi! She's so polite, she has this superserious work ethic, and she's cute, too! It's gotta be against the law to be this cute! She's a national treasure! They should make her a World Heritage Site!"

"S-Suzuki?!"

"Hey, Rika, you're scaring Chiho..."

"Yeah, and it's so *cuuute!*"

"Come on, Rika, you're acting like some drunk at two AM!"

"Ohhh, all riiiiight. Sorry I got so excited, Chiho."

"Gah... It, it's okay...I think..."

Released from her grasp, Chiho panted for air as she tried to gain a bead on her surroundings.

"So, did you find any good work leads?"

Watching Chiho squirm in Rika's presence to the side, Maou turned the topic toward the silent Suzuno. She hesitated for a moment, surprised at being spoken to.

"Not yet, no..."

"Oh? Well, looks like you enjoyed the trip around town, at least. That's good."

Between the kimono and the balloon still floating above her bag, she looked like someone out on vacation.

"It, it was a social-study excursion!"

Suzuno pleaded her case helplessly, her cheeks turning a tinge pink.

"Social study? Yeah, great, great. Just make sure you keep your purse strings tight, okay? I know it's easy to get excited out there, but you're gonna go belly-up if you keep spending money like that."

Maou turned his attention to Emi next.

"And since she hasn't found any work yet, try not to turn her into some shopaholic secretary, all right?"

He tried to act as jaded as possible as he spoke.

This struck Emi as an incredibly unfair accusation out of the blue, but she was in no position to reveal Suzuno's true identity to Maou and his cohorts. *Why,* she whined to herself, *am I the only one forced to keep any secrets here while everyone else is running roughshod over me?*

"The way Ashiya put it, it sounds like you had some kind of trouble?"

"Like *you* need to know. There's no trouble at all, as long as you don't do anything to mess up her tranquil, *private* life."

Emi attempted to spike the point home upon Maou and Suzuno simultaneously, albeit in two different ways. Maou shrugged and laughed.

"See? I told you. Don't blame me if you wind up paying for it later."

The portent behind the simple observation struck a chord.

"Wait, what are you…?"

Emi felt a strange sense of disquiet at the advice. Rika cut her off before she could question him further.

"Hey, by the way, what are you gonna do about all this? Sure doesn't look like business is booming in here. Emi's surrounded by all these talented people, so I'm sure you aren't the lunkhead you're starting to look like."

"Oh, so now you're saying I look like a lunkhead? I don't really appreciate that kind of feedback from customers, thanks. Bring it up with the regional manager if you care that much."

"Hey, just think of it as some friendly sales advice."

There was no stopping Rika now.

"But, here, lemme just come out with it—I'm here because I want to see how you work."

"Whadaya mean, how I work? Who *are* you, anyway?"

"Oh, Emi's friend, Suzuno's friend, and the daughter of a company president."

"That doesn't exactly help me, miss! If you aren't here to eat something, then get out of here, okay? I may not look like it, but I'm pretty busy right now."

"You talked about 'hitting back at them' just a second ago. What're you gonna do, huh?"

"You aren't too gifted at listening to people, are you, lady?" Maou sighed sullenly.

Suddenly, another voice rang out from the entrance.

"You there, Maou?"

An elderly customer entered, carrying something large and green with him. Rika, Suzuno, and the exhausted Emi turned their eyes toward him.

Once he recognized the man, Maou left Emi's table behind and hurriedly walked over.

"Nabe! You didn't have to run all the way over here!"

"Didn't want to let you down, Maou! I figured the quicker, the better anyway."

The man called Nabe laughed a hearty laugh.

"Well, thanks, though. You know I could've picked it up. Would you mind propping that up against the wall over there?"

"Ooh, right. Shouldn't have brought this huge tree into the dining area, huh?"

"Nabe" slapped himself on the forehead before placing the green mass outside by the door.

"I spent the day clearing off all the small bits and the branches low enough to poke kids' eyes out. It's all ready to go! I got you the best one I could find, so have fun decorating it! And now that that's done, I better get going."

"What, already? You want anything to eat first? My treat."

Nabe shook his head in response.

"Thanks for the thought, but I got my wife cooking dinner tonight. Next cleaning run, maybe, eh? Say yello to Ms. Kisaki for me."

With a quick wave, Nabe turned around and strode confidently out the door.

As if on cue, the free staff on the MgRonald crew began to stream out the back, rolls of colored paper in their hands.

"Wow, look at the size of that thing!"

"We better get this all decorated before we hit rush hour!"

"Hey, I think we still have some of those tiny plastic cones with the tops missing back in the storehouse. You think we could tape 'em on the branches?"

They gathered in the dining area, excitedly talking among themselves.

"So…what's that big thing out there?"

Noticing Rika's voice, Maou let the crew do their work on the tree as he returned to Emi's table.

"What do you think it is? It's a *sasa* bamboo plant."

"Sasa?"

"It's almost time for the Sasahata Star Festival."

As she said this, Chiho took out several sheets of colored paper cut into thin strips, along with a black marker.

"Sasahata…Star Festival?"

Chiho continued as Emi tilted her head in curiosity. "Well, every year, the Sasazuka and Hatagaya neighborhoods work together to hold a summer festival. That's where *Sasahata* comes from—it's just the two names put together. We're actually a little late on decorating, but what goes better with a Sasahata festival than a real *sasa* plant?"

"I asked the store manager to put in a request with the regional office as a special favor. Kids aged twelve or younger can write their wishes on these colored strips of paper and tie them to the tree to decorate it, and we'll give them a free small drink in exchange."

"The Star Festival gets into gear at the end of next week and we'll have a ton of customers that weekend, so Maou thought this would be a good way to get a leg up on Sentucky Fried Chicken."

Chiho held her chest out high, justifiably proud.

"Huh. *You* did that?"

Rika sounded impressed.

"We usually have a plastic bamboo plant we bring out each year, but I figured that doesn't have the kind of natural attraction to people that something like a Christmas tree does."

"Maou gave us all these ideas for decorations to make, too!"

The strips of paper had been made into all sorts of decorations, from streamers and origami cranes to little pouches and nets. Considering they were all handmade, the staff had done a remarkably thorough job. Rika carefully scrutinized the example Chiho gave her.

"Wow, this is pretty. But wouldn't a real-life *sasa* bamboo plant be expensive? No way they'd spend that much on a part-timer's request. Or is that your own?"

Now it was Maou's turn to puff his chest up.

"Heh-heh! You'd think so, right? But these are the kinda things an assistant manager has to charm his way through, you know? That guy earlier… Mr. Watanabe's his full name… He's a guy I came to know while I was volunteering with the city's urban cleanup campaign, and he's got a ton of those in his garden."

"You…volunteer with the antilitter guys?"

"Heavens! Donating one's time for the sake of the community? Sadao, you actually perform such deeds?"

"Huh. So you actually care about the neighborhood you live in."

The surprise exhibited by Emi and Suzuno was quite a different beast from what Rika exhibited.

"Yeah. Our last cleanup day was yesterday morning, actually. He said yes immediately when I asked, and I was supposed to come over to pick it up, too… I feel kinda bad about making him come here instead, though. He stops by sometimes for a bite with his grandson."

Now Emi understood why Maou was up so early and out the door yesterday morning. It saved her from a trip to the hospital, that was true, but the idea of the Devil King becoming a model citizen around the neighborhood was not something she found particularly pleasing, especially when faced with this reality in public with all her acquaintances watching.

"So anyway, we can't keep this tree around until next year, of course, so on the day of the Star Festival itself, I figured we could cut it up into little saplings and give them out to kids. Kind of a mini festival tree, you know?"

"Hmm! You think that'll pay off, though? I dunno if kids these days would care about something like that."

Maou waved his finger at Rika's criticism.

"Well, the sort of kids who'd write their wishes and tie them on the tree would dig it, wouldn't they? Adults like us, we tend to buy into this idea that all kids care about these days are video games. But, you know, every one of those Star Festival wishes has meaning to it, just like every ornament on a Christmas tree. And it's having all of that together in one common place that makes it so pretty. It's a living bamboo plant, so they can decorate their rooms with it and stuff, and if they get sick of it or it dies, the tree and the paper decorations are all burnable, so they can just toss it in the recycle bin."

In the Shibuya ward of Tokyo, you were allowed to put out small amounts of yard waste with the trash as long as you cut the branches into thirty-centimeter segments first.

"There's no guarantee this'll attract customers, of course, but I figured that, instead of the same old generic decorations whenever the season came around, it'd be better to have something that helped connect us to our customers and the area around us."

"Wow, you've really thought this through."

Listening to the explanation, Rika's eyes darted excitedly between Maou and the *sasa* tree. Finally, she turned straight toward Emi.

"He's *good.*"

It was pure, unadulterated praise.

"Ooh, did you hear that, Emi? Your friend just said the assistant manager's *good!*"

Maou readily took the compliment, standing defiantly over Emi.

"Hee-hee! Don't make her take that back, Maou!" Chiho tittered at Maou's all-too-predictable response.

Emi, watching Maou like one watches a toilet flush after emptying one's stomach into it, scrunched her face tightly.

"..You apply yourself to your work" was the only thing she finally managed to expel.

It pained Emi deep down to do, or say, anything that might paint Maou in a positive light when the man himself was around. Rika, not quite aware of the extent of this neurosis, gave a satisfied nod.

A crew member ran up to the table, carrying two large plastic objects with both of his arms.

"Maou! I found the broken plastic cones. That, and here are some of the no-parking poles, the kind you fill with water on the bottom to keep them upright. We could probably stick it on these to make it more stable."

"Ah, perfect! Thanks a lot! Now we just need to decide on a location!"

Picking up the cones and poles, Maou darted outside.

Emi watched him go. Seeing him excitedly direct the crew around as they prepared the Star Festival decorations, fighting tooth and nail to get customers through the door, it seemed utterly impossible for her to see any ulterior motive, any malicious intent to it.

All she could see was an assistant manager who had the trust of his employees supporting him.

"Are you feeling okay, Yusa? You don't look too good."

Chiho felt obliged to speak up as Emi wrestled internally over this. Emi smiled, unable to hide the complex feelings welling inside.

"Oh, no, I'm fine. Just thinking about something."

Her eyes never removed themselves from Maou's back.

Chiho seemed like she was about to open her mouth again, but another employee chose that moment to call her over to the register.

"Well, if you're tired, try not to overdo it, okay? I'll yell at Maou for you after we're done."

With that final turn of kindness, Chiho returned to work. Taking her eyes off Maou, Emi watched as the two employees behind the counter performed maintenance work on one machine or another.

The work atmosphere around here, she thought, was something "Ms. Kisaki" must have created. But now Maou, in a position of responsibility, was still perfectly friendly and cheerful, even with customer numbers as far down as they were. It was the truth, one she couldn't ignore.

All of the crew—not just Chiho, who smiled around Maou for different reasons—were in an equally festive mood as they tackled the project Maou gave them, even though a Star Festival bamboo plant didn't seem to have much to do with selling hamburgers.

Satan, the Devil King, was a foe that needed to be vanquished. But Emi, watching as Maou tried and failed repeatedly to keep the plant upright next to the door, had other thoughts on her lips.

"But he's…he's just not doing anything *bad* here…"

She didn't want to admit it. She *couldn't* admit it, in her position.

Even if a criminal admits his guilt, serves his time, and becomes a rehabilitated member of society again, that doesn't make the crimes he committed disappear forever.

She noticed that Suzuno, too, was watching Maou's back with a puzzled expression on her face.

Even after witnessing the scene for herself, Emi wondered if Suzuno still thought Maou had some kind of master plan for world domination in mind.

Just when he had succeeded in keeping the plant from tipping over at the slightest breeze, Rika noticed something.

"Huh?"

The voice jarred Emi out of her solitary thoughts.

"Rika? What's up?"

"Well…it's just they're kind of getting this huge onrush of customers all of a sudden…"

Rika pointed an unsteady finger out the door. Following it, Emi was shocked. The waves of people flocking toward Sentucky Fried Chicken seemed to magically dissipate. In its place, another wave began to push into MgRonald in droves.

Maou noticed this just when his valiant fight against the *sasa* plant came to a satisfying close.

"Dude, dude, dude!!"

A surprised smile crossed his face as he half ran back inside.

"They're here! They're here! All hands, battle stations! It's time to rock 'n' roll!!"

Before Maou had a chance to be clearly heard, the human wave crashed through MgRonald, leaving the automatic door open behind them.

The tables quickly filled up, an air of excitement suddenly filling the dining area.

"Holy... Are you *kidding* me?! What kinda feng shui did that bamboo give him, anyway?" Rika couldn't help but laugh at the absurd scene.

"How could this even...?"

Emi found it less than amusing.

"......"

Suzuno focused on the bamboo plant instead of Maou, her face hardened.

"Hello and welcome! Please form a single line in front of the register once you've decided on your order!"

Maou's sharp, ever-present customer service echoed above the din, well across the building.

THE DEVIL
AND THE
HERO RISK
THEIR LIVES
FOR THEIR
WORK
RESPONSIBILITIES

Being on top has its advantages. That was no doubt why the council decided to place full judgment responsibilities upon her for the crisis one of their own had triggered.

Her, former inquisitor and current Reconciliation Panel investigator.

It was true that she was on good terms with Olba Meiyer, Church archbishop and director of diplomatic and missionary operations.

A worker calling the directorial responsibilities of his manager into question was one thing, but in an organization like the Church—one reliant upon the faith of the people in order to establish its truthfulness and righteousness—having the highest of officials force responsibility for the failures of one of their closest confidants upon a subordinate and otherwise attempt to cover up their own faults was simply unthinkable.

Archbishop Robertio, after recovering from his fainting spell, had given her the order:

"Within your rights as a member of the Reconciliation Panel, I command you to find a way to deliver judgment upon him while damaging the authority of the Church as little as possible."

It was always like this.

They always treated themselves with kid gloves, in fear of their own reputations being damaged. They were unwilling to dirty their own hands, basking in the peace they themselves made no effort to attain, and took all the credit afterward.

When Lucifer's forces threatened to storm across the Western Island once upon a time, it proved frustratingly impossible for the Church forces there to build a unified front.

The knights of the Church Guard squabbled with those affiliated with the Unified Kingdom Guard over who should take the initiative in the upcoming battle.

The kingdoms that dotted the Western Island saw the invasion as an opportunity to unshackle themselves from Church influence, a chance the Church was eager to deny them.

Despite the overwhelmingly poor odds against them, it was not uncommon for mankind to fight among themselves for the crumbs they managed to win back against the demonic hordes. Lucifer was all too quick to seize on this weakness. As a result, the Western Island found itself all but handing over half its landmass to Lucifer's army, unable to even put up a coordinated resistance.

Even as they faced the specter of total annihilation, the political infighting among the power brokers of the Western Island only served to further decimate the population.

She was already a full-fledged member of the Council of Inquisitors by that point. Following the orders of Olba, her direct supervisor, she orchestrated a purge in the form of an inquisition.

In a place like the Western Island, where the teachings of the Church held great influence with the people, being branded as a "heretic" essentially meant one's departure from society.

Exercising the extensive knowledge of divinity and common law that was drummed into her in the Diplomacy and Missionary Department, she ruthlessly pursued the leaders that waged political battles, lowered the morale of the troops on the front lines, and thrust their own armies into chaos.

Until Emilia the Hero arrived to dispatch Lucifer once and for all, she and the inquisitors who worked for her went hardly a day without seeing bloodshed.

Flare-ups between the owners of holy Church lands and the neighboring kingdoms were as bloody as they were frequent. No matter how long she kept hunting them, whether holy or secular, the foolish leaders who failed to understand the crisis facing mankind continued to well up like a gushing spring.

She was as human as they, but she was hunting them down for the sake of justice. The cross of the Church was their eternal weapon, and it allowed them to even perform above-the-law assassinations.

She herself carried out much of this dirty work, using her Light of Iron as she did. That holy magic gave her the ability to transform anything shaped like a cross into a weapon.

It was all part of her job in the Council of Inquisitors, a job driven by the holy desire to spread peace and prosperity worldwide.

Things began to change when the empire of Saint Aile, the kingdom that boasted the largest territory on the Western Island, fell to the demonic forces, its top leaders captured by Lucifer's demon hordes.

Losing the most powerful kingdom on the Western Island meant that the Church was the only organization of any great size that could muster a front. The remaining kingdoms, fearing more Church inquisitions, soon fell over themselves to form a unified force, one under the ultimate guidance of the Church itself.

And with Emilia taking command of this force, the inquisitors quickly found themselves with very little of the "work of the gods" left to handle.

Thanks to Emilia and her companions advancing seemingly unopposed against the Devil King's forces, it was no longer difficult to instill a firm sense of unity that rang true across the entire human army. That, and the leaders who once squabbled and lashed at each other with impunity were now fully cowed into submission, falling into line underneath the flag of the Hero.

Mankind could hold its own against the demons after all. It was a simple hope, but one that only Emilia had the power to instill in the people.

But once word that Emilia had lost her life defeating the Devil King spread like wildfire, the world that once was so united under the Hero fell to pieces in the blink of an eye.

After the Devil King's defeat, the kingdoms of the Western Island began to hold criminal hearings against the inquisitors that demonstrated particular zeal in judging heretics during the war.

Seeking to avoid this, the Church dissolved the Council of Inquisitors, establishing the Reconciliation Panel in its place in a move to hold "more open" proceedings against those who defied the way of holiness.

It was a farce, one she found hard to stand for.

If the people of the Western Island had united against the Devil King's forces when they still had the chance to, there was no telling how many senseless deaths could have been averted, how many needless judgments could have gone unexamined.

Without the Council of Inquisitors, the Western Island would have been burned to the ground long before Emilia appeared.

"We did not execute people because we *enjoyed* the task!"

Her voice went unheeded.

The concession to the united kingdoms helped retain political equilibrium, but to the former inquisitors, it made them feel that their pride, their faith, everything had been stripped away from them.

And now, with the world dazzled by the light of a new myth, a Hero who sacrificed her life to bring peace to the land, the Church and the kingdoms simply turned their back to the past, unable or unwilling to admit any of their faults.

The world was in the process of returning to what it was before the Devil King's advent.

Was this the kind of world Emilia staked her own life to protect?

It couldn't be.

The peace that so many had sacrificed their lives to gain hold of couldn't be a simple extension of the corrupt, stagnant world from before.

Thanks to her extensive behind-the-scenes work for the Church, she had been granted a position heading the new Reconciliation Panel. A panel meant to reconcile the world with its past.

Then let it be done.

Instead of a peace roiled by the hideous machinations of a handful of old men, let us find a peace where the flickering light of life can burn brightly with hope once more.

"Reconcile...the world."

She opened the gate and let her body slide into another world.

Crestia Bell.

That was the name of the engineer of purges, the hunter of countless heretics in her tribunals, the executioner feared as the "Scythe of Death," and a woman of the cloth who thirsted for peace over anything else.

✳

"Well, I'm off."

The clock struck nine PM. Chiho, already changed out of her uniform, nodded at Maou from beyond the counter.

"Sure thing. Great job today. Thanks for the bento meal, too. I'll wash the box and get it back to you tomorrow."

"M-Maou, you're being too loud!"

Chiho was even louder as she tried to stop him, but the rest of the employees did not seem to notice the conversation.

"Boy, tonight sure was a relief, though, huh? I'm sure glad we saw a steady stream of customers through the dinner hours. Hopefully that was enough to prop the final numbers back up to what they should be."

Maou and Chiho shivered as if on cue, the image of Kisaki and her Arctic-blizzard smile flashing across their minds.

"Yeah. Sure wouldn't want to get deported to Greenland before I graduate from high school."

"It's kind of hard to tell when Kisaki's joking and when she isn't, huh?"

The pair exchanged dry, cracked smiles with each other.

"Well, be careful on the way home."

"Yep! And, uh, sorry I took your bike this morning."

"It's fine, it's fine. Oh, hey, Emi!"

Removing his gaze from Chiho, Maou noticed that Emi and Suzuno were behind him, a distance away.

"You guys are free, aren't you? You sitting at that table all night messed up our turnover ratio, so you could at least repay me by walking home with Chi, okay?"

He was hardly in a position to boss them around. He did anyway.

"Well, fine, but we *did* place orders, you know. I don't think you have the right to scold us like that."

Emi was just as sulky in her response.

Ashiya may have been long gone, but Emi, at all costs, wanted to avoid owing any kind of debt to demons. Two women spending upward of two thousand yen at MgRonald had to go a long way toward that goal.

"Watching Maou really puts my mind at ease."

Those were the words Rika left as she departed, just before the peak dinner hours began. She was the one who sparked all of this in the first place, but at least Emi was reassured that she didn't have to erase any of her memories in the end.

She hoped to leave with Rika, but Suzuno intervened.

"If possible, I would like to inspect you on the job for a little while longer, Sadao."

Maou, brightened by his apparent newfound success as assistant manager, readily accepted.

Emi didn't know what drove Suzuno to make the request, but Emi was in no mood to leave her alone. There was still no telling what kind of disquieting things Suzuno might attempt.

That was why she stayed so late in the dining area. It wasn't until Chiho hung up her apron for the day that Suzuno finally got the picture and stood up.

"…Tell Ashiya that we're even now, okay?"

"Huh? Why should I care? That's *your* fault for getting in a position where you owed him one."

Maou retorted snappily at Emi, making shooing motions as he did. "What's past is past, all right? Just get out of my sight. And I want you to see *Chi* all the way home, got it?"

Emi found it impossible to understand why Maou placed so much emphasis on "Chi."

"Of course. You don't have to tell me. Come on, Chiho."

"Okay. See you next time, Maou."

Chiho, well familiar by now with the way Maou and Emi sniped at each other, paid the banter little mind as she walked after the departing Emi.

Watching on from across the dining area, Suzuno remained where she was, not bothering to approach Maou at the counter.

"...Excuse me."

Her voice was just barely audible as she bowed at Maou and left.

"Thank you very much! Come again soon!"

Maou replied with a warm smile and the standard workplace-video line.

"So, where do you live, Chiho?"

Chiho turned toward the direction of Sasazuka.

"Um, it's pretty much on the opposite side of Koshu-Kaido Road from Maou's apartment, but are you sure you want to walk all the way over with me?"

"No problem. I was planning to take the train from Sasazuka anyway, so it's not that far of a detour from there. Not that I'm doing this to please *him* or anything, but it's night and all, so...I wouldn't want a girl to just go off by herself."

"Aw, you're a girl, too, aren't you, Yusa?"

"Yeah. Just kind of a special one. But let's get going."

Emi, Chiho, and Suzuno accompanied each other down Koshu-Kaido Road. Car traffic was still heavy this time of night, too early to be called "late night" but too late to be called "evening."

Not many other pedestrians were on the sidewalk. Most shops had their lights shut off, making the walkways notably darker than expected.

With the Shuto Expressway towering above them the whole way, the effect was akin to walking down a tunnel that pierced through a mighty mountain of concrete and metal.

They reached the intersection bordering Sasazuka, the Hatagaya Land Bridge spanning high above, when a red light stopped them.

"Ah, but I'm still happy we got all those customers in."

Chiho stretched as she spoke, as if to herself.

"Was it that bad since morning?"

"I think it may have been the slowest day since I began working there."

It really was breathtaking. One minute, emptiness. The next, a tidal wave of customers descending upon MgRonald, filling the air with crackling excitement.

Maou's Star Festival make-a-wish drink giveaway was a massive success. By the time Chiho left, the bamboo plant was covered from tip to root with small tied-up pieces of paper.

"Maybe that feng shui stuff isn't as stupid as it sounds, huh? I don't really believe in horoscopes and stuff like that, but you have to admit, that sort of thing makes you think a little."

The light turned green as Chiho spoke. She began to walk toward the curb.

"...But was it truly a coincidence?"

Suzuno's low voice stopped her.

"Huh?"

Emi turned around as well.

"Oh! That reminds me. What did you think of Maou's work ethic and stuff, Suzuno?"

Chiho cheerfully tried to change the subject. Suzuno ignored them both as she spoke to Emi...using a different name.

"Did you not notice, Emilia?"

"...Uh?"

"Emilia...?"

The green light began to flash, leaving the three of them flat-footed on the sidewalk.

"Emilia's...Yusa's real...? Suzuno, don't tell me you're..."

Chiho brought a surprised hand to her mouth. Suzuno glared at her before turning her attention to Emi.

"I had had my suspicions, but Chiho is fully aware of the Devil King as well, is she not?"

The sharp glint to her eyes pierced through Emi.

"I know, Emilia, that you have your own motives. That you aim to defeat the Devil King on your own terms. But, watching 'Sadao Maou' handle his assigned tasks today, I have come to the conclusion that we must dispatch the Devil King as quickly as humanly possible."

"Wha?! Wha—Suzuno?!"

Chiho, agitated, began to lean toward Suzuno before Emi stopped her.

"What are you talking about? I don't have any idea where this is coming from."

"Have either of you given a moment's thought about why the Devil King is acting like a fine, sensible Japanese youth?"

Suzuno spoke slowly, allowing the atmosphere to ooze between her words, like a priest reciting Holy Scripture to his flock.

"Have you ever thought about what may happen if he continues being promoted, if he begins to wield influence within societal systems here? A Devil King with the full trust and acclaim of the people behind him?"

Suzuno spread her arms wide.

"Have you ever imagined what the moment might be like when he reveals his true intentions? When he finally betrays the world and makes it his own?"

"Sorry, but no."

Emi sliced right through her speech.

"No offense, but what is getting promoted at MgRonald's gonna earn him? I mean, yeah, it's a big company, but even if he goes insane and torches their headquarters or whatever, that's really not gonna hurt the world much! Maybe it'll make stock prices go down or shake up the fast-food industry, but it's not gonna make the world flip upside down or…"

"We *reside*, may I remind you, in a nation where people with nothing more than an elementary or technical school education have become prime ministers that sway the very direction of the world. Do you honestly believe that the Devil King's bloodlust will be sated within the structure of MgRonald alone?"

"Oh! You're talking about Kakuei Tanaka, right?"

Chiho's interjection, like a student waving her hand excitedly and stammering *Me me me me me!* in class, was not enough to lighten the mood.

"It would be much more logical, I think, to see it as a ruse to throw us off. This cruel tyrant who laid waste to so much of Ente Isla, now a cheerful, hardworking frontline employee. Demons have long lives to work with, Emilia. There is no telling what manner of intricate schemes he has unfolding in his mind. That is why we must strike *now*, while we can! This is no longer simply an Ente Isla crisis. The safety of Japan, and the Earth itself, is at stake."

"N-no! You can't! Maou's doing really great as a shift supervisor, too!"

Chiho, finally realizing this apparent new visitor from Ente Isla was seriously contemplating Maou's murder, hastily came to his defense. Suzuno glared at her over Emi's shoulder.

"And the fact she still retains her memories is another issue we have to tackle. If it becomes more widely known that the Devil King is alive, there is every chance of more visitors coming to Japan— visitors seeking the simple glory of defeating them, not the loftier callings that drive you and me. Do you think such people care at all about what happens to Japan and its people in the aftermath? They may even try to use Chiho and the people around her to hurt you or the Devil King. Before that happens, we must erase the memories of everyone who has interacted with the Devil King and strike the final blow to end all of this!"

"No! You can't! You just can't *do* that!"

The stoplight turned again, bathing Suzuno in bloodred light as it went through yet another cycle.

"Chiho, do you know what the purpose of the Star Festival decorations are in Japanese culture?"

"...Huh?"

The sudden change of subject caught Chiho off guard. Emi's face tightened.

"The five colors that those paper strips people write their wishes upon represent the five elements that control the spirit in Chinese philosophy. The leaves of the *sasa* bamboo tree are fabled to house the souls of one's ancestors, while its straightened twigs and branches contain the power to ward off evil. There is, of course, none of those forces at work in modern-day Star Festival decorations. But did you see it? The moment the Devil King installed that tree out front, MgRonald was immediately overrun with guests. What do you think that means...?"

"...You're saying his bamboo tree *attracted* people?"

Suzuno replied with a heavy nod.

"The *sasa* tree, long associated with the spirits of the earth and the power to cleanse it of evil, is infused with the souls of the people who look to them for seasonal décor. The Devil King unconsciously infused the tree with his demonic power as he decorated it. That is the most natural explanation."

"Considering how much of a shock a flat-screen TV was to you, you sure know a lot about Japanese customs."

"I would be a failure at my missionary work if I did not research the religious customs of the lands I travel."

Suzuno, completely ignoring Emi's sass, took a step toward both her and Chiho. The two of them glared back, unable to move since walking backward would put them in a car lane.

"So do I have your understanding here? This is no longer merely an Ente Isla issue. If we do not hurry, then Chiho, MgRonald, and soon this entire land will find itself awash in a whirlpool of chaos. Failure to take action, and quickly, will cost us dearly later."

She focused her sharpened gaze upon Emi.

"And besides, you have already been attacked by an unknown

third party. I must keep this world safe, but I must also bring you back to Ente Isla. I understand it may be a painful decision, but these are people you should never have met, in a world you should never have needed to visit. We must erase Chiho's memories and eliminate all traces of Ente Isla that exist in Japan."

Emi glared back at Suzuno, the humid night forming sweat beads upon her brow.

Suzuno's stance was substantially persuasive. If it were a year ago, when Emilia the Hero was still a recent visitor to Earth, she would have eagerly agreed to Suzuno's proposal.

Internally, Emi had found herself supremely lost. And while she may not have intended it, Suzuno was helping Emi solve the question that bothered her the most—why, if she had access to her powers again, did she find it impossible to will herself into slaying the Devil King?

But before Emi could fire back at Suzuno, a shakier voice made itself known.

"...No."

It was Chiho.

"No...you can't. I, I don't want to forget."

"Chiho..."

"I don't want to forget. About Maou, about you, about Ashiya, about Suzuno... Okay, and I guess Urushihara, too, but..."

She tossed her head back and forth to emphasize the point.

"We're all friends, we've spent all this fun time together...and you want to make me forget all of it just because of stuff going on in another planet? That...that's just mean!"

"...I know there is no way to fully apologize for it. But...Chiho, this is for your own safety as well."

Suzuno averted her face, looking honestly conflicted. It wasn't enough to convince Chiho. She continued, almost shouting as tears welled in her eyes.

"I don't want to forget about Maou! No matter what!!"

But Suzuno, a touch of resolve painted on her serene face, returned fire with another punishing barrage.

"Chiho, the Devil King Satan will use those feelings of yours to his own advantage. He must. And the fact that you are attracted to him may even be part of an elaborate plan he has concocted to make us hesitant, unwilling to combat the Devil King…"

This, again, was something that the Emi of old would have enthusiastically agreed with. But…what could it be? The thought seemed impossible to her now.

And if it didn't move her, it certainly wasn't going to move Chiho.

"It is *not*! Maou isn't that kind of person! Why do you have to say all those horrible things?! He's working really hard, he's so nice to everyone… Why are you saying all of that?!"

The normally calm and composed Chiho was allowing her emotions to explode.

"…He is the Devil King. He allowed his demonic hordes in Ente Isla to conduct untold atrocities. He made everyone on the world suffer. He is the leader of all demons!"

The spite was becoming clear in Suzuno's voice as she tried to wrangle with the unwavering Chiho.

This was the pure, unvarnished truth, a matter of common sense to anyone from Ente Isla discussing the Devil King.

But Chiho refused to blink.

"Well, before he became Sadao Maou, did you ever even *meet* the Devil King Satan, Suzuno?!"

Several silent moments passed.

Both Emi and Suzuno had difficulty immediately understanding what Chiho had just asked. It was something nobody—especially not Emi, watching on from the side—had ever thought of before.

"What do you mean…?"

To them, Chiho was making so little sense that they couldn't answer the question with anything but another question.

Chiho's teary eyes swiveled toward Suzuno.

"All of you are going on about Maou like, *ooh, he's the Devil King, he's the Devil King*, but if he's really a demon thinking all those bad things, why would he do stuff like fix up the destroyed Shuto Expressway and erase all those terrible memories of the scene from everyone's minds?! When he got all of that massive power back, he could have mind-controlled the prime minister or the US president or whoever and taken over the whole world! Why didn't he *do* that?!"

Now it was Suzuno's turn to hesitate.

"I…I did not witness the battle Olba Meiyer perpetrated with my own eyes. But I am sure the Devil King had his reasons. Some deeper explanation only he would…"

"Is there any *other* reason, except he's a nice guy who wants to help people?! If you cause trouble for other people, then you're supposed to apologize and make up for it! That's common sense! And Maou was just doing the obvious thing!"

"……"

"I learned how to do my job from Maou. He went through all the steps with me. If I messed something up, he always brought me to task about it. He always had my back when I was still new and inexperienced. Whenever I need to talk about something, he's always there. Even when he turned into the Devil King Satan, he kept his promises. He taught me how to clean the ice-cream machine. On the same day! If someone like that really wanted to summon his demon hordes or whatever and conquer the world, then how would you explain all of that?!"

"So…so you are bidding us to simply let the past go and forgive him?!"

Suzuno exploded as well.

"How many innocent lives on Ente Isla do you think were snatched away by the demonic armies?! Do you think those people would accept it if they heard the Devil King has mended his ways?! You live in a nation at peace. One where you may never be exposed to mortal danger during your entire natural life. And I will *not* have someone like you question the will behind our quest to slay the Demon King!"

Chiho remained steadfast.

"What would *you* know?! You just fought those demon armies. You never even *met* the Devil King himself!"

"…What?"

Suzuno fixed her gaze upon Chiho, too openmouthed to respond.

"Even if Maou turns into Satan again, I *know* he's a good person! And I also know that that big church in Ente Isla tried to kill Yusa for no good reason!"

That experience composed the brunt of what Chiho knew about Emi's homeland.

"You never met the Devil King before you stormed the Devil's Castle, either, right, Yusa? You talked about how Satan's armies invaded the land and did all these evil things, but that's it. Do you even know what the Devil King was *doing* before then?"

"…You would make a gifted court attorney someday, Chiho. By my name as a former member of the Council of Inquisitors, I guarantee it. The way you turn people's words against them is breathtaking."

"Suzuno! Don't dodge the question! Please, answer me!"

"He was their commander! He bears full responsibility for what his armies did! Do you think a man who orders massacres should escape fault because it was someone else who actually committed them?"

"Hey, can both of you calm down a little? We're not gonna accomplish anything arguing out here."

"Wait!"

"But we must!"

The two of them protested in unison at Emi.

"Suzuno… No. Crestia Bell. I think everything you're telling us is correct. Really. But I just want to say one thing."

Emi brought her hands behind the back of Chiho, whose face was reddened with tears by now.

"Yusa…"

"The peace I fought for is the kind of peace were people feel like smiling again. Not a peace where sacrifice is viewed as a necessary evil, where I have to turn my eyes away from something that makes my friends cry."

Suzuno's appalled face shot upward.

"I want to slay the Devil King in a way that everyone can smile about at the end. The idea that we don't want to get Japan caught up in this just shows how arrogant we are, coming from Ente Isla. We have our thoughts about the Devil King, and other people have theirs. We don't have any right to make one-sided decisions for them."

"...Do you truly believe that?"

Suzuno's voice was shaking as she asked.

"I sure do."

Emi's was clear and defiant.

"It is a pipe dream. Do you want the permission of every man, woman, and child on Ente Isla and Japan before slaying the Devil King? Such an approach is impossible. There are always going to be sacrifices that must be paid."

The energy seemed to drain from Suzuno's eyes and voice as she spoke.

It hurt her deeply. How could her own words stab so deeply into her heart?

She had searched for Emilia precisely because she wanted to rid the world of "sacrifices that must be paid," because she wanted to do away with a world so willing to turn its back to those sacrifices and the reasons they were made.

"But that's what I have to do. I am Emilia, the Hero. The hope of mankind."

Suzuno knew Emilia would have understood that. Just as she did back in her own world, a world that tried to bury her in the darkness once.

Emi lightened her expression for a moment before continuing, her words aimed squarely at Suzuno's heart.

"And there's a more present problem, too. If we meddle with them too much and the Devil King, Alciel, and Lucifer all awaken to their true natures at the same time, the two of us would be at a serious disadvantage. The skill that mystery attacker showed off to me... That wasn't the Devil King's style, either. If we hurried along with attacking the Devil King, we'd simply find ourselves in a two-front war without enough manpower or information. So…"

Emi placed her hands on Chiho's shoulders.

"Right here, right now, I just want to keep you smiling, Chiho. I won't erase your memories, and I won't let the Devil King die. And if you insist on pushing the point, you'll have to fight against me first."

She held her hands against her chest.

"The holy sword… Are you serious?"

Her right hand lit up as her holy energy resonated with the Holy Silver within her body, the core of her weapon.

That tiny release of power was enough to send a powerful flash of light across the deserted evening intersection, dark except for the streetlights and flashing stoplight.

"You are a citizen of Ente Isla. I protect you, just as I protect everyone else. But if you want to do anything to Chiho because of all those pretexts you spouted off, then I will fight it. I will fight for Chiho's memories, for her indelible past. She is a friend, a precious one, who I need to protect."

"Yusa…"

Chiho's voice was laden with pure emotion.

"Besides, you came to Japan because you didn't like having to cover up things that were 'inconvenient' for your mission, right?"

"……"

Suzuno put up a brave front as she stared at Emi, but the bravery was brittle and fleeting, liable to crack at the slightest shock.

"If all you cared about was the good name of the Church, you would have tried to cover up Olba's crimes the moment you found out about them. That would have created the ideal postwar scenario in the Church's eyes, right? Me and the Devil King being dead would let them build the legend of this great Church guard knight who sacrificed her life to defeat the ultimate evil."

Suzuno gritted her teeth, eyes turned downward toward the street.

It was exactly the scenario all the old sanctuary archbishops wanted.

"But even though you worked for Olba, you weren't satisfied with that. That's why you're so preoccupied with bringing me back home, isn't it? You want to reveal Olba's crimes and the dark side of the Church to everyone, so it can purify itself and become the proud beacon of faith that a peaceful Ente Isla deserves."

Emi stepped away from Chiho and approached Suzuno, whose eyes were pointed squarely downward.

"You are, after all, chief of the Reconciliation Panel. The Church wing whose mission it is to spread it the Church throughout the world. To portray it as a just faith."

Emi extended a hand, attempting to touch Suzuno's shoulder. Suzuno twisted her body to avoid it, staggering backward as she did.

"Whoa! Be careful!"

But Suzuno paid the red light no mind, darting into the intersection. The loud car horn didn't stop her, either, as she plunged into the darkness, attempting to flee the scene with all of her shopping purchases.

Emi, to her, had accused her of being just the same.

She made her realize that she was no different from those monstrous old men, the very ones she judged as being so below her.

Those ugly, twisted powermongers, unable to protect those who needed protection the most, who saw sacrifice as a necessary evil, the "evil" of which should be shunned and ignored.

The skidding tires of the screeching cars sounded like the howling laughter of the "heretics" she had cleansed from the world during her long career.

Emi watched on, her face gravely concerned as Suzuno continued her dangerous escape.

"I'm sorry. I think I probably went too far."

Chiho was behind Emi, tears still rolling down her eyes.

"I don't really know much about Ente Isla. Everything I do know is secondhand knowledge. But all I cared about was myself, and Maou, and...and I was so mean to Suzuno..."

Emi, conflicted internally, patted the sniffling Chiho on the head.

"It's all right. You can't choose who you wind up liking."

"Yeah, but it embarrasses me, you saying that…"

Emi gently hugged Chiho as she tried her hardest to choke back the tears.

"Yusa…"

"It's hard for her, too. I'm sure she has a lot to think about. So try to remember that, too, all right?"

"All right…*sniff*…I better apologize to her later…"

"Sure. And make sure it's a nice, long conversation next time. She's a lot more open to other people than it looks."

"…All right."

Chiho returned the hug, a little more tightly than Emi.

"You're like a big sister to me, Yusa."

"I don't think we're really that different age-wise." Emi flashed a deliberate smile as she ran a hand through Chiho's hair. "But…I think we'll all need to be on guard from now on." Her smile tightened as she whispered.

Suzuno seemed to cozy up to Emi's story in her own chaotic way, but her anxiety toward Maou had hardly vanished. There was no telling what she would do next.

That, and there was that scythe-wielding freak who messed around with Emi earlier.

That was obviously a targeted strike. An assassin from the Church, perhaps, as they took action in response to Olba in their own way.

There were all these unpredictable elements running around unfettered, and she had no idea what they would do next. It wasn't good.

Her mind heavy with thought, Emi emitted a long, troubled sigh.

It was probably time to tell Maou and the others about the attacker, and about Suzuno's true colors. They needed to be prepared for the unexpected, and Emi needed to ensure she could slay the Devil King on her own terms.

She was reluctant to do anything that seemed like she was looking out for Maou's safety, but knowing that his next-door neighbor was a powerful Church figure was the perfect way to ensure the demons, already mostly robbed of their strength, would stay in line. In that regard, it wasn't all bad in the end.

She kind of had to think about it that way in order to drum up the willpower for the task.

"Well, so be it… I really hate this. It's like I'm helping him or something."

"You know, if you and Maou are being nice to each other, that'd make me happy, too."

Chiho chimed in, taking advantage of the now somewhat lightened atmosphere.

"Sorry, but if you want us to be friends, that's one request I'm *definitely* not taking."

She liked Chiho, but not enough to do *that*.

"But if you're gonna tell him, then probably the sooner, the better! If you leave a text and a voice mail on his phone, he'll probably return it once he gets off of work."

Chiho took a step away from Emi before removing her cell phone from her bag and searching for Maou's number from her contact list.

"But when did you find out, Emi? About…Suzuno, and stuff?"

"It was just this morning, actually. She told me everything after breakfast at Sasazuka station, and then…"

Then Emi noticed.

"Sorry, Chiho!"

Her voice ratcheted up in intensity.

Chiho was struck dumb on the spot. Then Emi leaped at her from the side. Then, a loud crashing sound.

"Huh? What…what…?!"

Chiho had trouble understanding why Emi just knocked her over.

"…Speak of the devil, as they say. These stalkers must really love me."

Emi whispered in response, the anger clear in her voice.

The figure was about the height of Suzuno or Urushihara. The black ski mask made a return, as well as the plastic rain poncho and camouflage-print pants. The lack of paintball stains on the mask made Emi conclude that her attacker had purchased a new one.

In both hands was an enormous scythe, as if the attacker had plucked the evening's crescent moon straight from the sky.

"Y-Yusa, this guy…"

"Yep."

Emi kept Chiho behind her as she steeled herself for a fight.

"The Ente Isla assassin. The one who crashed into the convenience-store door in Eifukucho before getting driven away by that clerk's paintball arsenal."

"……"

Chiho's eyes darted between Emi and the scythe-wielder.

"Is that…really an assassin?"

"Well, I can't think of any Japanese people who fall from the sky spinning that thing around."

"Y-yeah, I guess…"

"You know, it was the same thing before. Why's this guy always attack me in public streets? We're gonna have a ton of witnesses!"

The three of them had just held a heated argument a moment ago. That could be ignored. Bladed weapons, on the other hand, generally wouldn't be.

The area seemed deserted at first glance, but once things actually got started, someone would be calling the cops within a couple of minutes. Emi found that out for herself two months ago.

Considering this was a foe perfectly willing to involve other people in battle, she would need to make this an extremely short conflict, both to keep Chiho safe and to keep her name off the arrest records for a change.

"I can't spend a lot of time on this. It might get a little messy."

This time for real, Emi focused her energy on her right hand, binding the Holy Silver with the divine power within her body. The Better Half holy sword formed in an instant, shining in the night as it filled with holy force. That should be enough power to deflect at least one or two of those violet beams.

The next moment, a flash of purple shot out from the holes of the attacker's ski mask.

Emi darted to the side, predicting the direction of the beam. The light barely whizzed by her chest, striking an intersection guardrail before disintegrating.

Emi and Chiho both shot a look toward the rail. It wasn't twisted, warped, or otherwise damaged at all.

It confirmed that the beam caused no physical harm, but interacted with holy energy in some way that gravely affected Emi.

"Heavenly Fleet Feet!"

Focusing the Cloth of the Dispeller on her legs, she was face-to-face with the masked opponent in the blink of an eye. There was no time to let Chiho escape, so Emi had to keep her foe from striking instead.

Since this attacker's scythe had a longer attack range than her holy sword, she needed to settle this with close-quarters combat.

The darkened intersection sprang alive with the shrill sound of metal against metal as sparks flew through the air. To Chiho, looking on from afar, it seemed like the two combatants had only just begun to wage their pitched battle.

But while Emi succeeded in closing the gap, she was surprised to find this match to be a great deal more even than anticipated.

To combat the purple light, she had powered her holy sword up to maximum, a feat made possible by her now-regular 5-Holy Energy β habit. This sword, and the Hero's lightning-fast advance, had been stopped front and center by the scythe's handle.

No matter how much power she put into her blade, it didn't seem like she could put even a nick on the weapon. In fact...

"I'm...getting pushed back..."

Even with the Cloth of the Dispeller granting her enhanced speed, she was finding it difficult to advance upon her foe. Unable to support herself against the scythe-wielder's oppressive attack, Emi was slowly, but surely, giving up territory.

"Who *are* you...?!"

Somewhere along the line, the match had gone from an even battle to a matter of the scythe-wielder completely outclassing Emi. Then a voice rang out.

"Didn't I tell you? Men like to seize upon weak women."

"...!! You...!!"

The voice within the mask, close enough that it seemed to touch her, made Emi instinctively open her eyes wide.

"Ngh...! Divine Flying Blade!"

A flash of white ran across Emi's sword.

The move was originally meant to dispatch faraway foes with a leaping slash. At such close range, it was entirely possible Emi would be caught in the shock wave as well.

But there was no other way to break through this. Just as she was ready to release this potentially self-destructive blast, another purple beam glowed before her.

"None of that. Nothing that would make a woman hurt herself."

The violet beam released alongside the breezy, unhurried words and struck her glowing sword. Then:

"Wha...!!"

Emi's shout betrayed her honest distress. Just before she could release it, Divine Flying Blade had been completely annulled. In fact, the holy energy inside her sword, brimming with her bodily strength, was rapidly ebbing away.

She groaned as she felt her enemy grow even stronger.

"This is my power. The Evil Eye of the Fallen. The power to overwhelm all wielders of holy magic. It's mine, and mine alone."

"The Fallen...?! You couldn't be...!"

"Oh, I am. I'm here to release you from the cruelties of our mission. Sleep well."

As the silky voice continued, violet light began to gather toward the center of the mask.

"I'll be taking that holy sword back now."

"What are...!"

At that moment, a completely different kind of light whooshed past Emi's line of sight.

"Yusa!!"

Chiho's warning scream was an instant too late.

A huge, gold-colored streak advanced upon Emi from a place unseen, sending the pinned Emi flying with the force of a massive shock wave.

"Gahh!!"

Her body was steeled against one attack, only to be struck by an even more punishing one from another direction. She groaned as she flew through the air.

Blown like a cannonball right past Chiho, frozen in fear and quivering, she slammed against the side of a building and immediately lost consciousness.

The holy sword dropped out of her hand as she did.

The scythe-wielding maniac watched on as it did.

"…!"

But the metallic-looking sword fell softly, like a feather, down to the ground, before disappearing into a million particles of light.

Like a huge swarm of fireflies, the particles rushed toward the fallen body of their master, emitting a soft glow as they completely covered her. Then they flickered out of sight.

The scythe-wielding maniac greeted the sight with an annoyed clicking of his tongue.

"Yusa! Yusa!!"

Chiho, meanwhile, was half-crazed as she shook Emi's body.

Emi was on her stomach and unresponsive. Chiho was unable to lift up her loose, limply sagging body with her thin arms, leaving her to clutch Emi desperately while glaring at the other attacker, the one who wielded the golden light.

"Why? Why did you have to *do* this?!"

Chiho was screaming.

"Suzuno! Why?!"

Suzuno's hair, usually held together by her hairpin, was for some reason down to her waist as she carried a large war hammer in her hands.

"You were just like them all along, Suzuno, weren't you?! Yusa's just an obstacle in the way to you, just like she was to Olba!"

"......"

Suzuno looked down upon Chiho, a pained expression on her face.

"This...this isn't even fair! If Maou is a demon, what does it make *you*, stabbing Yusa in the back right when she's fighting for all of us?!"

Suzuno shut her eyes, no longer able to withstand Chiho's verbal attack, and shouted.

"Silence!"

Chiho froze in shock and fear, letting Suzuno advance upon her in a moment. Suzuno placed a finger on Chiho's forehead.

"Maou...h...help..."

Her consciousness fell into darkness.

The pink cell phone in her hand clattered noisily to the ground.

✳

"Ooh, there go the cops."

Maou noticed the shrill sirens of the emergency vehicles as they zoomed down the Koshu-Kaido Road. Night was finally starting to settle in, and as he pored over his cash-register printout, he anticipated that, while the customer stream went back to normal around dinner, it wouldn't be enough to make up for the damage done in the morning and afternoon.

The Greenland demotion was a joke, presumably, but Maou knew there was every chance Kisaki actually *would* dock Maou's hourly wages. His only choice was to attempt a catch-up tomorrow.

The tree-decorating gimmick had done wonders, though. It had attracted more families and large groups than usual, and—even more unexpectedly—a fair amount of couples and young women were interested in placing wishes on the tree, not just the children Maou anticipated.

Thanks to that, the bamboo tree was now completely swathed in colorful strips of folded paper.

The Star Festival decorations Maou had directed his staff to make were all things he learned about as part of his investigations into planet Earth's magical and occult folklore.

He had conducted a wide range of research in areas like religious ceremonies, alleged sources of magic, spiritual philosophy, and ancestral spirits. The bamboo décor was nothing if not authentic as a result.

It also gladdened Maou to have a teacher, one who said she worked at a nearby preschool, ask him to show her how to make Star Festival decorations. This kind of professional compliment was a real source of pride for him—she must have already known how to make simple origami for the class curriculum, after all.

Maou vowed to pick up a fresh tree from the Watanabe residence as soon as possible, hopefully tomorrow. He put together a rough schedule for the next morning in his mind as he directed his crew to prepare for closing procedures in between orders.

Then the phone rang.

Not Maou's cell phone, but the MgRonald office telephone.

Maou quizzically glanced at the clock, but picked up the receiver before giving it any further thought. The customer-service manual said never to let the phone go past two rings, and if the manual said it, it was law to Maou.

"Thank you for calling MgRonald at Hatagaya rail station. This is Maou speaking. How can I help you?"

"Hello? Oh, dear, hello!"

It sounded like a middle-aged woman, one who seemed bewildered by the fact that anyone had picked up.

"Is this Sadao Maou, perhaps? The shift supervisor and assistant manager?"

Who's this weirdo who knows my entire job title? Maou's eyebrows arched up incredulously, but he didn't let it show in his voice.

"Yes, this is Maou, shift supervisor for the evening... May I ask who's calling?"

"Oh! Well, my goodness, I'm very sorry! I was just surprised...

I didn't think you'd actually be the one answering the phone! Hee-hee-hee-hee!"

Maou silently begged the woman to stop laughing and just get on with her request.

"This is Chiho Sasaki's mother. Thank you for taking such good care of her in there!"

"Uh..."

Maou could feel the muscles in his back twitch like a tightly wound spring as he let out a short groan.

"W-well, thank you very much. You're Chi...er, Ms. Sasaki's mother, then? It's good to hear from you!"

He folded his upper body into a bow as he spoke, even though she wasn't actually there. It almost made him bang his head on the drink dispenser.

There was no need to get worked up. It was just the family of one of his employees calling.

It's not like he had some kind of especially close relationship with Chiho. Well, okay, they *were* pretty familiar with each other. But they definitely weren't a couple or anything. ...But, considering that Chiho's home cooking was apparently parent-approved, Maou found himself unable to figure out how to approach Chiho's mother, or even what he should call her.

The slight quiver in Maou's voice as his entire body erupted in a cold sweat must have been clear across the phone line.

"I do have to apologize, though. I understand Chiho's been causing assorted trouble for you as of late? Let me tell you, it was quite the surprise this morning, her coming home with a bicycle I'd never seen before!"

She almost seemed to be enjoying this.

"N-no, it's no trouble at all. Chiho is a wonderfully talented crew member, and...well, not to speak too personally here, but I'm on a rather tight budget at the moment, so I very much appreciate the large breakfast she prepared this morning."

"Ah, well, Chiho, you know... It's not that she never helps out around the house, but she's certainly never prepared that much food by herself before, so, you *knoooow*, if anything was undercooked or tasted off to you, don't be afraid to come out and say it, all right? Because I taught her everything I could think of, but whenever I offered to help, she turned all red and said she didn't need me around, so I just kind of let her do her own little thing!"

"Ah...yes... Well, I do appreciate it immensely. It was a truly delicious meal."

"Oh, my, my, my! I do apologize if I'm making you feel, you know, on the spot or anything! I know it's not a, ah, *serious* relationship or anything even *close* to that, but that girl, you know, she's always taken to her father, and it's not that she's never been friends with another boy before, but I tell you, I've never *seen* her work so hard on something like that before, so... Well, it makes a mom proud, you know? Seeing that. Oh, but I'm sorry, you're still working, aren't you?"

"No, er... I apologize."

That was the best Maou could manage. He had done nothing wrong, but the anxiety was making his entire body shiver.

But when Chiho's mother turned off the mom-of-a-girl-in-her-prime smarm and got down to business, the anxiety disappeared, replaced with something even more unpleasant.

"Is Chiho still working over there?"

"Huh?"

Maou peered at the clock. It was just past ten in the evening. Over an hour would have passed since Emi and Suzuno escorted her home.

"Is...she not home yet?"

"Well, I told her to go buy some milk for us at the convenience store on the way home, but she still isn't back yet, so I thought she was just, you know, hanging out over there after work again."

Maou could feel his mind freeze.

He'd never visited Chiho's house before, of course, but it couldn't have been that far away.

She seemed on pretty good terms with Emi, and it looked like she was opening up to Suzuno as well. Maybe the three of them went off somewhere else for a while.

But Maou wasn't feeling optimistic enough to believe it.

A thought that bounced around Maou's mind ever since Suzuno first moved in began to sound an alarm bell.

If Emi was with them, he doubted their being together would lead to any weird, out-of-control misunderstandings. But maybe that was just wishful thinking.

Ugh. That Hero is so useless.

"Um, Mrs. Sasaki?"

"Oh, dear, there's hardly any need to be so formal! Ooh, I've never had a young male friend of my daughter call me *that* before!"

Resisting the urge to ask Chiho's mother what the hell she found so joyous about this, Maou took a deep breath and plunged forward.

"I'd like you to just relax and stay at home until your daughter gets back."

The sound of his voice was transformed into digital signals and ferried over to the ear of Chiho's mother.

She grew quiet, the previous cattiness now very much a thing of the past, and hung up without another word.

Maou mentally patted himself on the back. Long-range demonic hypnosis was always a bit tricky.

A crew member called to him as he hung up the phone.

"What's up? Chi isn't home yet or something?"

"Doesn't sound like it. She's probably just out somewhere, I bet."

"Yeah. She had those friends with her, too, right?"

That was enough to put the employee's mind at ease as he ventured into the kitchen area, alcohol-based disinfectant and dust mop at the ready.

Maou flew into the staff break room, taking his cell phone out from his personal belongings. He sighed painfully once the screen came on. A call had come in nearly an hour ago.

It was from Chiho.

The phone had rung for ninety-nine seconds, the longest his provider allowed. Maou was far too cheap to sign up for something like voice mail, and his phone didn't allow him to automatically record calls to the internal voice-memo function.

If it was clear Maou wasn't going to pick up, Chiho was always polite enough to leave a text or call back some other day. And if someone like her was letting the phone ring for a minute and a half, something was definitely wrong.

He tried giving a call back, but her voice mail picked up after half a minute or so. The same thing happened on the following two attempts.

Stricken by anxiety, he next tried placing a call with Emi, the woman she was theoretically together with.

After several more attempts and banal voice-mail encounters, Maou jammed the END CALL button with a vengeance.

"Crap…!"

Emi's lack of responsiveness only served to further ratchet up his sense of dread.

Hopefully this wasn't anything more serious than the Hero ignoring his call.

"Maou? Oh, Maou?"

The employee from before was in the break room, apparently searching for him. The portable handset from the office telephone was in his hand.

"There's a phone call for you."

"From Chi?!"

The sudden, urgent response made the staffer shake his head in alarm.

"N-no, uh, it's from a Mr. Urushihara."

"Huhh?!"

Maou couldn't hide his surprise. Of all the people to be calling right now…

"…Hello?"

"Oh, Maou? Yo, it's me!"

But there he was, the former fallen angel and current Devil's Castle parasite, on the other end of the line.

"What the hell are you calling the office phone number for?! Where are you even calling from?"

Urushihara was under strict instructions not to venture outside unless absolutely necessary. There were no public phones anywhere near walking distance of Devil's Castle. So why was Maou faced with his nasal, whiny droning right now?

"Well, what? I know you never pick up your cell phone during work. I'm callin' from home, what's so bad about that?"

"From home?! When the hell did you buy a phone?! You *had* that kind of money?!"

"I don't have a phone, dude. You think I'm loaded or something? I'm using SkyPhone. You know, SkyPhone?"

"What's SkyPhone?"

"Basically, it's a phone you can use over the Internet. It's practically free to use, and you can even call landline phones with it. Like, signing up with a phone company is *so* last year, you know?"

Maou internally marveled at how Urushihara thought he knew everything after two months of life as a Japanese shut-in.

"All right. Fine. As long as it's not messing up our finances. So what do you want?"

"Jeez, you don't have to be so passive-aggressive like that. Ashiya asked me to find some inside info on Sentucky Fried Chicken, so I found it. You happy?"

Urushihara's own attitude wasn't much better. To the impatient Maou, this call didn't seem like much of an emergency.

"Yeah, yeah, sorry. But I'm kind of busy right now. I'll ask you about it at home."

He tried to hang up. Urushihara shouted at him before he could.

"Wait! You sure about that? You know, Sentucky... Something's really effed up about it."

"Ah?"

Maou could hear someone clicking away with a mouse on the other end. The audio quality was clearer than he'd expected.

"That location's managed by a guy named Mitsuki Sarue. The one with the Hatagaya address is, anyway. That's the one, right?"

"Yeah, I suppose."

"Well, the employee profile on the site says that Sarue's five

foot eleven and used to play rugby in college. He look like that
to you?"

"...It said what?"

Maou was too thrown to shoo him away now.

"That's gotta be someone else's profile. He was this little shrimpy
dude, just about as tall as you are. He looked like he'd be more at
home trying to hook up with chicks at a sleazy Kabukicho bar than
stiff-arming dudes on a rugby field."

"Oh, so you're calling me shrimpy now? Thanks a lot. Anyway,
Sarue's a pretty rare last name, so when I checked the personnel logs
on Sentucky's HQ site based outta Shibuya, that was the only Sarue
on the whole list."

"Uh...wow, what the hell kinda sites were you accessing?"

"And that's not all. According to the HQ logs, Sarue's supposed
to be working for the advertising department. Those logs list someone totally different as the manager at Hatagaya. Someone named
Tanaka. A girl!"

"Hohh..."

If Maou wasn't focused on other crises at the moment, he
could have just written that off as an inconsistency with SFC's
record-keeping.

But considering the events at hand, was it really safe to let this Mitsuki Sarue guy, manager at the Hatagaya Sentucky Fried Chicken, go
ignored when his very existence was now being called into question?

And then there was the missing-in-action Chiho, the unusually
silent Emi...and the girl who was with them.

"Hey, uh, is there any way to, like, look up where somebody is right
now if you have their cell number? Anything as useful as that?"

"Why d'you ask? I guess so, but I'd have to look."

"There *is*?!"

The twenty-first century was still news to Maou in countless ways.

"But I don't have anything like that right *now*, and figuring that
stuff out is probably gonna take a ton of time. I don't even even know
if this piece-of-crap PC can handle it or not..."

"All *right*! Sorry it's such a piece of crap! Jeez!"

It was a piece of crap Urushihara hadn't spent any of his own money on. Maou felt justified taking offense.

"But, like, what, you want to know where somebody is?"

"Yeeaaahh, kind of..."

"'Cause if it's Emilia, I could probably tell you."

Maou stopped breathing for a moment.

"What?!"

"Well, yeah. I kinda stuck a tracker in her shoulder bag. A hidden GPS transmitter."

"A hidden...GP...what?"

All this rapid-fire lingo was too much for him.

"Uh...well, just imagine one of those little bugging devices you see in movies. They use 'em to track wild animals and migrating birds and stuff, you know? They tell you what kind of path whoever's carrying it is taking, and how much time it took to do it."

There was no doubt Emi was a far more fearsome presence in the demons' lives than some collared wolf or bear. Tracking her was a brilliant idea.

"When did you do that?"

"Back a coupla days ago. I put it under the bottom layer of her bag so she wouldn't notice it right away."

It made sense. Maou recalled how Urushihara picked up all the purse contents scattered across the ground after Emi's flying leap off the stairway.

"Plus, you had to have noticed by now, right, Maou? Like, how Suzuno's not exactly a normal Japanese woman?"

Urushihara made it sound like the most obvious thing in the world.

"You didn't say anything, so I figured I'd play along, but you know, what reason would anyone have to move into this building unless they were seriously short on cash? I mean, there's *nothing*."

"...You're more observant than I thought."

"I don't know if Emilia's noticed, though, and that's why she's getting chummy with her. But our landlord isn't really normal, either, right? A regular human being signing a lease with that lady and moving right next to us… You'd have to be crazy to think that was just your typical tenant."

When Suzuno moved in, Maou wasn't concerned about the sort of things Ashiya mentioned—acting like a decent neighbor, being part of the community, blah blah blah.

His sole reaction was that anyone willing to sign on with *that* landlord could very well be from Ente Isla.

"So…the udon noodles and other stuff Suzuno made for us…"

"Well, duh, I'm half-angel, remember? Holy power isn't gonna mess up *my* body. I ate everything you gave me. It didn't hurt you at all, Maou?"

That must have been what put Ashiya down for the count—the assorted food Suzuno brought into Devil's Castle.

Both on Earth and in Ente Isla, food played a primary role in the sacred ceremonies generally known as "consecrations."

On Earth, the food involved was usually bread or wine, placed into special holy vessels for use in religious rites.

Ente Isla, meanwhile, often used special ingredients, grown within Church grounds, raised with the help of holy water, and instilled with the power of the gods themselves.

All of the food Suzuno brought with her must have been consecrated on Ente Isla.

And it was easy to imagine why Suzuno was so generously sharing it with Maou and his cohorts. She was an assassin—one whose approach chiefly differed from Emi's in its leisurely pace.

Consuming purely cultivated, consecrated food could indeed be hazardous to the health of a lesser demon. But…

"Hey, the worse it is for you, the better it tastes, right?"

"*That's* your take on it?"

Maou's utter indifference exasperated Urushihara.

A higher-level demon eating consecrated food was essentially the same as placing holy force directly into their body. It would hurt him in the long run, but only in the same way trans fats and "bad" cholesterol would hurt a normal person. It wasn't something that would drain his strength and shut down his bodily functions with a snap of the fingers.

In Ashiya's case, the cause was partly that he'd all but used up his demonic power in the battle two months ago and partly that Suzuno's cuisine simply didn't agree with his stomach.

"It's not like she's flailing away at us the way Olba did. I'm not enough of a prick to complain about whatever someone feeds me, and hey, it helps us save some cash. I figured we'd use her for as long as we could get away with it."

"Yeah, but isn't it kind of like that documentary about the guy who ate burgers every day just to see what would happen?"

"You know, Ashiya used to bring up that film all the time when he lectured me. I think he's a huge fan or something."

Maou chuckled to himself.

"What's he doing right now, by the way?"

Ashiya seemed unlikely to remain still if he discovered his next-door neighbor was his mortal enemy.

"Well, he got home, ate some udon, and now he's grunting and groaning on the crapper."

"...Oh."

The mental image of his beloved general and tactical genius meeting his match against indigestion almost brought tears to Maou's eyes.

"I think he was getting pretty suspicious of Suzuno, too, though. It's just that you never said anything, so I guess he kept quiet because it was helping keep the lights on."

"...I'm glad he's got faith in me, but dude, he doesn't have to ruin his health just to save a few yen."

"Yeah, seriously. So that's why I snuck that GPS transmitter in there, but Emilia hasn't done anything suspicious at all, really, so I turned off the tracker a while ago."

"Huh. All right. I gotcha. So you can use that to see where she is now?"

"Probably. The battery's gonna run out pretty soon, I think..."

Maou heard Urushihara tap away at the keyboard for a moment.

"Whoa."

Some surprising turn of events stopped his fingers.

"Whoa, what?"

"So she was at this intersection between MgRonald and our place, then all of a sudden she's moving in this straight line. Like, right though buildings and stuff, like she's flying or something."

"Where's she going?"

Urushihara's reply was short and to the point.

"Tokyo city hall, it looks like. The GPS signal's been hovering around building number one, the main one, for a while now."

"…Great. That's all I need to know. Way to actually help out for a change."

"'For a change' is kinda mean, you know."

Maou nodded before bringing up something else that crossed his mind.

"By the way, how much did that track editor or whatever cost you?"

The moment he asked the question, there was a flushing sound over the phone line, followed by the old, sticky door opening. Ashiya was out of the john.

"It's a *tracker*, dude. Uh, Ashiya's back out now, so I don't really want to say, but…"

"I got your back on this one, I promise. Just tell me."

Maou could feel the hesitation over the phone.

"I got it from an Akihabara online store for…uh, forty thousand… on your card."

The sound of something heavy falling echoed across the line.

Through the phone's audio, Maou easily pictured Ashiya fainting in shock from Urushihara's extravagant purchasing habits.

"Well, at least you're honest. I don't know what Ashiya's gonna say, and I'm not sure I wanna know what you bought that thing for in the first place, but you got my permission. You really helped me out tonight."

"I'd kinda appreciate it if you could get home ASAP and tell Ashiya that. I'm a little scared…"

"Can't. Not done working yet. But thanks. See you."

"Whoa, wait, Mao—"

Ignoring Urushihara's pleas, Maou hung up the phone.

"I don't want you bums following me, either. Not with all your demonic energy drained. You'd just get hurt. A good supervisor needs to watch over the condition of his staff."

After whispering it to himself, Maou took a deep breath, almost choking on the grab bag of powerful odors that pervaded the break room, than slapped his cheeks a bit to wake himself up.

"If this is still just Emi getting sidetracked, she's gonna have some *serious* explaining to do."

He took a look around the room before his eyes stopped on the cleaning-supply closet.

"Huh? Are we cleaning the floors already, Maou?"

One of the crew members noticed Maou leaving the break room with a mop in his hand.

"Well, uh…yeah. I need to go out for a bit."

"What? With a mop? Where?"

Maou had trouble responding for a moment, but drummed up the most stoic look he could.

"There's something annoying me that I need to clean up."

"Um, I'm not quite sure I know what you… Ah! Maou, wait a sec!"

Ignoring the employee's cries, Maou ran across the dining area.

"Maou!"

"Don't worry! I promise I'll come back!"

"I don't care about that! Just don't leave us in here!"

The employee's shout sounded like a battle horn to Maou's ears as he boarded his trusty two-wheeled Dullahan and flew off.

Dullahan's bell rang its approval at its master's burning spirit, its staccato ding-a-ling now a beastlike roar.

Like a cavalryman of old, Satan, lord of the demon realms, held his mop firmly in hand as he galloped down a side road removed from Koshu-Kaido to avoid police attention, heading straight for the city center in Hatsudai-Shinjuku.

*

"Hmm… So the angel refuses to fall that easily."

A cross floated in the sky, emitting an eerie purple light. The creepy scythe-wielding maniac looked up at it, and the body of Emi that was crucified upon it, as he muttered softly. Suzuno, standing right next to him, had her eyes cast upward as well.

Emi, hair blowing in the wind, glared downward upon the pair, even as her body remained limp.

Above them, an enormous crescent moon, far bigger than anything seen on Earth, showered its white glow upon Emi and the entirety of Tokyo city hall's main building below.

The area within the light was cut off from reality, much as the Devil King could wrangle with his magical barriers.

The heliport at the top of the towering building, the one point in Shinjuku closer to the moon than anywhere else, seemed utterly detached from the hustle and bustle of the city below. It was quiet, with only the howling wind present to witness this otherworldly scene and its denizens.

"Just…give it up already."

Like a holy warrior awaiting her judgment, Emi had been bathed in that purple light again and again, her body now nearly bereft of holy energy.

The light that scythe-wielding maniac wielded really did have the power to drain her strength, after all.

He was apparently after the Better Half holy sword within her body, but no matter how often the light coursed across her, the Holy Silver that resonated with her inner strength to form the sword refused to budge from within.

"I'm not resisting you. You just can't do it. So can you try again some other time?"

Emi was recognized by the Church as the Hero with the power to slay the Demon King. They presented her with the Holy Silver, which she blithely accepted into her body with the help of the Church's holy energy. But she had never given a single thought to how, exactly, this Holy Silver was stored within her.

The Better Half itself seemed to present itself as a physical weapon, one forged in some heavenly foundry somewhere, but the Cloth of the Dispeller that protected her was composed strictly of light, having no physical presence whatsoever.

Which meant, as she now questioned within her mind, that the Cloth wasn't powered by Holy Silver, perhaps.

Robbed of the abilities she deftly harnessed in her war against the demons, her current state made her realize for the first time just how little she knew about her powers.

"Just...give it up already. Release me and Chiho."

The words weakly spilled out of Emi's mouth.

Chiho was still unconscious, tossed to the ground behind the scythe-wielding creep with her hands bound behind her.

"I'm afraid that won't be happening. In fact, I plan to have this lovely little lady help me out in more than a few ways."

The maniacal, scythe-wielding, convenience-store robber's shoulders pulsed up and down as he laughed.

"...You worked in front of MgRonald so you could hit on women, Sarue?"

Emi summoned up all the sarcasm she could. The scythe-wielder's shoulders stopped cold.

"Ah. You noticed."

"Women are a lot more sensitive to stupid men and their exhibitionist streaks than you think."

Even captured and depleted of strength, Emi still never shut up. The scythe-wielder laughed again.

"Fair enough. I did call myself Sarue. However..."

He raised a hand to remove his ski mask.

"My true name is Sariel. Sariel the archangel."

Now he was revealed—his well-ordered, boy-like visage, his purple eyes, and…

"I didn't know orange eyeshadow was all the rage in heaven right now."

The orange paint around the angel's eyes was clear now as he introduced himself.

"Heh… It's proven to be quite obstinate."

The angel called Sariel shrugged and laughed to himself, as if wistfully complaining about bad weather outside.

The mask was off, but the plastic rain poncho and camo pants were still on. The well-defined features of his face, now bedecked in bright orange, made for an almost clownish sight.

A heretofore unknown enemy revealing himself was usually meant to be a dramatic situation. For Emi, it took some effort to keep from cracking up.

"Wouldn't be much of a crime deterrent if it came off that easily, you know?"

"Hmph. It is of no great concern to me. I needed those sunglasses to hide my purple eyes anyway."

"You got a lot more issues to tackle than *that*, I'd say."

The overpowering cologne he had on was no doubt meant to conceal the odor from the antitheft paintballs.

But his equally overpowering approach to chatting up women was likely more a permanent part of his personality.

Emi knew Sariel's name well.

It was a name that appeared frequently in the Church's holy texts. Several departments of the Church, including the Council of Inquisitors themselves, venerated him as an angel symbolic to their cause.

He was among the upper echelons of heavenly dwellers, enough so that he bore the title of archangel.

The purple light was the Evil Eye of the Fallen, a force that allowed him to defeat even high-level angels, sending them reeling down into the mortal world below.

One story even pinned the blame on Sariel for the fall of Lucifer.

"You know, you really had me concerned. Such a powerful weapon, being bandied around on another world. And now I reek and my beautiful face looks like an orange panda's. I honestly considered taking my own life at one point."

Emi rued his inability to go through with it. She had no idea Sariel was such an immature, narcissistic, smelly archangel.

"I failed to defeat you, I allowed you to regroup with the Devil King, and I almost had to miss work on our opening day. Quite the ordeal, I can tell you. But!"

Sariel the orange panda smiled, then turned toward Suzuno.

"Thanks to *you*, I managed to capture her without even breaking a sweat. And look at the lovely bonus prize I found!"

Emi followed Sariel's eyes. Suzuno hung her head low, teeth still gritted.

"Chiho Sasaki. Quite a valuable sample, you know. A girl from another world who knows of the Devil King, and yet desires nothing more than to be close to him. She will provide us with untold research into how the Devil King's powers affect the human mind!"

Emi rolled her eyes.

Sariel's villainous, almost cartoonlike manner of speaking was one thing, but his current act was nothing short of unbelievable.

"You were listening in on us at that intersection?!"

She had noticed nothing suspicious near her at the time.

"Psh. You could at least be kind enough to call it 'spying.'"

Sariel was overly eager to confess to his stalker tendencies. Emi wrinkled her nose in response, apparently enough to merit another blast of the Evil Eye of the Fallen from Sariel.

"Nngh!"

Emi groaned. It didn't physically hurt her at all, but whenever she was exposed to it, the discomfort made it feel like her stomach was going to turn inside out.

"The holy sword is not something meant to be wielded by a human. Before it returns to the people of Ente Isla, we must pluck it out from you with our own hands. Such is the consensus of all of heaven, you see."

"Aaaaaahhh!"

A particularly strong blast of light almost made Emi lose consciousness.

"Hmm. No dice, then? ...Oh?"

Sariel halted the barrage to think for a moment. He walked toward the edge of the heliport.

He looked down, across the nearly eight hundred feet to the ground. Then he found something. He laughed.

"Well, well! Look at the little gnat who blundered his way in here."

Suzuno's head darted upward. Emi, too, lifted her head an inch or two.

"Ma...ou..."

Chiho, still unconscious, called his name as she struggled in her sleep.

"I couldn't say how he penetrated my barrier, but there's no need to show him an improper welcome. Is there, Bell?"

Suzuno's body convulsed at the sound of her name.

"He doesn't have any of his putrid little underlings with him. Even you could defeat the Devil King easily enough at this point."

"...!"

She flashed an uneasy look at Emi, but her limp head, and the hair blowing wildly around her, made it impossible to gauge her expression.

"There's nothing to fear. This building is bathed in the glow of my moonlight. There is none of that nasty negative energy for the Devil King to harness. Go."

Even as her face remained pale, Suzuno dejectedly followed his words, walking to the edge of the roof.

As a member of the Church, there was no way she could defy the order of an angel, one very much a target of worship in her domain. To both the Council of Inquisitors and the new Reconciliation Panel, Sariel was undeniably an object of veneration.

The weight of her resolve groaned heavily on her back. The voice that followed made it all the heavier.

"...This is what you want?"

"!"

Suzuno gasped as she stood motionless.

"You want the Hero with the Holy Sword and the Devil King to meet their end on an alien world? For Ente Isla to be the exact same as it was before you came here? For peace to reign as if nothing happened? Does that work for you?"

It was the strong wind that made her legs shake. Suzuno forced herself to believe that. If she didn't, she would have to admit otherwise.

She would have to admit that she was an agent of evil in the end, one of many tentacles writhing in the darkness that lurked at the very core of the Church.

"What could be troubling you? What you are doing is right. It is just. I, the symbolic leader of the Reconciliation Panel, guarantee it. Now, go. A word or two from me, and no one in the Church could ever lay a finger on you. You have nothing to fear."

Sariel stood defiantly behind Suzuno.

"Besides, this was the plan from the start, wasn't it? We're just a bit behind schedule, is all. Ente Isla will enjoy an era of peace. One free of the Devil King's looming presence. One where the myth of the Hero with the holy sword shall be passed down for generations to come. You and I, Bell... We merely came to tie up the loose ends. There is no need for the audience to see all the furor and confusion behind the curtain."

His tone was casual, as if they were discussing where to go for lunch.

It is true. I know I am in the right. What problem could defeating the Devil King possibly pose to us?

It's not that Sariel is here to kill Emilia, besides. World peace, and my own goals... We can achieve both, without a single hitch.

"Suzuno..."

The papier-mâché fortress Suzuno attempted to build in her heart instantly crumpled at the sound of her voice.

"…Chiho."

Chiho, bound and lying on her side, watched Suzuno as the tears streamed down her face.

"Why…why…?"

Suzuno couldn't will herself to look. Her eyes darted around the night sky.

Her kimono flapped haphazardly in the rising gale. Bringing her right hand upward, she removed the cross-shaped hairpin from her head.

Her hair spread forth like a pair of jet-black wings in the wind. The hairpin began to shine.

"…Light of Iron."

A glowing, golden hammer of war materialized with her voice, the "hammer of justice" that served as the Scythe of Death's most notorious symbol during countless cruel, heartless inquisitions.

With hammer in hand, Suzuno shot toward the ground like a golden comet.

"Please…help me…already…"

Droplets of silver from her eyes and flew into the night sky.

"I don't want to sacrifice anyone else!!"

"Whooaaarrghh!!"

The man at Suzuno's upcoming landing point was startled to notice the girl above him.

Aiming squarely at the man as he was about to park his bicycle, Suzuno swung her hammer downward. The pathway crumbled with a roar, the man reduced to smithereens…it seemed at first.

"Damn! That was close! What the hell! You want me to die here?!"

Sadao Maou was on his rear end, mere inches from the edge of the hammer, as he griped. Then:

"Ah."

He looked at the flattened mass underneath the hammer, stretched out like a steamroller had run over it. His face tightened.

"Du…"

"Du?"

"Duuuuuuuuuullahaaaaaaaaaannnnnnnnn!!!!"

Sadao Maou's woeful wail echoed off the high-rises of western Shinjuku.

Maou clutched at the metallic hulk that used to be his trusty Dullahan as he glared at Suzuno.

"Suzuno, you incredible, incorrigible incompetent! What the hell did you do *that* for?! Do you have a grudge against Dullahan or something?! Give me back the two months I spent with this guy! And after that, give me a new bike, too! And the registration fees! And help me pay the bulk-garbage fee to give this guy a decent burial!"

"Shut up!"

"Agh!"

Suzuno, paying him no mind, fixed her next swing squarely upon Maou's head.

Maou dodged in a panic, but the sight of the hammer whizzing by a few inches from his nose made him break into a cold sweat.

"Whoa, whoa, wait! Time out!"

"Silence!"

"Dude, dude, listen to me for a…"

"Silence, silence, *silence!*"

"Aaagggh!"

Faced with a war hammer swung at full force, Maou turned his back and ran.

"Halt! Devil King Satan!"

"The hell I'm halting! *You* stop first! Please!"

Running at full speed, Maou finally managed to open some space between himself and Suzuno.

"One minute! C'mon, just one minute!"

Maou held his index finger in the air.

"…?"

Suzuno stared, temporarily bewildered at the sight. But:

"!!!!!!"

Maou must have mistaken her indecision for agreement to his request. She gaped silently.

His mop was now on the ground as he slowly, deliberately, began to remove his clothes.

He took off the trademark MgRonald red polo tee, revealing the running shirt below, its colors faded from overwashing. His belt followed, accompanied by his work pants, allowing his world-beating UniClo sweat-wicking boxers to say hello to the outside world.

Once the cap went off, Maou wore nothing but his undies, a T-shirt, and a smile as he folded up his uniform and pants, dropping them off on the side of the pathway. Then, picking up his dingy mop, he turned to Suzuno.

"Okay, now I'm ready."

"Wh-what are you *doing*?!"

Suzuno simply had to ask.

No matter what world he was in, a Devil King never stripped to his skivvies before battle.

But here he was, this deviant sporting boxers, fake-leather shoes, and a grimy mop, snorting derisively at Suzuno like she was an idiot.

"Hah! Like some unemployed ditz like *you* would ever understand."

Maou's eyes flashed toward the folded uniform off to the side.

"Listen, I don't *own* those. MgRonald *loaned* those to me! If I get 'em messed up for nonwork reasons, I'm gonna have to pay restitution, all right? And the Devil's Castle kinda doesn't have that sort of surplus cash sitting around right now!"

"Wha...!"

Maou exuded devilish majesty as he spoke. Despite everything that happened so far, Suzuno couldn't help but blush.

"Also, what are *you* doing, huh?! Where do you get off, getting my employees caught up in this?!"

He boldly pointed straight at Suzuno with his mop.

"I didn't want to go hard on you. You had guts, moving in right next to me like that, and you're a hell of a good cook. But if you screw around with my job and hurt my crewmates, you're gonna have one pissed-off assistant manager to deal with!"

For an instant, she wavered in the face of such overpowering impact.

"What...!"

Then, in an instant, Maou was upon her.

"Ngh!"

She tried to duck down, avoiding the handle of the mop as he swung it, but then fell back in a panic as the mop head, swarm of fluffy, black pieces of mystery garbage stuck to it, flew straight at her face.

Suzuno was amazed to see how Maou handled the mop, like a certain amphibious ninja with a *bo* pole. She finally managed to deflect the head away with the middle part of her hammer, preparing his backswing to be countered with a swipe of her own.

"Oop!"

But the swing was again just a moment too late, as Maou made a grand leap backward.

It was no regular jump. One leg was all he needed to jump high, and fast, straight up before landing on a streetlight. Suzuno was thunderstruck, eyes wide-open as she looked upward at his body— the lower part—and once again felt her cheeks turn red at the sight.

"This...this is no time for *that,* you perverted monster!"

"You don't like it? Blame yourself!"

Maou's running shirt, perhaps grazed by the light from Suzuno's hammer, ripped apart from the stomach out, flying into rags in the night air.

Now Suzuno was looking up toward a boxer-clad Devil King in severe danger of exposing a little too much of himself.

"So you retained some demonic power all along. Did you not, you sexually deranged Devil King?"

"Yeah, well, there was no telling when someone like you would come along. They call it a trump card because you don't show it until the very end."

"...When did you notice that I was not Japanese?"

Maou sighed like an embittered bus driver.

"The moment I first saw you, when did you think? No Japanese person in her right mind would start caring for this bunch of destitute schlubs living next to her the moment she moved in! Not even some samurai-era Japanese beauty like you! And sure, it made me happy, but before that, it was incredibly sketchy, you know?"

In the end, Suzuno was the only one out of all of them with zero doubts about her act.

"What...what do you care about Chiho, then?!"

"I taught Chi everything from A to Z about the job! She's my right-hand girl now! And if you thought it was just some kind of thin, fragile relationship, you've *seriously* got the wrong idea!"

Maou jumped down to the ground, keeping a polite distance away from Suzuno.

"But it's too bad, huh? I thought you had some potential, trying to take us on by yourself and getting all chummy with Emi. But you're just another Olba, aren't you?"

Suzuno's back teeth gritted against each other.

"Long as you can score some power, you don't care what sacrifices you have to make along the way, yeah? You don't care how much of a hypocrite it makes you. If I let someone like *you* slay me, the sheer patheticness of it all would make me cry. What makes you guys different at all from us demons?"

"S-silence...!"

"Not gonna happen. I'm a demon, and I just *love* making people despise me."

Maou's eyes were pointed straight toward Suzuno's.

"So answer me! Tricking Emi, getting Chi involved... Aren't you even a *little* ashamed of yourself?!"

"Siiiilennnnnnnce!"

"Yeoow!"

"...Wha?"

She had swung her hammer, fully expecting him to dodge again, only to find she made a clean hit.

The boxer-clad Maou was a tough sight to watch. He was on his hands and knees a distance away, groveling like a crushed spider.

"Damn...that hurt... Rngh!"

"What are you doing?! Why did you not dodge that?!"

Flustered, Suzuno ran up to Maou, despite having just sent him flying.

He was now covered in abrasions from head to toe, a side effect of his free-love approach to mortal combat.

The puddle of blood he had coughed up indicated that the hammer's shock wave made it to his internal organs.

"I, I tried to, but, but I exhausted my demonic force... I couldn't release as much power as I thought..."

"Whaaa?!"

"Before I came here...I hypnotized someone over the phone... and I had to get through the barrier over city hall, too... Ah, crap, I totally miscalculated this. I thought it'd hold out a little more than that."

Maou finally propped himself up, but quickly fell facedown on the ground, unable to gather any strength whatsoever.

One more full-swing blast from Suzuno right now would send Satan, the Devil King, to wherever his beloved mount was enjoying the afterlife right now. But:

"...What? Not gonna do it? It's your chance...*cough, cough*...to be a hero."

Standing in front of Maou, who was still grinning defiantly even as he grunted in pain, Suzuno could do nothing but cast her eyes downward in shame. There was nothing, no final trump card, the Devil King could use to corner Suzuno any longer. But she couldn't do it.

"Must've been real embarrassing for you, huh?"

"...What?"

"You want to beat me fair and square, then go home in triumph with Emi. That's why you used Chi's phone to call me. You wanted to have me defeat an opponent you were powerless to defy."

Maou raised a shaky arm toward the skyline, and the Tokyo city hall building that dominated it.

"You...realized that...?"

The golden hammer disappeared from Suzuno's hand. She fell to her knees next to the fallen Maou.

A cross-shaped glass hairpin fell from the hand that once held the hammer, plinking against the ground.

"Well, it wasn't hard to guess. You were proceeding along with your plan, gradually weakening us with your food. You weren't gonna suddenly go dirty and kidnap those two. If you were gonna do that, you could have just poisoned us the normal way. Or, hell, you could've killed us any number of other ways and just gone home. You didn't have to care about Emi."

A pink clamshell cell phone, one Maou was familiar with, fell out of Suzuno's kimono sleeve. It was Chiho's. The strap with the cartoon clip art of MgRonald menu items on it was a telltale sign.

"Someone able to kidnap the Hero without a struggle wasn't going to just sit pretty while Chi tried calling me for a minute and a half. Whoever *did* call me, had to be capable of doing it. Jeez, you really hammered me, you know that? You better pay my medical bills if you broke any bones."

Maou slowly checked over his body as he pleaded his case. He tried to painfully ease himself upward, but was interrupted.

"...The angel is here."

Suzuno picked up the flagging Maou's hand. Maou readily accepted it.

"Huh. Yeah, I guess you couldn't defy an Ente Islan. What's he here for?"

"...To recover Emilia's holy sword, he said."

"Huh? Without killing me first?"

This confused Maou. Why would the angels want their sword back from the Hero if the Devil King was still alive and well?

"I do not know why... He said it was nothing a human should wield..."

"Well, we can let him deal with that on his time. What about Chi?"

Blissfully kicking away the topic, one that could very well decide the fate of every human being on Ente Isla, Maou pressed forward. To a demon, the farther away the Better Half was, the better.

Suzuno hesitated for a moment before continuing.

"A valuable sample, is how he put it. He wants to make her into a research subject...someone with feelings for the Devil King, despite a full knowledge of his deeds... He wanted to examine her heart, and her mind."

"…That bastard…"

At that instant, Suzuno instinctively looked upward.

Maou's voice was darker, grittier, and angrier than she had ever heard it.

"You."

"Wh-what…?"

"Who was it? Who was the puke-ridden psycho-freak bastard who did it?"

"Um…puke-ridden…?"

Maou grabbed the confused Suzuno by the shoulders, shouting at her.

"I *said*, gimme the name of that angel bastard who's trying to kidnap a member of my effin' *staff*, dammit!"

"It, it's Sariel."

The sheer forcefulness of the tirade made Suzuno dribble out the name.

"…The Evil Eye of the Fallen, huh? Hell, no wonder Emi couldn't take him."

"You…know of that?"

Maou's apparently intimate familiarity with archangels surprised her.

"Yeah, we got some history. It just had to be that womanizing freak, didn't it? I *knew* it—Mitsuki Sarue!"

Finally, that flamboyant store-manager wannabe connected himself to the current state of affairs in Maou's mind.

"W-wait! Are you going now? You are injured!"

Suzuno tried to stop the snorting Maou, all but ready to sprint into city hall.

"Of course I am! My precious coworker is quaking in fear waiting for me!"

"You can't! You'll be killed! Sariel's force grows stronger the closer he is to the moon! There's no way you could defeat him up on the roof, bereft of—"

"So you think I'm gonna run instead?"

Maou's quiet reply stopped Suzuno's panicked advice cold.

"It's my job to handle crisis management for the crew on my shift.

Chi's a valuable employee. I have to protect her. It's basically my fault anyway that Sariel chased Emi into this world. I'm not dumb enough to foist that responsibility on someone else and run for the hills. That's just *shameless!*"

"!!"

Suzuno froze, caught off guard by this unanticipated speech.

"How the hell am I supposed to conquer the world if I can't take care of business here? I can't! So I'm going! And, worst-case scenario, if I can't beat Sariel, I might be able to get Chi out of there!"

Then, with a demonic roar, he brought his pained body to a frenzied run.

"Hyaaahhh! Hang on, Chi!"

He was inside City Hall before Suzuno could stop him. She stood dumbfounded for a moment, but quickly snapped out of it as she turned up toward the roof.

Sariel had closed off the entire area from the outside, which meant nobody was going to stop Maou's mad rush, but the elevators weren't going to be operational. The climb to the top would sap even more of his energy.

And even if it didn't, this was a wounded man in his drawers. It was hard to see how he'd possibly win this.

"Why…why are you doing this? You are a demon!"

Suzuno wailed at the heavens above.

"You are the Demon King… How can you even *say* things like that?"

Then she picked up Chiho's cell phone and returned to her feet. There, on the screen, was the word *Maou*, followed by a modest heart symbol.

"If that is the Devil King's stance, I could hardly allow myself to remain as shameless as I was."

Wiping her accumulated tears, Suzuno took a deep breath, feeling her pulse calm down.

Never misunderstand what needs to be protected. Never allow yourself to lose sight of the justice that must prevail.

As head of the Council of Inquisitors, as a proud member of the Church, it was a credo that always reigned over her heart.

Was there any other reason that she traveled so far away, all the way to Japan?

Suzuno racked her brain, searching for a way to open up a larger hole for the justice she needed to push through to the surface.

Then she recalled a passing observation from Sariel.

Negative energy for the Devil King to harness.

Lifting her head, Suzuno grasped the hairpin that fell to the ground, turned away from City Hall, and, in a flash, flew into the night sky.

"Hmph… It doesn't fill me with joy, but so be it. I hate to perform such a grave disservice on a lady, but forgive me. It is simply part of my appointed task. I was expecting my Evil Eye to make the Holy Silver simply divorce itself from your body, but I suppose I will have to directly take it from you instead."

Sariel's face was pained as he spoke to the limp, exhausted Emi.

"Directly…?"

Repeated exposure to the Evil Eye of the Fallen had robbed her of nearly all her stamina, but the sensation of Sariel suddenly reaching for a blouse button sent emergency signals across her entire body, making her open her eyes and bite back.

"Hey! What're you doing?!"

"Harvesting the Holy Silver from your body. Oh, but this won't be a horror-movie scene, so try not to worry about that. Think of it as a type of surgery, one where my holy force will provide all the anesthesia you need…"

"That's not the problem! I… Stop it! I'll kill you!"

Emi screamed as she flailed her head around, the only free part of her body. But Sariel paid no heed as he calmly, efficiently removed the buttons on Emi's business-casual blouse from the collar.

"Wh-what are you doing to Yusa, you weirdo?!"

Another voice of dissent echoed behind Sariel's back. His hand stopped for a moment as he turned around.

"Trust me, I would never want to do anything to humiliate a woman. The present situation notwithstanding, I am considered quite the gentleman up in the heavens. But if I had to place my good name against the recovery of our Holy Silver, I'm afraid my mission must take priority."

"That's awful! Just awful! Why do all you angels have to be these absolutely horrible people?!"

Chiho Sasaki, the girl Crestina Bell brought up to the roof, focused upon Sariel, her eyes filled with as much hatred as she could manage.

She had awakened just before Bell had gone off to eliminate their recent intrusion. Ever since, she had been savaging the archangel with as much abuse as her creative mind was capable of generating.

"Well, considering your position near the Devil King, I suppose Lucifer is your primary experience with them, is it not? I would prefer you not to lump him in with the rest of us, thank you."

"Urushihara's a self-serving shut-in creep, but at least he's not a molester like you!"

There was little love lost for either of them, apparently.

"Yes, yes, all right. I'll be happy to listen to your running commentary after we return. So would you mind being quiet for a moment?"

"Whoa, not so fast there! What're you gonna do to Chiho?!"

Now it was Emi shouting out in protest.

"You aren't gonna take her back with you to Ente Isla, are you?!"

"But of course. I have to, if I want to research her."

"Oh, yeah, that's a *totally* normal thing to say... Hey! Don't touch me!"

"I am a gentleman. I will do my best not to look, so please be quiet. Besides, I am not a fan of, shall we say, 'petite' women."

Sariel did not hesitate to say one of the few things no man should ever say to a woman, ever.

Emi's emotions exploded to the point where they almost blew her into next Tuesday. She quickly regained her senses as she directed yet more vitriol at Sariel.

"Oh, you are *dead*! You are *so* dead! And I'm not gonna let you take Chiho away, either! I'll make sure you regret every single thing you're doing right now!"

"My, you certainly do make a lot of noise, don't you? Did you think I was going to take a scalpel to that girl like a lab animal?"

Sariel's face tightened, as if hurt by the rebuke.

"I have nothing but high praise for her beauty. Once my research is complete, I would be more than happy to promote her to the echelon of the angels and greet her as my wedded wife."

His face, and his face alone, was the very definition of angelic. But the juxtaposition with what he was saying transformed his smile into something downright indecent.

"I'd rather die!"

Chiho opened her mouth as wide as possible as she turned down the proposal.

"But, of course, I will need to examine her in great detail, from head to toe, before that. I need to know how building a close relationship with the Devil King affects a human being, both in body and in spirit."

"You're a hopeless monster! D-don't touch me! You make me sick, you freak!"

"Molester!"

"Pervert!"

"Die!"

"Psychopath!"

"False angel!"

"Peeping tom!"

"Panty raider!"

"I didn't go *that* far!!"

Being sandwiched in by Emi and Chiho's bashing was finally enough to make Sariel snap.

"Quit it! Now! Both of you! Don't you understand how easy I'm making this for you?!"

Sariel removed his hands from Emi's chest long enough to thrust them high, the anger writ clear on his face.

From out of thin air, the scythe from earlier materialized. Holy Silver must have been at its core as well. Letting his rage drive him,

Sariel took the tip of the scythe and pressed it against the blouse over her chest.

"If I may say so, I am allowed to place the Holy Silver above Emilia's life if need be! I had pity on you, and you repay me with nothing but this incessant blather! I have no qualms with slashing it right out of you, you realize!"

Chiho gasped at Sariel's fearsome tirade. Emi refused to back down.

"So? Go ahead. I don't how the Holy Silver's fused into my body, either. It's just too bad I wouldn't get to see you all heartbroken after the Silver disappears along with my body."

Emi was drawing a line in the sand. Sariel ejected an irritated grunt.

"In that case, I'd be happy to work on this girl first."

Sariel's purple eyes turned toward the fallen Chiho, scythe still pointed squarely at Emi.

"A human intimately tangled with the demons. Transporting her to Ente Isla and examining her body may offer us a way to rescue those tormented by the demons of our own land."

Chiho's face drained itself of blood. Her eyes were still determinedly fixed upon Sariel, but she was still just a teenager, one with no special powers save a half-angel friend who was currently affixed to a cross. If she were tossed into an unknown world by herself, she'd be well and truly helpless.

"I dare you to lay even a finger on Chiho. You'll be sorry!"

Sariel cackled as he turned back toward Emi.

"Well, I appreciate your spunk, but what exactly do you think you can do now?"

Emi's dark eyes focused themselves upon Sariel. The frustration was palpable.

"Not me."

"What?"

Her hatred bubbled, even outclassing Sariel's, as she seethed.

"I said, if you lay a finger on Chiho, the Devil King's not gonna let that go."

"The Devil King?"

The sheer hilarity of the idea outshone any surprise Emi intended. Sariel laughed, loud and mocking.

"So *that's* your big reveal? The Devil King? Emilia the Hero pinning her hopes upon the Devil King?! You've been in collusion with him this whole time, haven't you?"

"No, I haven't. Didn't you notice? You were across the street from MgRonald."

Emi spoke with a firm voice, even as she felt a damp haze gather over her heart.

"That girl's an employee over there, and the Devil King's her assistant manager and shift supervisor. If an employee's in danger, it's the boss's job to step in."

"Have you lost your mind, Emilia? Do you truly believe the Devil King would stay beholden to the laws and practices of a human world? You are fully aware of the Devil King's current state. A puny weakling with only the barest flicker of demonic force left. Even if he came here, what could he manage against an archangel like myself?"

That much was true. Maou was just another young man, one with no more evil force than a low-level demon grunt back in his own realm, if even that. But even if his goals and behavior had gone off on a pretty massive tangent as of late, the trademark Devil King pride he retained hadn't faded one iota.

"He's not beholden to anything. He *protects* it all, all by himself. That's Sadao Maou for you. Shift supervisor at the Hatagaya rail station MgRonald."

"Yusa..."

Emi's eyes met with Chiho's, seeking her approval.

Chiho, face wet with tears, gave her a firm nod.

"This is a perfect farce! The Hero, trusting in the Devil King! Heh-heh-heh... Well, where is he? I want to see this human-loving Devil King for myself! Let him take the stage whenever he likes! Not that he even exists! And not that he could even fly up here anyway. Bell's Light of Iron would have pounded him to ash by now."

"I think I have my doubts about that."

Emi flashed another look at Chiho.

"Chiho, have you ever thought about why you were taken up here?"

"Because Bell followed my orders and took her hostage so you would obey me. What other reason is there? That's why I made her take everything else from the scene, too, so the police wouldn't catch our scent."

Chiho's and Emi's belongings had been stacked on the far side of the heliport.

Emi chuckled at Sariel. It almost seemed like an expression of pity.

"Then shouldn't Bell have taken Chiho someplace where I couldn't see her? She'd be a much more effective hostage that way. She kind of loses her value if I don't have to worry about her safety. Bell isn't stupid. Everything she does, she does for a reason. That..."

Not even Emi was completely sure of this. But the agitation she displayed at the intersection seemed to provide the answer she was looking for.

"That, and she heads the Reconciliation Panel. The council that reconciles the false teachings of the past. Better watch that your faithful guard dog doesn't bite the hand that feeds it."

"What if she does? Then I'd punish her. Simple. And I hardly need to worry anyway. As long as I am an archangel, there isn't a cleric in the Church who would dare defy me."

Building one of the Tokyo city hall is 797 feet tall. It was high enough that the air turbulence was blowing gale-force winds across the roof.

A particularly strong gust had tossed Emi's long hair toward the heavens when he finally arrived.

"Hahh...hahh...hahh... S-sorry to...to interrupt... Urrgghh..."

The soft voice all but disappeared beneath the force of the wind.

But it still rang true to the three people who heard it.

"Why...the hell...isn't...the elevator working...huff...huff..."

There, by the penthouse that served as the roof exit, was a man who couldn't look more out of place on a high-rise heliport.

"Ah... Ah!"

The surprise and joy Chiho felt brought a wide smile to her tearstained face.

"Maou!"

He had a grimy old mop in his right hand, he was topless and decked out in a pair of boxers, and he was also covered in scabs and scars. But to his damsel in distress, he was as a knight on a white horse, confidently galloping to her rescue.

Emi, meanwhile, was greeted with the forlorn sight of a near-nude Devil King clambering to the rescue on a rattly used bike.

"Don't look at me!"

"*That's* how you say hi?!" Maou coldly interjected, even as the fatigue almost made him lose consciousness.

"Also, don't look like *that*! Why are you dressed like that?! Get out of my sight!"

Emi, in the unenviable situation of being restrained by Sariel and on the precipice of being undressed herself, didn't have much recourse apart from shouting.

"...Well. This is a surprise."

Sariel closed his gaping mouth, then repositioned his scythe from Emi's chest toward Maou.

"You appear quite human to me. Bereft of all your demonic powers. You couldn't have defeated Bell."

"...Does it look that way? She beat the crap outta me. And who knows what she woulda done *next* if I let her."

Maou certainly didn't sound like he was enjoying the evening's events much.

"This is bewildering to me...but you are far from well, I see. It is an unbelievable sight indeed, but here it is! You are truly no longer the Devil King I once knew, Satan."

"Yeah, well, I wasn't expecting the limp-wristed freak across the street who stank of cologne all day to be the Evil Eye, either. Still chasing after all the lil' girl angels up there?"

"...What?"

A deep rumble tempered Sariel's voice.

"Yep! Heard you've been harassing a lot of people. Not that I'm gonna say who."

Without explaining further, Maou turned toward Chiho and Emi.

"What did I just say? Don't *look* at me!"

Ignoring Emi's singularly out-of-place protest, Maou steeled his gaze back upon Sariel, the two now facing each other.

"'Course, I don't really care what's going on with you guys up in heaven anyway. What I'm worried about right now is the fact that you hurt one of my coworkers. You put Chi through a lot of crap, you bastard."

"Maou!"

Chiho was choked up with emotion.

"Listen. As far as I'm concerned, until you get back home, you're still on the clock!"

"...Maou?"

Chiho froze. It wasn't the gallant reassurance she expected.

"A manager needs to take responsibility for the safety of his employees when they're in transit, too! And I'm gonna make you *pay* for getting my precious staff involved in all this Ente Isla BS!"

"...Maou..."

This time, Chiho's voice was filled with disappointment.

"I'm the assistant manager right now. The safety of my crew at work is priority number one! Chi here is a valuable member of my staff! And no Devil King, no shift supervisor, *ever* abandons his crew!!"

"...Ngh."

This was Maou's final blow to Chiho's self-consciousness. Her head slumped as she held back the tears.

"I'm afraid I have no clue what you're talking about. But there is one thing I know for sure..."

A sharp sparkle formed in Sariel's purple eyes.

"And that's how foolish you must truly be, attempting to stymie my mission with that fragile husk."

A hazy aura of gold flowed out of Sariel's body. It was an onrush of holy power riding on a sudden torrent of wind, one so intense that the restrained Emi next to him had to close her eyes.

"I don't give a crap about your Holy Silver and swords and stuff. In fact, if you'll help keep that crazy Hero in line for me, go right ahead. All I care about is getting Chi out of here…"

The shock wave of holy power would have been enough to vaporize your typical demon. It was still enough to make Maou break into a sweat.

"But it looks like that's not gonna happen… Jeez. Well, *this* is great."

Beams of crackling light coursed around Sariel's body. Without any demonic force backing him up, Maou couldn't even lay a finger on him.

All he thought about was how he was going to carry both Chiho and the mop with him as he ran away. But then:

"?!"

It was difficult to describe how the atmosphere changed in that instant.

The air around the heliport, arguably the most purified place on Earth thanks to Sariel's holy energy, suddenly grew heavy and humid.

Then a blindingly dark cloud began to form over the landing zone, pushing the holy energy back as it blinded everyone standing upon it. There was a prickly feeling on Sariel's skin, like his hand was on a static ball.

"Wh-what is…?"

The eerie presence was enough to even make Sariel waver.

"This is…making me sick…"

Chiho sounded out of breath as she groaned. Emi swiveled her head around, straining to see what was happening.

Only Maou remained serene. More than serene. In fact, both of his eyes were now the color of blood, as if fighting back against Sariel's aura.

A flash of bewilderment crossed his face, but only a flash, as he realized what was behind this phenomenon.

"Oh, hell. I didn't really feel like helping Emi, but…whatever.

Listen up, Sariel. You scared Chi and put a blemish on my potential career track. Those're both high crimes, you know."

Suddenly emboldened, Maou took a single step toward Sariel.

That enough made the atmosphere all the more oppressive.

Sariel screamed, the appalled shock obvious on his face.

"This...demonic power! You! Why?!"

Until this moment, he was Sadao Maou, just a normal young man.

But in mere milliseconds, the air that surrounded him had transformed into something grotesque.

That overwhelming sense of intimidation. Those bloodred eyes. The demonic uncanniness that now pervaded the air.

"Whoa! Devil King! Knock that off! If you do that now..."

Emi tried to warn Maou about his upcoming transformation, but Maou shook his head, a defiant grin on his face.

"Quit worrying."

He snapped his boxers against his hip.

"These underpants are supposed to stretch to the contours of your body. They ain't gonna rip, I promise."

Then, as if the statement was the catalyst that sparked it, a rapid metamorphosis took place.

"Who the hell was asking about your boxers, you dumbass?!"

Emi's scream was muffled by the violent, otherworldly gale that stormed across the heliport in an instant.

A supernatural red glow enveloped Maou's half-naked body. His muscles expanded, his legs becoming gnarled and beast-like. And the UniClo undies, built for hot summer nights like this one, deftly handled every change in size and shape. Particularly size.

The one-horned Devil King, with his bloodred eyes and cloven hooves, had descended upon the Tokyo sky.

"Whewwwww..."

The transformation complete, the boxered Devil King Satan began twisting his neck, as if performing calisthenics.

"Ahh, feels great. The hell did that bastard *do*, anyway?"

He stretched out the rest of his limbs as he spoke. The answer was provided to him shortly.

"You transformed while leaving Chiho in her current perilous state?! You fool!"

She flew in like a shooting star from the direction of Shinjuku station, her hair flowing in the wind as she wielded her golden war hammer.

"Bell!"

Suzuno, better known as Crestia Bell to Sariel, alit next to Chiho as he watched, a look of malice on his face. The first thing she did was create a barrier of holy energy around herself and Chiho.

"Pffahh!"

Chiho immediately exhaled, as if ejecting the dark, grimy air from her lungs.

"Whew… That was rough."

"Are you all right?"

"Y-yes… Oh! Suzuno!"

Chiho, who had witnessed the moment Bell sent Emi flying, tensed up for just a moment. Then her eyes opened wide at the sight of the cell phone thrust before her.

"I apologize. I will explain later. For now…"

Bell turned toward the demon and his terrifying crimson eyes.

"Allow me to take advantage of the one you hold dear, Chiho."

"Bell! Have you gone mad?!"

"You are the only madman here, Sariel."

Suzuno stood strong, keeping Chiho behind her back.

"Pushing a false peace upon our people; planting the seeds of chaos in another world; backstabbing the very people whose faith we rely on, and must protect… Is *this* the truth the gods hold for us?! As chief inquisitor of the Reconciliation Panel, I refuse to overlook such a shameful, deceitful truth!"

"And you would even link hands with the Devil King for it?! Your 'reconciliation' means nothing to me! You are a demon yourself! A tainted demon, driven by your inquisitor's thirst for blood!"

"Silence! The Devil King's life on Earth as Sadao Maou, at least, does not run afoul of the justice that we seek!"

"Whoa, thanks. Guess I'm the big man at MgRonald after all, huh?"

Satan looked on as the argument raged between divinity and follower, taking abject pride in his comparatively puny assistant-manager position.

"You know, though, I'd say the Hero and the angels have been the real villains here lately. I'm just sittin' here living life day by day, you know?"

Satan took another step, boring a hole into the heliport.

That small move was enough to put Sariel on guard, halting the argument and flying backward to safety. Satan chidingly watched him go.

"Bell...what did you have to do to gather all this evil force...?"

Not even Satan was expecting this tsunami of demonic power to flood through Sariel's barrier into this space. At best, he was hoping he could get Chiho to safety somehow.

Bell turned around and gazed at the nightscape before her.

"Tonight...the men and women using Shinjuku station have my pity."

"Uh?"

"Wha?"

"Huhh?!"

Chiho and Emi both looked straight at her.

"What did they call them? Electrical transformers? There were these power lines between the tracks that led to all of those, and I sliced a few of them in half. I figured stopping the trains would create a storm of anger across the area..."

"Dude, that's a terrorist attack!"

Even Satan, and his visions of conquering the world, were thrown.

"Do...do you have any idea how many trains go through Shinjuku?! Like, even if you count the Japan Rail lines alone, that's gonna affect nearly every single service in greater Tokyo!"

"Ah. I see. Then my guess was correct. I am glad to see my missionary training wasn't for naught. It is quite annoying if the transport wagons in Ente Isla fail to arrive at their appointed times, after all, yes? I assumed that delaying so many trains at once would create an aura of rage that could transform into demonic force..."

"I'm not praising your analytical skills, okay?! I've never even *been* on one of those dumb wagons!"

Satan's alarmingly dynamic comeback was enough to send another shock wave of evil force across the area.

"Aagh!"

The barrier protecting Chiho wavered at the impact, almost knocking her off the heliport entirely.

"M-Maou! Please, be careful!"

"Sorry, sorry..."

"Oh, but now, Maou...or Devil King, maybe? Or Satan? Ooh, I don't even know what I should be calling you!"

Maou tried to ignore Chiho as she blushed, starting to feel quite out of place.

"We, uh, we can figure that out later. Yo, Sariel. Little freak over there. Nobody's gonna accuse me of being merciless tonight. Lemme give you a choice."

Satan now stood high and mighty above Sariel.

"Either you turn your tail and run back home, or you accept your punishment and let me beat the tar out of you. Which is it?"

"It's obvious."

The archangel, great scythe in hand, spread his white, swanlike wings wide as he glared at Satan.

"Devil King Satan! I will defeat you and fulfill my mission!"

In an instant, Sariel was in the air, focusing his holy magic as the moon framed his body.

"What do I have to fear from a Devil King who can only regain his powers after getting doped up on the negative energy of humans?!"

"Man, shut *up*, happy hands."

Sariel's wings shone across the night sky like a pair of crescent moons.

"Thunderwing Moonlight!!"

A laser-like beam of light navigated its way among Emi, Chiho, and Bell before boring down upon Satan. He may have been enraged, but he had not forgotten his mission. Satan had to appreciate his twisted sense of feminism, too.

"I wouldn't sass a Devil King at full power, man."

Satan raised his arms against the advancing bolt of moonlight.

"Nngh!"

A simple moment of concentration was all it took to repulse it.

"Wh-what...?!"

"Pfft. Bet you're missing your home-field advantage right now."

Satan snickered at the flabbergasted Sariel.

"Something tells me you've sorely overestimated our strength. Let me show you what you're *really* worth."

The lightning that Satan repulsed was now balled up in a single palm. He handled it effortlessly, like he himself had conjured it up, despite being a product of Sariel's holy power.

"Guess that Evil Eye of the Fallen made you feel a lot more powerful than that, huh? You never fought against anyone who *didn't* run on holy power, did you?"

As if throwing a ball and chain, Satan tossed the small mass of energy right back at Sariel, using nothing but pure brute strength.

"What?!"

Sariel hurriedly tried to cancel the attack, but with the ball of lightning right before him, he fired a bolt of purple from his eyes to send it scattering.

"That ability of yours makes you pretty much invincible against any holy force user, I'm betting..."

From his hand, Satan summoned a ball of black fire. It was only the size of a baseball, but with the form of a Major League pitcher, he hurled it toward Sariel in the sky.

"But when you're faced with some other kind of power, you're utterly clueless. Should've chosen someone else to pick on, huh?"

The moment the mass reached Sariel, it grew into an enormous fireball, large enough to envelop his entire body.

"Grraaaghhhh!!!"

"I'd suggest you sell those chicken wings of yours, but it'd probably make Sentucky's sales plummet."

Sariel's pained scream echoed within the blazing ball of dark flame.

Satan snapped his finger once. The mass of hellfire disappeared in an instant, revealing a Sariel who was plainly charred, his holy protection failing him.

"Oop."

The moment he appeared, Satan nonchalantly swung his mop down upon the back of Sariel's neck.

"Gahahhh…"

It was enough to break the mop at the middle of the handle. Sariel's eyes rolled back as he lost consciousness, falling downward through the air.

"Agh!"

As he fainted, the purple cross Emi was bound to dissipated, sending her hurtling toward the heliport.

Sariel, for his part, slammed helplessly against the pavement.

"And…oop."

Satan caught Emi, robbed of her strength and unable to even prepare for impact, just before she reached the landing zone.

"Whadaya think, Emi?"

"…Think of what…"

Nearly out of breath, a depressed-looking Emi looked at Satan, helpless in his arms.

"I'm here to catch you. You could appreciate that a little, huh?"

"……………………"

Emi, all too aware of what he was talking about, groaned and contorted her face into a thousand combinations, as if chewing on a faceful of something awful. Then:

"…I have to. I can't do anything else."

The Hero always had to get in the last word.

Satan chuckled to himself, then quietly placed Emi on the ground.

"Hey. Emi. Your top."

"Huh?"

The Devil King was patting his own chest as Emi howled a response, shoulders still tensed from the strain.

"Dude, your top. Button it up. Pff…!"

A beat, and then Emi finally realized what he meant. She took off one of her pumps and throw it straight at Satan's face.

"Oww! Look, demon or not, that still hurts! ...Agh!"

The other shoe hit him square on the forehead.

"I *told* you not to look!"

Emi wrapped an arm around her chest, face beaming red. Satan turned around long enough to let her redo her blouse's buttons.

The anger quickly returned to his voice.

"That's *your* fault for spacing out in the first place! I was kind enough to warn you, remember! Besides, it's not like showing them off is gonna make 'em even smaller, so—*gaghhh*!!"

Emi, out of ammunition, didn't deliver the final, merciful blow that stopped Satan's cruel rant cold. That honor belonged to Bell and her war hammer.

"You...bast...ard...!"

"My apologies. I simply found that too difficult to listen to."

Bell couldn't have said it more matter-of-factly as she placed her hammer back behind her shoulder.

"Uhmm, look, guys, you beat that creepy guy and all, so could you stop arguing for..."

Chiho tentatively spoke up from behind the holy barrier that protected her.

"What?!"

"What do you want?"

Emi and Bell were oddly curt as they turned toward her. Chiho wondered to herself why they weren't looking her in the eye, instead gazing right at her chest.

"Um...I'm sorry."

She decided to diplomatically step away.

Emi, realizing that Bell was preoccupied about the same thing she was, felt a bizarre sense of kinship.

Satan was less than thrilled at any of this.

"Man, why did I even both rescuing either of you, huh? I shoulda just snatched up Chi and hightailed it outta here! Boy, did I blow it!"

He began to visibly pout, ignoring his own tirade of just a few moments ago.

Then, in a very undemonic, dejected tone:

"Gate, open!"

Suddenly, a Gate erupted to life before him, just large enough for a single person to venture through.

"Whoa, whoa, whoa! You aren't going back now, are…"

Emi, shocked to see Satan so casually open a Gate before her eyes, tried to stop him.

"Yeah, I'd sure like to! But you know that's not gonna happen!"

With that, Satan picked Sariel up off the ground and tossed him in the Gate, like a MgRonald customer throwing his refuse in the garbage container.

"Ahhh!!"

"Devil King! What are you…"

"Maou?!"

This exceedingly rough treatment of the archangel was enough to amaze even his victims.

"I'm not gonna kill him or anything. He's still got most of his power left. Maybe he'll wind up someplace livable, if he's lucky. Who knows if he'll make it back to Ente Isla from there, though?"

Satan shrugged.

"Gate! Close Sesame! Or whatever!"

With that un-incantation-like incantation, the Gate popped out of existence.

And with its conjurer out of the picture, the holy force field that covered the building must have disappeared as well. Soon, the nighttime murmur of Shinjuku ward could be heard once more. Satan turned back toward the others as they looked down at the city and its cacophony of neon and ad jingles.

"You aren't blaming me, are you? Keeping him around would just cause more trouble for us, but killing him would bring even more trouble down on *me*. That was the best way to do it."

"Yeah, but…he isn't just some pile of garbage…"

"I'm not too interested in killing an archangel and setting off a full-scale war with heaven quite yet. And if they take this as Sariel screwing up his mission and getting stranded somewhere, then everything works out. Everything except his rep, I guess."

Nobody could deny that, but was this really an issue that could be resolved so easily? Emi and Bell stood there, mouths agape, unable to react.

"So! Now for the real problem."

Satan clapped his hands once, Sariel already apparently a thing of the past for him, and gave Bell a stern look.

"We gotta clean this whole thing up. Let's move, Bell."

"Clean up?"

"Don't just go, *Cleanup in aisle seven*, dude! You can't stop every train in Tokyo and go, *Oops, sorry!* afterward! There's gonna be a ton of electrical lines and transformers to repair, and now that Sariel's barrier is gone, someone's probably gonna be up here before long. So let's go! I need to get back anyway. I can't leave MgRonald before closing it!"

Satan, sounding exactly like Sadao Maou despite his current dreadful form as king of all demons, was too much of a sight for Bell to avoid being flummoxed.

"Oh, right. Emi?"

"Wh-what…?"

Satan snuck a look at the teenage girl who had been staring at him through the holy energy barrier the whole time.

"Get Chi back home. For real this time. Her mom's worried about her."

It was Bell, not Chiho or Emi, who was the most surprised.

She looked up at Satan, an alien creature now more than twice her height.

Only Chiho was serene, flashing a small yet undeniably triumphant smile.

"I always knew you were a good guy, Maou."

"Ah, jeez, get outta here."

Satan shooed them away with his hands.

"I'm royalty, you know? Kind of a big deal? I like to treat my underlings right, and if I'm gonna conquer this land, I wanna make sure it's all nice and neat first."

"That all sounds fine to me for now."

Chiho nimbly flashed a smile back at him. He stiffened for a moment, embarrassed.

"Ugghhhh! Let's just go, Bell!"

"Ah, wait, where are you grabbing me—*aaaaaaahhhhhhhhh…*"

He had grabbed her by her kimono's collar, lifting her up before flying off, as if fleeing Chiho and Emi.

Chiho finally escaped the barrier after they departed off the edge.

"Hey…Yusa?"

"……"

Emi watched Satan and Bell fly off for a little while, hands still folded over her chest. She furrowed her brows at Chiho.

"Let's just leave it at that for today. But only today, all right?"

Her defeated voice was nearly a whisper. Chiho snickered a bit in response.

"In that case, could I ask you a favor, Yusa?"

"…What's that?"

She looked a bit concerned as she turned away from where Maou left, looking at the skies over Hatsudai-Hatagaya.

"Maou said he left the MgRonald open. I think he'll probably be in trouble. *Big* trouble."

✳

"Ugh… Why'd you *do* all of that…?"

Sadao Maou lumbered groggily out of the taxi in front of Hatagaya station, near the Keio line entrance.

"Ha-ha…ha-ha-ha-ha! Well, you see… I mean, Chiho mentioned that the Devil King restored the entire Shuto Expressway back to normal, so I wanted to be sure I had a widespread impact. That way, I could be certain you would expend as much demonic energy as possible."

"You liar. There's no way you could've planned all this!"

Suzuno Kamazuki laughed shrilly as she broke out in a nervous sweat.

The Shinjuku that Satan and Bell were greeted with was an unprecedented traffic disaster.

The way Bell had worded it, Satan wasn't expecting much more than a few downed power lines here and there nearby the rail station. Said expectations were dashed when he found she had all but leveled an entire transformer building.

"Yes…well, I cannot easily slice through wiring with my hammer, so I am afraid blunt trauma was the order of the day…"

Satan saved her the trouble of coming up with any more namby-pamby excuses by flicking her on the forehead. With demonic power behind the blow, it got the message across.

First, the transformer station had to be fully restored; next, he had to unravel the chaos unfolding on the rails across all of greater Tokyo. Then came the repairs on all the cascading damage the haywire transformer caused to the city's electrical grid. The demonic force that was his all the way up to tossing the archangel through the Gate was running on fumes by the end of it all, transforming the Devil King Satan back to Sadao Maou, part-timer in a set of stretchy boxers.

Bell was no help at all during the repairs, either.

Considering she hadn't consumed a great deal of her holy force in the battle, burning through all this evil power in front of her actually put Maou in life-threatening danger, now that he reflected upon it. But nothing happened. She merely sat and watched on as Satan worked to bring everything back to the status quo.

And once Maou was utterly exhausted of power, she was kind enough to pick up the uniform he left on city hall grounds and grab a taxi for him.

He had little idea what sparked this change in heart from her. But instead of trying to fish an explanation out of her, he decided to think over more pressing issues.

It was already near midnight, closing time for the MgRonald in front of Hatagaya station.

"Devil King! What is wrong?"

Suzuno chased after Maou as he tried to toddle away once the taxi left. But there was no time to deal with her. Every minute, every second counted as he made his way back.

But there was no avoiding punishment for his crime of ditching his shift for nearly two hours.

Maou found himself frozen in the glaring light as a familiar vision marched in front of him.

"...Now just *what* is going on here, Marko?"

"Ms....Kisaki..."

The expression on Kisaki as she stood tall in her business suit, staring down at the emasculated Maou, was hidden by the glare. But, just the same, he could tell how stern, how judgmental, it was.

"I mean, just...why?"

"I had a phone call... Something happened to Chi."

Kisaki's gaze, just as sharp and stabby as the Hero's, crashed down upon Maou's face like comets of white-hot light.

"Yes. And it sounded like you took a mop, ran out, and never came back. You caused a lot of trouble for a lot of people."

"I... No, but..."

Maou's face twitched as he leaned away from her. Suzuno stood motionless next to him, perhaps just as awed as he was.

"You got a lot of guts, you know that? The shift supervisor, one who *still* hasn't made up for the morning's losses, cutting work for two hours without telling anyone where he's going. What is this, a date? Well? *Is* it?"

"That, uh..."

His brain was running in circles. This couldn't be more awkward.

Maou wasn't expecting Kisaki here, but looking back, he must have really freaked out the staff. After all, he ran right out of the place with barely a word after Urushihara's phone call.

Since repairing the train system took longer than expected—and took far more of his demonic strength than expected—he wound up having to waste more time waiting for Suzuno to go fetch his uniform for him.

And with him reporting back to work with a girl in a kimono, it wasn't outrageous to imagine the idea of Maou shirking work to hang with the ladies for a while.

Kisaki didn't seem too open to the real reason behind his disappearance, and he didn't have any other useful excuse for her. Giving her even more transparent lies would only make her angrier...

"Mr. Maou rescued me, madam."

"What?"

Kisaki looked up at the unexpected voice, noticing an unfamiliar woman in front of her.

Where did she come from? Maou briskly turned around, never expecting to hear *this* voice right now.

"...Can I ask who you are?"

"My name is Yusa. I'm friends with Chiho Sasaki, and..."

She froze for a moment, taking the time to gauge the ball of sweat and nerves in front of her.

"And Mr. Maou, too."

There. She said it.

Maou was already sheepish enough before. Now, looking at Emi, he felt like an entire flock of them.

Emi averted her eyes, focusing on Kisaki alone.

"Marko's...friend?"

"Yeah. When we were returning home with Chiho and Ms. Kamazuki over there, we were stalked by a molester. We hid, and Mr. Maou wound up rescuing us."

"A molester? Oh. You know, I *did* hear about something happening at an intersection in Sasazuka."

"We were just three women, and we didn't have anything to defend ourselves with. It was all we could do to keep ourselves unseen..."

Kisaki listened on, still dubious. Then Suzuno decided to board the roller coaster for herself.

"Yes...she's, er, Yusa is correct."

"Suzu...uh, Ms. Kamazuki..."

Maou barely avoided revealing his familiarity with Suzuno. That was how unexpected her follow-up was.

"M-Maou chased the stalker away for us, but he, er, he needed to return to MgRonald because he'd left it empty, so I reasoned, uh, I thought I should accompany him back…"

It was an awkward performance, but the tears Suzuno somehow summoned to her eyes did wonders to sell it.

Maou had to resist asking whether she'd made up that character herself, or she was imitating someone on TV.

Then Emi gave him an even bigger fright.

"…Sadao."

"What…?"

It was the first time Emi called him by that name in front of anyone else.

"We wound up bringing Chiho back home. Her mother was waiting for her."

"Oh? Oh. Well, great. Sounds, uh, good."

Maou found himself unable to form a coherent sentence. He decided to nod lightly instead.

Kisaki watched all of this in silence before speaking up.

"…Well, I suppose it's not your fault, then."

She sighed, eyebrows still slanted downward, as if resigning herself to the "truth."

"I guess I knew I shouldn't have had teenage girls working dinner alone. You never know what kind of people are out there, waiting to prey on them."

She placed a hand on Maou's shoulder, plainly a level calmer than before, even as she ruefully reflected on her scheduling practices.

"Listen, Marko. You're a really important part of the team, both for me and the rest of the staff. So try not to get yourself hurt, okay? I'm glad you were brave enough to protect Chi and these other two friends of yours, but if you were injured out there, that'd really hurt me…and them."

"Ms. Kisaki…"

"I hope that today's been a constructive experience for you…and I hope you understand how these girls feel, too."

Then Kisaki finally rested her eyes upon Suzuno.

"Thank you for bringing Marko...I mean, Maou...back for me. Why don't you take a break inside? I'll get some coffee going. You, too."

She gave Maou another friendly pat on the shoulder as she called for Suzuno and Emi.

"What do you think?"

"Oh, I think we should..."

Suzuno and Emi looked at each other hesitantly.

"Ah, just have a drink."

Maou abruptly stopped them before they could refuse.

"It's weird how good the coffee at the Mag tastes when Ms. Kisaki makes it."

It came out more awkwardly than he'd hoped. Suzuno and Emi exchanged another glance.

"Ahh, don't be silly. The coffee tastes exactly the same no matter who prepares it."

Kisaki lightly chided Maou before turning toward the girls.

"How about it?"

"Well, if you're offering..."

The pair entered the dining area, not wanting to put Kisaki off too much.

"Ms.... Ms. Kisaki!"

But as they did, a crew member dashed out into the room, his face pallid.

"Oh, Maou, you're back! Oh, uh, but we got another problem right now!"

He was waving his hands all over the place, in a state of near shock. A simple order from Kisaki was enough to bring him back to military discipline.

"Calm down! Nobody on my crew needs to get all panicky like that! Just tell me what happened, and keep it short!"

The ramrod-straight crewman replied to the battle-hardened sergeant's command.

"Yes, Ms. Kisaki! Someone fell out of the refrigerator!"

"Wha?"

Kisaki, Maou—even Suzuno and Emi—reacted in such unison that it sounded almost like a choir..

"There was this guy in the fridge, and his clothes are all charred and stuff! I think he's unconscious, but what should we do?"

"Oh, no *way!*"

"Hey! Marko, hang on!"

Brushing Kisaki away, Maou flew into the kitchen.

"Gehh!"

The sight prompted him to shout out loud.

Sariel, the archangel he had just tossed through a Gate to parts unknown, was lying on the floor, halfway outside the industrial refrigerator used to store MgRonald's ingredients.

Given how there wasn't much space for Sariel in between the bags of potatoes and chicken parts, he must have "fallen out" just like the crew member described.

"Wh-what the hell?!"

Kisaki and the others were equally shocked when they took in the scene.

Suzuno and Emi in particular, naturally.

"Maou! That *sasa* tree…"

Suzuno turned back toward the entrance.

It couldn't have been mere coincidence that the Devil King's Gate connected to someplace like this. The only explanation was that the bamboo tree he'd unwittingly placed right by the front door, now a manifestation of Maou's demonic power, had somehow resonated with the demonic power Satan used to open the Gate.

The tree had attracted a litany of customers, including some who never should have been customers at all. But uprooting it now wouldn't make Sariel go away.

"Gnh…nngh…"

But before the chaos could subside, Sariel slowly began to groan and wriggle on the ground, struggling to regain consciousness.

Having him stir up trouble here would cause nothing but despair.

Sariel had merely been knocked out in the battle before. His powers were still very real. His Evil Eye would render Emi and Suzuno all but powerless, and Maou—the only one who could hurt him, really—had just exhausted his demonic strength.

There was no time to have Suzuno wreck the train system all over again. As Maou's mind blanked out on him, Sariel's head rose upward.

"Who...might *you* be?"

It was Kisaki that dared to confront him, the only one in the group Sariel didn't know. She was preparing to deal with the intruder, no doubt. The Devil King, the Hero, and the Reconciliation Panel chief all began thinking in unison about how they'd ever keep her safe.

"...You're...beautiful..."

It sounded like the ramblings of an alcoholic, and Sariel's drugged facial expression looked the part.

"...Pardon?"

It took a moment for Kisaki to parse what he'd said. She smiled awkwardly, not wanting to rile him.

"The goddess of beauty... She existed in another world..."

"...I'm afraid I'm not quite sure what you're saying."

Not even Kisaki could hide her bewilderment.

"Sariel, you couldn't have..."

Maou groaned at the fearsome prediction that crossed his mind. The frenzied scream Sariel erupted into a moment later confirmed it.

"Ahhhh! Such sweet destiny! Such a wondrous miracle! Here, in Japan, I've stumbled upon the goddess of beauty! Oh, by all the gods in heaven! My body burns with the flame of forbidden love! I am about to fall from my angelic heights!"

"...................................."

Maou, Emi and Suzuno froze, unable to figure out how to react.

"Who's *this* idiot?"

Kisaki, alone, snapped out of her friendly business face, sneering at the pathetic figure before her.

Suddenly, Sariel came to his knees, shouting as he pressed his still-charred body against Kisaki's legs.

"Ahh, that worshipful face, looking down upon me from such

lofty heights! It makes my heart pulsate like the great bell tower that governs the passage of time in the heavens!"

"Can anyone explain this? Who *is* this weirdo?"

"...Well, he's kind of the manager at the Sentucky across the street."

Sariel nodded briskly at Maou's introduction, pointing wildly out the window.

"My beloved icon of beauty, my name is Sarue. I am manager of the Sentucky Fried Chicken location in front of Hatagaya station. The two of us, from two rivals doomed to compete with each other... Truly, we are the Romeo and Juliet of the fast-food industry!"

"...Freak."

"No matter how vulgar and abusive the words that spill out of your supple lips be, they ring like the great orchestras of heaven in my ears! I would gladly fling my body into the fire and brimstone of hell if it would make your eyes turn toward mine! What kind of fragrant rose would possibly serve as your equal, my sweet flower of love?"

It was quite a feat of improvisation.

"...Can someone translate this guy into Japanese for me?"

"I, uh, I think he's saying that he'll do anything you say, Ms. Kisaki."

Sariel nodded proudly at Maou's expert interpretation. Kisaki closed her eyes and sighed.

"...All right. Get over here."

At that moment, Sariel's orange-encrusted eyes gleamed like a full moon as he dragged himself before Kisaki's feet.

"Aaaaahhhh! The height of ecstasy! Oh, may all the gods in heaven forgive me! I remove myself from your flock and fling myself into the pyres of passion!!"

Kisaki's heel embedded itself into the face of the advancing Sariel. He howled like some otherworldly beast, then fell.

But even with this rebuke, the Evil Eye–wielding archangel's expression was one of sheer ecstasy, even as it was warped and twisted by the MgRonald manager's heel pressing into it.

"You think I'm playing around? Franchise management isn't some kind of *game*, you know! What is *with* that loony panda makeup? And what's with the oil drum of cologne you threw over your head?! Is *that* what Sentucky expects from its managers?!"

Kisaki's heel dug itself further into Sariel's face. Sariel greedily accepted his punishment.

"Ahh, the lure of the fallen! Such a sweet, fetching scene, one I am no longer able to resist!"

"Shut *up*, you perv!"

Kisaki glared at Maou, eyes open wide, as she kept up her barrage of abuse. Her gaze, sharp enough that even the Evil Eye was reluctant to focus upon it, made not just Maou, but Emi and Suzuno gulp nervously as well.

"Marko…are you telling me we placed second in customer draw to *this* idiot?"

"Uh…well, no, I…um."

"Huh. Hope you and everyone else won't complain when I send you all off to Antigua and Barbuda, then."

"I, I don't even know where that is, Ms. Kisaki…"

"Well, that was my and your problem to deal with, and we blew it. We'll both have to volunteer to return our salaries for the day. Ugh. Guess I still have a lot to learn, don't I? Serves me right for whining about that manager training session."

In one fell swoop, Kisaki had pieced the situation together in her mind, expressed regret, then made Maou join her in the punishment. The sheer speed made the blood rush from Maou's head.

"W-wait…you're joking, right, Ms. Kisaki?!"

"I thought I told you, the only time I tell jokes is when I want people to laugh!"

"I'll laugh all you want! Please! Just tell me you're kidding!"

Now it was Maou throwing his body upon Kisaki, not altogether unlike what Sariel attempted.

"Ugh! Enough! You're a man! Just accept it! A true samurai would rather starve than allow his honor to be tarnished in public!"

"But this is the twenty-first century! I'm just a simple commoner, Ms. Kisaki!"

The twenty-first-century commoner and lord of all demons begged Kisaki for a change of heart he knew was unlikely to come.

Emi and Suzuno, watching the part-timer and location manager's aimless argument, their sexually overactive archrival prostrate before their feet, exchanged glances at each other.

"...Quite a joke, indeed."

"*I'm* sure not laughing."

Yet the Hero of Ente Isla and head of the Church's Reconciliation Panel both smiled giddily as they looked on.

"Me, being Maou's friend... Ugh. That isn't funny at all. Why did I have to call him by his first name, even?"

✳

"S-Suzuno!! What are you doing in here?!"

Chiho shouted out loud upon opening the door to Devil's Castle and finding Suzuno already inside.

"Ah, welcome, Sasaki! Just the person I needed. I was attempting to make a tea-flavored pound cake with this rice cooker. Would you like to try some?"

"Ooh, thanks, Ashiya! I'd love to! ...Wait, no!"

Chiho noisily stormed into Devil's Castle. Suzuno was facing Maou across the domain's sole table, pointing a pair of food-laden chopsticks at him.

It looked like the classic *open your mouth and say ahhh* trick, but considering how the chopsticks were attempting to bore their way through Maou's cheek at the moment, there seemed to be a communication breakdown in progress.

Inserting herself between them, Chiho glared ruefully at Suzuno.

"What are you doing? Could you avoid being in my way, please?"

"No, what are *you* doing?! And why are you just taking that from her, Maou?!"

"Uhh..."

Maou cast his eyes downward, plainly just as sick of this as Chiho.

"Aren't you two supposed to be enemies, Suzuno?! Where do you get off, inviting yourself into his place and trying to feed Maou like that? It makes me so…jealous…"

"Chihooooo, you might wanna filter yourself a little…"

"You stay out of this, Urushihara!"

Urushihara meekly closed his mouth. Now Chiho's eyes were locked with Suzuno's.

"Yes. It is as you say. I am, at the core, the enemy of the Devil King."

Suzuno repositioned herself, back straight up, face cool and composed.

"But, while the Devil King may not have intended it at first, he has also performed a great service for me. Thus, I am doing my best to prepare my consecrated ingredients in the most taste-tempting ways possible and pretend to repay his efforts with food while secretly filling the demons' bellies with damaging holy force…"

"Suzuno, I have no idea what any of that means! Ashiya! Don't you care about what she's saying?!"

"I know full well how you feel, Sasaki. Too well, in fact…"

Ashiya's eyes darted over to Urushihara as he showed Chiho a college-ruled notebook.

"But thanks to Lucifer's unplanned shopping spree, our budget for next month will be firmly in the red. It is truly a gut-wrenching travesty for me to witness…"

Looking at the last page of the notebook labeled, DEVIL'S CASTLE ACCOUNTS on the front, Chiho saw a line reading *Card payment: 40,000 yen; User: Dumbassihara.*

"Forty thousand…? What on earth did you buy, Dumbassihara?"

"Quit calling me that, man! I know Ashiya's pissed off 'n all, but if I *didn't* buy it, you might've been in Ente Isla with Sariel right now! You could try thanking me a little, for a change!"

"…But it was Maou's money, right?"

Ashiya approached Chiho, whispering in her ear, "And what's more, the money was for a hidden GPS transmitter he slipped into Emilia's shoulder bag."

"…That is *so* creepy."

Her reaction was one of utter disgust.

"You guys are *so* unfair! This is BS!"

Urushihara resentfully tried to defend himself, showing no sign of regret.

"...But, regardless, we are now firmly in negative territory...so we've been forced to grudgingly accept Crestia's attempt upon our lives via her dietary support..."

"You don't have to wreck your health just to save some money! Please!"

Chiho rapped the notebook in her hand against the table.

"But we do! Now that we are unable to return home, bringing ourselves back into the black is my utmost priority!"

In the end, the customer numbers for the week that Maou served as shift supervisor lost out to Sariel's Sentucky Fried Chicken location...but only by the slimmest of margins.

Perhaps Kisaki had awoken something within Sariel. For reasons only he could understand, he officially became a full-fledged employee of SFC the following day, serving as the Hatagaya location's permanent manager.

Maou was wary at first, fearing he would go back to his nefarious, disturbing, womanizing ways, but Sariel—aka Mitsuki Sarue—had become an honest, hardworking fast-food employee. Apart from the bouquet of roses he sent Kisaki on a daily basis, he was just another manager striving to boost sales at his franchise, a far cry from when Maou first met him. In fact, one of the message cards included with the bouquet read:

I look forward to visiting on the day when we finally surpass you.

Kisaki was deeply offended, of course ("Do I really look that weak to him?!" were her exact words), but since none of it was the flowers' fault, she decided to place them outside to provide some store décor, along with a sign inviting anyone interested to take them away for free.

Urushihara reasoned that, besides his sudden infatuation with Kisaki, Sariel was sticking around because he had no way to return home.

He had failed in his mission, after all. Flying back to the heavens after a painful loss to Satan, the Devil King, could apparently place him in serious danger of being banished from his native domain.

Sariel hadn't infiltrated SFC for any strategic reason. In the end, he simply lacked anything he could sell for money, the way Suzuno did. So he took a job to support himself, just like any other destitute urban outcast.

And as for Suzuno…the scene playing out before Chiho's eyes told her all she needed to know.

"What are you even doing here, Suzuno? How can you just sit here and relax inside enemy territory like this?!"

"I am here to fulfill the justice that must be done."

Suzuno smiled at her—this smile laden with hidden meaning, one unlike anything she showed her before.

"I desire to slay the Devil King, of course. But, more than anything, I want to bring Emilia back home and reform the rotten and corrupt Church organization. The Church must remain an icon of truth, a holy place that mankind can confidently place its faith upon. But, as you see, Emilia refuses to return until the Devil King is defeated, yes? So I thought I would weaken him and his generals as much as possible, to make it all the easier for Emilia to strike the final blow when she deems it proper."

From the ever-prim and upright Suzuno, it sounded like a laudable pursuit. Chiho knew better.

"Ugh! And you think Maou isn't going to *do* anything about you?!"

Chiho waved her hands wildly as she spoke. The gesture was pointless, given Maou's obvious disinterest in moving away from the chopsticks jabbed into his face.

Between losing all of his demonic power and most of his stamina that fateful night, combined with the rigors of shift-manager duty and his bitter loss at the hand of Sentucky, Maou was physically and mentally defeated.

What's more, the police had found the antitheft registration label on the mighty steed Dullahan that Suzuno had flattened in front of Tokyo city hall, earning Maou another home visit from the cops.

The ensuing lecture was the final knockout punch at the end of an already-grueling bout.

In the end, he risked his life, blew his big chance to regain his demonic force, got raked over the coals by Ashiya…and now Suzuno was needling him with her sanctified, holy meals. It was enough to take the wind out of any demon's stygian sails.

"I'll cook for Maou, all right?! You don't have to worry about him, Suzuno, so please, go find a job or something instead of hanging out *here* all day!"

"I am afraid that proposition is a difficult one for me to swallow. This, right now, is my true calling. Now, when the Devil King is at his weakest, is the greatest chance we will ever have!"

"Are you being serious?! You can try to make excuses all you want, but you just want to have Maou eat your home-cooked food, don't you?!"

"Hohh? Is that how you see this? Do you think the heart I placed in his bento box is a sign of my true love for Maou, rather than its true origin as a symbol of the Holy Grail as it pervades and destroys the Devil King's body?"

"I… What? No! No 'true love' at all! Please! You're the one who thought *osechi* cuisine was standard bento-box food! Quit making all this junk up!"

"I do not understand what you mean."

"Stop playing dumb! Come on, Maou! You don't need to sit here and let your sworn foe try to kill you! I'll have my mom teach me how to make all kinds of dishes!"

"Oh? Well, well! We must come visit your mother to pay our respects sometime, Sasaki!"

Ashiya, ever the househusband, chimed in as he cleaned the kitchen floor.

"Think it over carefully, Devil King. If you refuse my food now, I will forever cut off your supply!"

"What, is that your attempt at *threatening* him or something?! Don't listen to him, Maou! I'll take *real* good care of you, I promise!"

"...Man. Weird how it's starting to look like they're fighting over him, huh?"

Urushihara lazily gave his own two cents, elbow planted on his computer desk.

"It's like he's some kind of hot-to-trot playboy or something."

The two girls paid no mind as their slightly off-kilter conflict continued to heat up.

"Well, which is it? Chiho or me?"

"Whose food are you gonna eat?!"

Confronted by the pair, Maou flashed an utterly exhausted look as he muttered softly.

"Please...just let me enjoy some breakfast, at least..."

His plaintive request was blown to bits in the next moment.

With a great crash, the door to the Devil's Castle was kicked open. The group immediately turned toward the front of the room, only to find:

"Luuuuciiiferrrrrr..."

Emi Yusa, angry enough to transform into demi-angel form at any moment.

Framed by the morning sun, Emi stomped into the room, all but breaking the floorboards underfoot as she grasped a small, boxlike object.

Urushihara grimaced when he saw it, sidling up against the wall in a futile attempt at escape.

"What the hell were you thinking?! Hiding this inside my bag?!"

It was the GPS device discussed just a moment ago, the one that pinpointed Emi's location.

"That, uh... You know..."

"No, I *don't* know! Why did you put this in a woman's bag? So you could find out where I was at all times, you stupid shut-in fallen angel?! You're gonna pay for being such a goddamn creep all the time!!"

The freight train of Emi's blitzkrieg attack struck Urushihara pallid with fear. The rest had already returned to the pre-Emi business.

"Hey! Ashiya! Stop Emilia for me!"

"It is not my business to."

"It kind of *is*, dude! Whoa! Jeez, c'mon, Bell!"

"If Emilia would be kind enough to dispatch all of you at once, our work is done here."

"You're freaking me out, guys! Chiho Sasaki! Get Emilia away from me!"

"C'mon, Yusa! Go get him!"

"This is *so* unfair! I hope you all go to hell! Dude, Emilia, calm down! I can explain all of this!"

"No more excuses! Kill yourself now, before I do it for you!"

"This is *insane*!!"

"Please…I'm begging you…let me eat in peace…"

Maou's pained whisper was muffled by the noise of the life-or-death struggle that shortly ensued.

Even with all the powder kegs and enraged intruders, a steady, if insane, sort of peace continued to rule over the hundred-square-foot Devil's Castle.

The sunlight pouring in signaled that the true arrival of summer was just around the corner.

THE AUTHOR, THE AFTERWORD, AND YOU!

PART 2

As I'm sure my readers are aware, royalties are an important part of an author's income. *Kojien*, the most authoritative dictionary of the Japanese language, defines the term as follows:

> **ROY-al-ties** (n.): Payments received by a copyright owner from a publisher or other entity for the usage of a copyrighted work, usually provided on a commissioned basis depending on sale price or circulation.
> —*Kojien, 6th edition, © 2008 Iwanami Shoten*

Not that this is paid out to the author in cash, of course. In Japan, what happens is that a company purchases something called a "revenue stamp" for the agreed-upon payment. This represents that the company has provided compensation for the work, for all official purposes.

This revenue-stamp system has its roots in how copyright and royalties used to work in Japan. In fact, the Japanese word for "royalties" is *inzei*, which literally means "seal tax."

You see, in ye olde Japan, the back page of every book printed would include an official seal stamped on there by the author. The royalties paid to him or her would be based on the number of seals the author stamped on his work.

This system has largely died out in modern times, but if you take a peek at the older books that occupy the dusty shelves of used bookstores or university libraries, you'll be able to see these official "stamps of approval" for yourselves.

Since this system of receiving royalties based on official stamps was the norm for the legal system that allowed publishers to handle author copyrights for publication purposes all the way to the modern age, we still call royalties "seal tax" in Japanese.

But, considering that system's a dead relic from the past, nowadays in the twenty-first century, why do we still use such an old-fashioned term like *inzei*?

I found out for myself the day my first published work, *The Devil is a Part-Timer!*, went on sale.

I was at my local bookstore in order to get an eyeful of my book lined up on the shelves. To my enormous surprise, I walked right past someone who had the first volume in hand as he made for the cash register.

The great majority of the royalties I receive for writing *The Devil is a Part-Timer!*, of course, comes from the money spent by my readers with every purchase they make.

I knew that, of course, but it was when I saw that man in the bookstore that I truly felt it for the first time.

The royalties that are paid to me, in exchange for the readers' expectation of the entertainment they will receive from reading my work, are what allow me to stay in this business.

So what would be the best way to use these royalties paid to me by these loyal readers?

We often talk about how people who work for the government bureaucracy are "living off the taxpayers' dime." I suppose that means writers like myself are "living off the readers' dime," then, the virtual seals we stamp on each volume the only thing keeping us clothed.

The "taxes" I receive in the form of royalties from my readers are what allow me to effectively invest in new projects. I have a duty to use that money to the hilt in order to repay the favor to the readers, in the form of my "work."

Amid all the momentous events that occurred in Japan and the world as I wrote this volume, I spent a great deal of time worrying about what a would-be author of light, entertaining fiction like myself should really be doing with his life. In the end, I came to the conclusion that reinvesting the "taxes" I receive in order to produce better "work" and entertain more of my readers was the most logical choice.

I hope I can continue working toward that goal, too—the goal of making those readers smile.

I apologize for continuing to irreverently talk about taking reader's souls and seizing their taxes and so on in these afterwords. I should probably know my place a bit more.

Despite the tremendously stiff and self-centered thinking that went into this volume, it's still filled with people living frenetic, exciting, fun lives.

Finally, I would like to close by apologizing on the Devil King's behalf to my faithful readers living in Greenland for all of the inappropriate comments he made about your country. Thank you.

THE DEVIL IS A PART-TIMER! 2
SPECIAL END-OF-BOOK BONUS

RÉSUMÉ
COLLECTION

← HA-HA, THE CHURCH CLERIC'S A LIAR! —MAOU ← Stop writing on my résumé! —Suzuno

NAME

Suzuno Kamazuki

DATE OF BIRTH	AGE	GENDER
October 1, XXXX	18	F

ADDRESS

Villa Rosa #202
Sasazuka X-X-X
Shibuya-ku, Tokyo

↑HA HA, THE CHURCH CLERIC LIED AGAIN! —MAOU

↑ How do you know it's a lie, you fool? —Suzuno

TELEPHONE NUMBER

I do not own one yet. ← Have you considered Dokodemo? —Emi

PAST EXPERIENCE	
19XX	graduated from St. Bluerose Academy Middle School
20XX	entered St. Bluerose Academy High School
201X	graduated from St. Bluerose Academy High School

QUALIFICATIONS/CERTIFICATIONS

Japan Kanji Aptitude Test, Level Pre-1

↑W-wow! —Chiho

SKILLS/HOBBIES

gardening, kimono maintenance, cooking, people-watching

REASON FOR APPLICATION

to become a contributor to human society and support my mother and father in my homeland

PERSONAL GOALS

If you want to give me a nickname, call me "Osuzu." ← You've been watching too many samurai dramas. —Emi

COMMUTE TIME	FAMILY/DEPENDENTS	NAME OF GUARDIAN
searching for live-in situation	All of mankind is a family.	Suzuo Kamazuki,
	↑That is such BS. —Urushihara	Suzuko Kamazuki

↑ You don't count. —Suzuno

↑ MAKE UP SOMETHING MORE BELIEVABLE... —MAOU

NAME
Suzuno Kamazuki

DATE OF BIRTH	AGE	GENDER
Fall XXXX, Ignora 1211	2~~X~~	F

DUDE, JUST WRITE IT. —MAou
↑
Silence!
—Suzuno

ADDRESS
Villa Rosa #202
Sasazuka X-X-X
Shibuya-ku, Tokyo

TELEPHONE NUMBER
I do not own one yet.

PAST EXPERIENCE	
199X	born as the second child of the Bell bishopric, Sankt Ignoreído, Western Island
200X	graduated from Sankt Ignoreído First Theological College (major: Church law)
201X	assigned to diplomatic/missionary department of Church
201X	
	JOBLESS. —MAou ← At least write "Searching for work." —Suzuno

QUALIFICATIONS/CERTIFICATIONS
Japan Kanji Aptitude Test, Level Pre-1; doctorate in theology; master of Church law; missionary certification; bishop certification

SKILLS/HOBBIES
gardening, kimono maintenance, cooking, people-watching

REASON FOR APPLICATION
world peace

PERSONAL GOALS
I want to fulfill my mission and return home.

COMMUTE TIME	FAMILY/DEPENDENTS	NAME OF GUARDIAN
It was about an hour from the Gate.	don't need any	Orgot Riddman Bell

NAME
HANZOU URUSHIHARA

DATE OF BIRTH	AGE	GENDER
I — dont — Know	doesnt matter	M

ADDRESS
Devils Castle
Villa Rosa #201   ← THAT'S "ZUKA." —MAOU
Sasa(zuka) x-x-x, Shibuya-ku, Tokyo

TELEPHONE NUMBER
050-xxxx-xxxx   ← Wh-when did you...! —Ashiya

PAST EXPERIENCE	
	angel
	fallen angel
	demon general
	part-timer ← YOU'RE A SHUT-IN. —MAOU He sure is. —Ashiya
	← Quite so. —Suzuno
	You're awful. —Chiho
	Dude! —Urushihara

QUALIFICATIONS/CERTIFICATIONS
none   ← AT LEAST TRY TO WRITE LIKE AN ADULT FIRST. —MAOU   ← I can read, and I have a PC. Who cares? —Urushihara

SKILLS/HOBBIES
Internet, google earth, street view. I want to fly around.

REASON FOR APPLICATION
whatever

PERSONAL GOALS
work I can do without leaving home   ← Help out with chores already! —Ashiya

COMMUTE TIME	FAMILY/DEPENDENTS	NAME OF GUARDIAN
I am never far from battle.	I can't read this.	Sadao Maou! ↑ I OFFICIALLY PROTEST. —MAOU